This first one is for me.
For my childhood self, who dreamed of the day she
would hold her own book in her hands.
We did it, Panda Bear.

YEARS *Between* YOU

MIRANDA MELANIE

AUTHOR'S NOTE

Years Between You is intended for mature audiences only. This book contains sexually explicit content and adult language.

There are also brief mentions of a cheating partner, absent parents, and our main character's struggle with anxiety.

Please take care while reading.

1

MILES

I don't think I've ever found myself this attracted to a complete stranger. Sure, I've noticed small details, a nice smile here or there, but it's never been anything like what I'm experiencing now. I haven't even seen the front of this woman across from me in this grocery store aisle. I haven't seen her face.

And yet I am so drawn in, by her laugh especially. The red dress she's wearing compliments her curvy figure. Her golden brown hair is long and wavy, falling to the middle of her back.

I stare for as long as I can without her noticing, but maybe it wouldn't be a bad thing if she did. Luck might be on my side for once, and she'll be available, and even interested. It's been a few months, but I think I'm prepared for that possibility. I think I could start dating again.

She turns as she talks, holding a phone to her ear. That explains the laughter. If there hadn't been a phone, if she were just laughing at herself, I'm not sure it would've changed anything. She could be completely crazy, it might do my boring life some good.

I'm briefly shown more than the side profile I was admiring before. I caught bright eyes, and pink cheeks covered in freckles.

It's not long before she's back to the shelf, pulling something off to read the label. A bottle of fancy coffee creamer.

She almost looks familiar, maybe something about her mouth, or her nose, or...

I get another short glimpse, and I force myself to quickly look away.

She actually looks a lot like a girl I used to know. There is *no* way it could be her, the resemblance is so small. Maybe she has a sister I never heard about? Although, as I think it, I know how unlikely it is. She would've mentioned a sibling at some point, given all the time we spent together.

I risk it and make my way further down the aisle, enough that I can look back and—

It's her.

Somehow, that's *exactly* who I'm looking at. I manage to keep my jaw off of the floor at the realization.

She looks *good*. Confident and happy. Such a change from the girl I knew.

She's definitely not a teenager anymore.

Guilt floods into me for the way I was looking at her a few seconds ago. It's not going to leave anytime soon either, because I find myself disappointed that she's not a prospective date.

I'm struggling to match what I'm seeing with the Autumn Owens in my memories. The short, straight, multi-colored strands, and mascara that was always smudged under her eyes. She smiles into the phone, and the dimples it creates are the key piece that have me sure that this isn't just a lookalike. They didn't come out often, but I used to feel so relieved when they did. There's no way I could forget that smile.

She notices me as I'm trying to pinpoint more details, and I blink fast enough that I'm sure I look like a fool. When her eyes widen, I feel like she can see every thought in my brain, every ounce of attraction I've been standing here in shock of. She mumbles something and promptly hangs up her call.

I can't help but wonder if it was a boyfriend on the other end, and want to smack myself at that thought. My head is not in the right place.

Not. A. Prospective. Date.

"Miles?" She smiles wide with perfect, white teeth.

I smile back, trying to appear casual, but I doubt that it works. I have this nervous, buzzing energy from the excitement in her eyes. I like that she looks happy to see me after so long.

"Autumn." I say it appreciatively, as I close the distance between us. I go in for a hug that's more of just a friendly pat on the back. "Long time, no see. I almost didn't recognize you."

"You're not kidding." She laughs a little and it's still just as pleasant when I'm not straining to hear it from a few feet away. "Did you move out of town or something?"

I'm not surprised why she would think that, given the way the last few years of my life have been. I shake my head.

"Nope. I actually bought a house recently, so I'm staying put for a while."

As much as I've wanted to leave lately.

"Wow, congrats on being a homeowner." I can see the questions behind her politeness. I'd have questions too about living in the same small town as someone for years and not running into them a single time. "How weird that we haven't run into each other."

Yeah. There it is.

She says it in a way that makes me feel like I should give her an explanation. I don't have it in me to bring up my divorce, or the way my marriage had isolated me.

I just shrug. "I'm trying to be less of a homebody these days."

She nods and I'm relieved that's that.

"I'm glad to hear it. It's so good to run into you! You look..." It takes her a second of hesitation to land on a word. "Well."

"So do you." It's an understatement. There are plenty of other adjectives I'd use to describe her, but it's in my best interest to stop thinking through them. I wouldn't want one to accidentally slip out.

She gestures toward her shopping cart. It contains nothing but snack foods and hard seltzer. Combining that with how she's dressed up, it looks like she's going to have a more exciting night than I've had in a long time.

"I'm in a hurry at the moment, but we should really catch up soon. Maybe grab dinner?"

My heart leaps, liking that idea a little too much. "Definitely. That sounds nice."

I pull out my phone and open it to a new contact before handing it over.

She puts her number in and I tell her I'll text her. I'm more excited than I should be about this little run in, but it's been a while since I've seen *any* of my old friends, and even longer since I'd seen her. She was my friend at one point, as complicated as it had been.

She apologizes, something about melting ice cream, before waving goodbye and heading away from me.

The interaction is way too short, and I know I'm going to make sure we do have that chance to catch up. Although, as I'm unable to keep myself from watching her walk away, I'm aware it's not my brightest idea.

2

AUTUMN

I'm not sure I'm breathing as I rush away from Miles. He's the last person I was expecting to run into on this last minute shopping trip. He's the last person I was expecting to see *ever*.

I'm grateful for the timing of it. That it was tonight while I'm all done up, and not yesterday morning when I was in this exact store wearing my sweatpants. Pretty sure the anti-gas medication I'd been picking up would have made our conversation a little more uncomfortable.

I don't think he'll text me. I'm almost positive he won't, but it was sweet of him to make the gesture. He was always one to try and cheer me up, make a bad day a better one. I guess he never got rid of that habit.

It worked for a minute. The way his small kindness made my heart feel like it was going to pound out of my chest. A side effect I wish *I* had gotten rid of. It makes me feel like a train wreck of a teenager all over again.

I sigh and try to shake it off. The moment has passed, and now we'll go back to forgetting the other exists. I'm sure he will at least, even though I've never been able to. Not a week has passed over the last six years without some reminder of him. Granted, some of those were reminders of his brother, but I chose to think of Miles instead. The sweet, helpful brother. The one I wish I could have met first.

It didn't help matters on that front when I wrote an entire book inspired by my little crush on him. Something I never would have done if I'd known I'd see him again, because just the idea of being confronted about it makes me feel nauseous. I really thought he was gone for good.

It's strange, how he's still been here all this time without me knowing. In a small town like this, it's inevitable that you'll run into everyone you know at least a couple times a year. I've seen glimpses of his family more than I'd have liked, usually attempting to hide or head the opposite direction to avoid any awkward encounters.

I wonder if this is his grocery store as much as it is mine. If we've always just missed each other, or if we'll bump into each other again.

Oh, I meant to text you! And some pathetic attempt on my end to appear casual, as if I didn't think about it for a second. I hold back on rolling my eyes at myself as I go through the self checkout.

Trying to distract myself, I make a mental checklist of what I need for this weekend's get together. If I missed anything that's currently in this store, it's forfeit. I won't be turning back, knowing he's still here somewhere. As far as things I brought from home... I can't remember if I grabbed a swimsuit, but I'll dive into the hot tub in my underwear if I have to.

I practically sprint out to the parking lot, only stopping to pull the bags out of my cart so I can drop it off in the designated area.

Except I'm horribly unsuccessful, and time seems to slow as I feel the bottom of one overstuffed plastic bag start to rip open. There's no chance for me to stop the six pack of glass bottles from crashing to the ground with my hands full. Other items dramatically fall to the ground, following the sound of glass shattering. At least none of the rest of it is breakable, I guess that's a positive.

I freeze for a minute and take a deep, but shaky breath. My anxiety can hardly handle the grocery store on my own, let alone embarrassing myself in a way that would have all eyes on me. I avoid looking up or around as I slowly bend down to see what can be saved from the mess.

I don't get a chance before a familiar, tattooed arm is before me, carefully picking it up.

Of *course* he was nearby.

Where's somewhere to run and hide when a girl needs it?

"Looks like you only lost the one," Miles says, pulling the remaining glass out of the dripping cardboard.

I just stare at him for a minute while my brain tries to get over the panic it's experiencing.

When did he start wearing glasses?

He stares back for a few seconds, like he's trying to figure out the thoughts racing through my mind.

"Are you okay?" he asks, snapping me out of it.

I shake my head– before realizing I should be nodding and switching to that. "Yep. Yeah... sorry. That was embarrassing." I take it from him with trembling hands. "Thank you."

"No problem." With that we both bend down to grab the remainder of my groceries off the ground. If two bags of mini donuts, plastic shot glasses, and a six pack of Gatorade count as groceries. Miles magically pulls a reusable bag out from under his arm and starts to set my things in it. Then he turns to me so I can do the same.

"This is what I get for leaving my reusable bags in the car," I try to say lightly, but I know I still sound distressed. "I can transfer this into one of mine and give this right back. I'm parked—"

"Don't worry about it, I've got tons of them." This time when he smiles at me, I'm completely caught in another trance. One of his dark curls falls onto his forehead before he runs his fingers through the front of his hair, pushing it back in place.

Is it hot out here?

No, it's definitely not that. The sun is hidden behind suspiciously gray clouds, and I want to get into my car before that becomes a problem. I dressed for plans that would be indoors.

"Thank you," I tell him again. "I'll see you around?"

"Definitely," he replies with a small wave.

Once I've loaded everything into the trunk of my car and slide into the driver's seat, I text my friend, Reya, to let her know I'm on my way.

Picking her up is absolutely necessary, otherwise there's no telling when she would show up. She's a professional when it comes to being late unless it's her actual job. I was happy to learn that recently, she's not completely hopeless.

We're headed to a house that my best friends and I rented for the weekend. All of us pitched in *eagerly*, due to the much needed hot tub. It's already been a particularly gloomy October, and we're all missing the warm weather.

I'm excited to relax, have some drinks, and be around my favorite people. Although, I *almost* don't want to mention running into

Miles. They've never met him, our friendships forming after that time in my life, but they've heard plenty. An embarrassing amount for someone I haven't seen since I was a teenager.

Reya has taken it upon herself to find me a love match, and if she thinks that simply being my upstairs neighbor is enough to knock on someone's door and ask him what he thinks about me? There's way too much ammunition here. A history. An old crush that I'm thinking might not be so old anymore.

He's gotten better looking over the last few years. The dark curly hair that he's grown out slightly, the tasteful shadow of stubble on his face.

Those black, square-rimmed glasses that fit his features so perfectly.

I wonder if Kara is still the lucky lady, or if he's moved on to someone that's better for him. I should hope so, but I can't ignore the tiny voice in the back of my mind that wants him to be single. Not that there is anything I could do with that fact.

Miles Cress is completely off limits.

3

AUTUMN

SIX YEARS AGO

I 'm sitting on a curb, crying my eyes out, and it's a very snotty ordeal. It only makes sense that Miles would choose that exact moment to pull up into the gravel driveway. The *exact moment* I wipe my snotty nose on the sleeve of my shirt.

It's just my luck. One would think that things couldn't get any more embarrassing than this, but I've had an extremely mortifying year.

It wasn't my plan to make a scene, but once my thoughts wandered I couldn't stop the tears from coming. Thoughts of him, his family, *my* family, my best friend. The list is a long one, and the thought of any of them is enough to send me spiraling.

I get a quick glance at him through the windshield, and he looks impossibly put together for someone who's been at work all day. I quickly hide my face in my arms, and rest them on my knees. I don't want him to see me like this.

Not more than he already has, anyway.

It's like I'm his complete opposite most of the time, and I wonder if he thinks the same. No one would ever describe him as a burden. No one would ever catch him crying at their front door. I can't even remember the last time I brushed my hair, and his looks like *that*.

Miles is definitely over my shit. I can see it on his face, hear it in every sigh. But he's the only person that's tried to be there for me during this whole mess. The *one* person that's made an effort with me over the last few months, and I'm so grateful for that. Grateful enough that I know I don't want to experience what the end of his patience looks like. If I don't leave, I know it'll happen. At least if I do this now, on my terms, I can hold on to that. The fact that there is one single person in this world that never gave up on me.

"You okay?" he asks as he approaches, his brows scrunched in concern. His tall figure casts a shadow over where I sit, making me feel even smaller than usual. He'd hate knowing that, but it's not his fault. It's impossible not to feel small next to someone who feels so big. Not just physically, he's bigger in the important ways. The ways that make you feel seen and heard.

I don't know why he still bothers to ask, he knows that my answer has been the same for a long time. Ever since my breakup with his brother I haven't come close to being okay.

After wiping the tears away and hoping I can keep more from falling, I finally look up at him. My face is surely all red and splotchy, giving him the answer. I just nod in response, because that's the easy thing to do.

"She— um," I motion towards the front door of *their* apartment. "She won't let me in, but I was just hoping to grab my things." The way my voice cracks makes me cringe.

I think Miles has always felt bad about the way his family has treated me. Bad enough that he offered up his spare bedroom when I told him my best friend, Jade, was moving across the country. I'd been living with her for years, and felt so lost when she broke the news. I had nowhere else to go, no family to fall back on.

He wouldn't take any money for rent, so I gave him what I could, even if it meant sticking the occasional twenty in the dryer with his clothes. I'd clean the apartment while he was gone, cook the couple meals I knew how to make when he was there. Anything I could think of to thank him, I did.

I was also scared he would change his mind at any second, and start siding with his brother over me. It's what their mom did, just flipped a switch one day. She was nice enough, *tolerant* enough of my overly emotional state, until she suddenly wasn't.

I've thought maybe if I had something to offer Miles, he'd be less likely to toss me out when that day came for him.

Not that it mattered. That day never came, but it didn't change my fate. His girlfriend did.

Kara didn't come over to his place often, but she made me uncomfortable whenever she did. She was always glaring, always whispering. Very clearly on *Team Justin*. It made me feel like I was dealing with high school mean girls all over again, except she was a grown woman in her twenties.

And then she moved in, because that's what girlfriends do.

Miles was oblivious until the day it happened. I didn't blame him, with his rose-colored glasses and all. He tried talking to her on my behalf, get her to understand my situation, but nothing changed her mind. They were arguing about it all the time, and I couldn't stand being the reason. I wasn't trying to complicate anything, I just didn't have anywhere to go.

Even with that being the case, it got to the point where leaving was easier than staying. I've slept in my car for three nights so far, and it's as miserable as I expected. I don't sleep well. My neck hurts and I'm always cold. I'm even getting complaints at work, because I can't manage to fake a smile for customers.

I'd been at work today, dejected and exhausted, when Kara texted me that I had thirty minutes to get my things out of their place. She also may have implied that they'd be in the dumpster if I didn't meet her requirements.

By the time my job let me leave with an emergency, I was five minutes late and she wouldn't let me in. I checked the trash, and was relieved when I didn't recognize any of my belongings inside of it. A small mercy.

I don't trust her. I've been sitting on the porch for an hour to make sure she doesn't toss it. I'm not much of a fighter, but I'll have to stop her somehow. I have nothing else to my name, it's not an option to let it go.

I wasn't sure when Miles was due home when I made the decision, but here we are.

"You still have your key, right?"

I pull it from the back pocket of my torn jeans, feeling a hole in there, too. I quietly thank the universe for not letting it fall through, and hand it over to him. I won't need it anymore, but I wouldn't put it past Kara to call me a liar if I lost it. I really hope she doesn't make him pay to replace their locks because of me. He's done enough already.

"I don't think it would've gone over very well if I used it."

He grabs it and takes a seat next to me on the ground, sighing on the way down. I can't be sure if it's because of her or me this time, but my gut feeling tells me it's the latter.

For a few moments, the only sound between us is my sniffling.

Why does crying have to involve so much snot?

"Where are you staying?"

I shrug. "My car."

"You can't stay in your car," he tells me like it's a fact.

I let out a dry laugh. "It's fine."

"You're going to freeze."

I shrug again. There's nothing to be done, but I don't want to sit here and convince him of that. He'd only argue, probably try to help me some other way.

He must read the resolve on my face, because I watch his shoulders sag in my periphery. "I can go grab your stuff and bring it out to you."

"That would be really awesome of you," I say.

"Yeah, I'm pretty awesome sometimes." I think he's hoping he'll get a smile at that, but the best I can do is a tight lipped imposter that doesn't feel like it belongs on my face.

He considers me for a minute, though I can't tell why. It's not the pitiful expression I was expecting but something more... sincere.

"Okay, I'll be right back," he says quickly as he stands. "You should wait in your car, it's too cold out here."

He's not wrong, I can see my breath cloud in front of my face. It's a gloomy day with thick clouds that cover the entire sky. If I wasn't already numb to everything going on around me, sitting here this long would've done it.

"It's cold in there, too. I'm fine."

He stops moving. "You don't even have heat in that thing?"

I shake my head. My Honda Civic is older than I am and I'm not sure how it's still running. It definitely looks as if it would have stopped by now with its peeling paint and bare tires.

"Damn it, Autumn."

I say nothing as he turns to go inside.

After a couple minutes, I can hear yelling. It's mostly Kara yelling at whatever Miles is saying in a voice that's too calm for me to make out.

"I told her she had thirty minutes!"

Pause.

"I'm sick of having her stuff here! She shouldn't have been here in the first place!"

Pause.

"Why bother? She doesn't care about anyone but herself! That girl has been nothing but drama since the second I met her."

I wince. She's not wrong about the last part. It doesn't matter that I seem to have no control over it.

She's wrong about the part before that. I care about Miles a lot. He's the best person I know. I don't blame him for any part of my current situation. I don't even blame *her*, as much as I don't like her. I try to put myself in her shoes, and although I'd definitely go about it differently, I can see her side of things. She signed up to live with her boyfriend, not some random girl she barely knows. A girl she's heard a lot of crappy things about.

I feel slightly bad for wishing Miles would just dump her and find someone who actually deserves him. Not for my sake, I'd still stay in my car and save him the trouble. I just want him to be happier than he is, but I also know how easy it is to look past someone's faults when you're in love with them.

When he appears at the front door there are two cardboard boxes stacked in his arms, and a big bag full of clothes hanging off of his wrist. Only two of those things are mine, and I give him a questioning look.

He doesn't say anything, just passes by me to get to the trunk of my car. I get a whiff of whatever cologne he's wearing, and feel a sharp pang in my gut. Not that we spend a lot of time close enough to smell each other, but it's all over his apartment. It's become something of a comfort to me, and it's a detail I'm going to miss.

It hits me that I have to manually unlock the trunk, so I rush over, feeling bad that he has to hold those while he waits. My anxiety about it only makes me fumble with my keys even more, dropping them on the frozen ground before I can get it together.

"What's that?" I ask as I finally turn the key and pull it open.

He shakes his head subtly and it makes me wonder if Kara is watching from the window or trying to listen through the front door. He sets them down, and arranges them in the least slidable way before turning to me.

I take him in for a moment, something I never let myself do. I never stare too long, I never say too much.

He talks quickly and quietly. "She'll be pissed if I give you a hug, I'm sorry. Promise me you'll text if you need anything?"

I stand there, now frozen for a reason other than the weather, and nod. I'm never sure how to respond to his kindness. Even after years of being on this end of it, it never ceases to surprise me.

I'm also not sure how to say goodbye. How to thank him for everything he's done, or tell him how much I'm going to miss him.

"Stay safe," he says, and then he's gone. So fast that I don't get the chance to say anything.

That will probably be the last time I ever see Miles Cress, and knowing it brings fresh tears to my eyes.

Later on that night, when I'm parked on the street of some quiet residential neighborhood, I pop the hood of my trunk and open the box that doesn't belong to me.

It contains a couple of fuzzy blankets, two pairs of men's sweatpants, and a big winter coat.

I stand and stare at the contents for a moment, trying to wrap my head around the fact that he *gave* me his stuff. He was worried enough about me freezing in my car that he threw these things in a box and didn't want Kara to know. I thought I couldn't possibly cry anymore today, but my vision blurs and I have to blink the moisture away.

I only snap out of it when I remember where I am, and that I don't want to attract any attention to myself. I quickly grab what I need and climb into my cramped backseat for the night.

I fall asleep much easier than I have previously, and it has everything to do with the smell of him on the blankets surrounding me.

4

Autumn

"Cheers to your twenty-seventh year!" I hold up the fruity, pink drink that Vic was making when we arrived. Knowing her, it has a whole lot of alcohol and enough sweet ingredients to make it a little dangerous. That's how it goes when we get together for a birthday. At first we'd make plans out in public, at restaurants or bars, but then we realized we all needed to let loose without the risk of getting kicked out somewhere.

The three of us haven't spent a single birthday apart over the last four years, and we wouldn't have it any other way. Especially because sometimes it's all we have, given how busy our lives are in such different ways.

Victoria, which we never call her, has two children and a husband to take up most of her time. Reya has a daughter, and an immature ex-husband on her plate. Neither of them ever has a complaint about motherhood, but I know they need an occasional break. They work so hard.

"Cheers to you babes for helping me get here!" Vic raises her cup along with the two of us, a huge smile plastered on her perfect face. I have a tendency to be dramatic, but calling Vic perfect is not an overstatement. Her deep bronze skin is truly without flaws, her curly hair always sits perfectly on her head, not a strand out of place. You'd never guess that her toddlers are constantly *pulling it out of her skull*, as she put it.

I'm right about the drink, and it's *delicious*. It is without a doubt the first of many, and the beginning of one hell of a hangover tomorrow. Another thing the hot tub will come in handy for. I glance over at Reya to see her chugging hers down at an impressive pace, until all that remains in the clear plastic cup is ice.

She notices my stare and grins. "What? That's how you do it." Her head spins followed by her body as she looks around the room in a circle that even manages to disorient *me*. "Where do I get another one?"

I don't wait for Vic to come to Reya's rescue, grabbing the cup out of her hand before she even registers the action. Then I do exactly what the moment calls for, and finish the rest of my drink even faster than she did.

Now I have two cups in need of a refill, and I'm saving my girl a trip to the kitchen.

"Nope," Vic's small voice comes from behind me. Her long arms reach around and snatch *both* of the cups from me.

I pout. "But I want a—"

"Yeah, so do I." She waves her hands in front of me, and she's not holding two, but three empty cups. The smile that breaks across my face means trouble.

"Can you make mine a bit stronger this time?" I challenge her. I know her answering grin means I'm going to get more than I asked for.

There doesn't need to be a single responsible one between us considering we have nothing to do tomorrow, and a checkout time that's over a day away.

Reya plops down on the couch across the room staring at her phone. She's surely too distracted by texts from her new girlfriend to request the same. She's going to get it anyway, if the gleam in Vic's eye is any indication.

I throw myself down next to her, and rest my cheek on her shoulder. I pull out my own phone, knowing perfectly well that everyone I talk to is currently in the room with me. I swipe away at pointless notifications, spam emails, a bill reminder, etcetera.

My mind is apparently working in slow motion already, because a few seconds after I swipe everything away I realize I just saw *Miles'* name.

I hastily open up my text messages, and sure enough there's a text from the grocery shopper himself.

Unknown: *Hey, this is Miles! It was good seeing you today.*

"Oh yeah, you guys?" I squeak, right as Vic places another beverage in front of me. "I have to tell you who I ran into."

Miles

It's nice to catch up with Autumn. She tells me about her friends, and her quirky cat. I talk about my dog, my new house, and I *don't* mention my lack of friends as of late. It surprises me how much you can get into after just a couple hours of messaging back and forth. I'm not usually the type to pick up my phone so much in one day.

I'd be lying if I said she wasn't coming close to getting some truth from me that I don't know I'm ready to share. Not because she's prying, but because it already feels easy to talk to her. As if there weren't years between the last time we'd talked about our lives and now.

I see that she's typing, the three dots moving on the screen. I should probably be doing something better with my time, but she's so quick to respond that it feels pointless. I'd rather be sitting here with Freddy in my lap, watching those dots than watching another show I've seen about a million times. That's all I do aside from work and family these days.

Getting divorced? Easy. Adjusting to being alone all the time, even though it's the peace you've been begging for? Not that simple.

The dots stop, and I take a moment to catch up with the change of my phone screen. Her name, big and bold.

She's *calling* me.

I hesitate, and let my phone buzz in my hand a couple times. I've never been a fan of phone calls, I don't even call my mother. I never called my ex-wife.

I don't know what possesses me to answer this phone call now, but that's what I do.

"Hello?" It's a question, because it's possible this was somehow an accident. A butt-dial. That makes more sense to me.

"How old are you now?"

Well, that sounds intentional.

"Old enough," I respond with a laugh.

"No, really," she says. I can hear a smile in her voice.

"Really."

"I'll tell you mine if you tell me yours." I realize she's slurring a little with that sentence, and hold back a laugh. I almost forgot she's at some party. That makes her random call even more amusing.

"That would be a fair trade if I didn't already know."

She scoffs. "Wait, what? How?"

"You're the same age as my brother, remember?"

The line goes silent for a moment, and I immediately regret mentioning him at all. It's no secret that he still exists and he's still my brother, but I wouldn't want the reminder if I were her either.

Before I can say something, anything, to fill the quiet, she yells. "Oh yeah!" There's laughter in her voice, thankfully. "Duh!"

It makes me smile. Her laughter used to be a very rare thing to hear.

"You sound like you're having fun."

A voice shouts something in the background, but I can't make out what they say.

"Wait for me!" Autumn yells back at them before bringing her attention back to her phone. "I have to go, so just hurry up and tell me how old you are."

"Thirty," I blurt out before I can think better of it.

"Huh. I didn't realize how many years ahead of me you were. How does it feel?"

"To be five years ahead of you?"

"To be thirty," she says with another laugh.

"Like everyone expects me to have my shit together more than I do." It's another thing I say without thinking, and feels like a good way to bring a mood down.

She hums as if she's thinking about my answer.

"I could see that," she mumbles. "What are you doing with the rest of your night?"

Great subject change.

"Going to bed. I work early."

Miserably early, but I would easily stay up to keep talking to her if she didn't have to go.

"Yikes. Good luck with that."

I note that she's still not a morning person. I never saw her face before noon during the time she stayed with me.

"Thanks, I'll need it. What about you?" I ask.

"I think it's hot tub time. Can't say I'm mad about it."

I chuckle. "Enjoy hot tub time."

"I surely will. Good night, Miles."

"Good night, Autumn."

When the phone goes quiet, it hits me that I feel much less alone than I usually do before bed.

I got my first friend back today.

5

AUTUMN

I consider myself a hopeless romantic, with emphasis on the lack of hope. I can think up scenarios all day, but I can't seem to manifest any of them into existence. I might stand a chance of spilling my coffee on a suit-wearing hottie if I wasn't too anxious to go inside the coffee shop, but I choose the drive-through every time. I try not to dwell on it, there are plenty of other things in my life to make me feel happy and fulfilled. I'm in plenty of committed relationships.

The only romance I've been experiencing lately is the fictional kind. I type up all the swooning, cheesy goodness, and live vicariously through my computer screen. Sometimes it's hard not to convince myself that I'm an imposter, creating stories that I have little experience to build off of, but I *have* read a *lot* of books.

Being cheated on as a teenager had residual effects that didn't go away as quickly as I hoped, if much at all. I was trying to learn how to trust *anyone* before Justin ever came along. I was a kid that couldn't even trust my own parents, so his actions were a big setback.

I've caught feelings more than once since then. I've also had fun, random sex, and tried not to take dating too seriously. None of it ever worked out for me, but not for my lack of trying. I gave into Reya's antics for years, letting her sign me up for dating apps, or take me out for drinks just so she could talk to the bartender about all of my endearing qualities.

I had a fling with one of my neighbors for a few weeks, also thanks to Reya. Ben was cute, and sweet, and had a nose ring. I understood why she tried to set us up, I might have even thanked her for it at some point.

But we had practically nothing in common. He was into sports, and cars, and lived off of his dad's money. We couldn't possibly be more different as people. I felt the attraction when I looked at him, and I enjoyed sleeping with him. I liked that he would always order takeout when I stayed over late, and remembered my order after the very first time I told him.

The moments in between having sex, and eating dinner, and going home, when there wasn't a sound coming from his television? There was no way to miss the uncomfortable silence, the lack of connection. It made me want to crawl out of my skin. It was everything romance novels told me I didn't deserve.

That was the first time I'd been the one to end a relationship, or a situationship, whatever we had. I should've known better, with him living right upstairs. I had given that to Reya as a reason why I shouldn't before I did. I had been so nervous that I didn't leave my apartment for weeks without a solid minute of listening for footsteps on the stairs outside.

We're on decent terms now, I might even say we've become friends. We share smiles on the days we're in a hurry, and catch up for a couple minutes when we're not. And yes, okay, we might have had a couple of drunk hookups since. I am not a perfect person, it gets lonely out here.

Before Ben, I had fallen for a guy named Lucas. We worked together for a few months at some real estate office. He had dark blonde hair, and a smile that melted panties right off.

Lucas was the first guy I opened up to after Justin, and we talked every day for months. He took me out to dinner all the time, he even introduced me to his family. Our chemistry was undeniable, and I was drawn to him like a magnet.

It took months for him to tell me he wasn't looking for a girlfriend. We had already spent so much time together, become so close, that it seemed silly to end things for that reason. And maybe... maybe I was holding out hope that he didn't really mean it, or at least that I could change his mind.

Spoiler alert: he meant it. I couldn't change his mind.

I needed validation and reassurance that he couldn't give me. I stooped as low as begging for it, which was new for me. A level of pathetic I didn't know I could reach, but I justified it at the time. I never asked Justin for anything, and that hadn't gotten me anywhere.

Lucas just wasn't the person to ask. He slowly, but surely shut me out. It started with shorter messages, seeming busier at work than he'd ever been. He needed his sweatshirt back, one that he never cared was in my possession before. He didn't have the decency to actually end things with me, or explain himself. I'm a smart girl, I didn't *need* him to. It just would've been nice.

A light social media stalking told me he got married a year later to the girl that replaced me when I left that job. I cried over him for a long time.

Those were the highlights of my dating life, the rest being inconsequential crushes and the occasional hookup. If I wasn't an author, and didn't have the outlet of writing love stories, I might have lost my mind by now.

I would be lying if I said I didn't find my run in with Miles romantic. It was a dream, the kind of meet-cute a really good romance novel would start out with. If this happened a couple years ago, I might be all over it. I might be acting before thinking, but now I'm trying my hardest to *stop* thinking about it.

This isn't my story. I don't get to fall for the guy and have everything work out, because this is *way* more complicated than that. There are some pretty big factors here, like the fact that he's Justin's brother, and would *never* be interested in me. This is the kind of story where the little girl has a crush, and the guy laughs it off if he ever finds out. Miles doesn't get to find out.

I couldn't imagine being shut down by him, the friend that never gave up on me. I'm still not planning on giving him the chance.

Hopefully I didn't blow it with the drunk phone call, but he didn't seem suspicious. If I didn't know better, I'd say he seemed to enjoy talking to me. Not that we've talked in the few days since, which makes me doubt we'll see each other again on purpose.

I'm already dreading the day that awkward run-in happens.

—*ele*—

I've never been good at night time routines, but I really want to be. I know from the rare times I have been successful, that it helps me destress after the long days. I fall asleep without all of the overthinking when I get to wind down with a bath and some soothing skin care.

I have a mental checklist that I've been trying to follow for a few weeks, but things keep getting in the way. Reya's daughter will FaceTime me, or my cat will have an accident on the carpet. A lot of the time I'll have an idea for my book that I have to start typing that very second before I forget it.

Tonight, however, I'm fully prepared to follow it step by step, and I start by scattering floral scented salt and soap in the bathtub. I don't even wait for it to be done filling up, the calming scents calling to me. It works wonders for the first few seconds, and I feel my muscles relax for the first time in days.

Then my phone rings.

I roll my eyes, already frustrated with whoever decided to have such terrible timing. This is supposed to be my time, but I should have known better than to set my phone within arms reach. There are only two people that ever call me, so I don't even bother to look at the caller ID when I pick it up. I greet them in the most annoyed tone possible, one that lets them know right away that they're interrupting something. My girl's aren't the type to take it personally, they'll dish the attitude right back.

"Uh, hi."

I sit up with a small splash. Whoever it is, they are definitely taking my tone personally.

"Sorry, is this a bad time?"

I pull my phone away from my ear to check, but it's a random number. Not saved in my contacts. "Who is this?"

"Miles?" He says it like a question.

Shit. I had forgotten he existed for a few minutes. I had also forgotten to save him in my contacts the other day, so now I look like a total ass.

I sit up even straighter.

"Oh wow, I'm sorry! Hi! That was so rude of me."

But why are you calling me?

"No, that's okay. I should've texted you. I can let you go if you're busy." He sounds about as awkward as I feel.

I can't explain why I don't want him to hang up, considering that fact, but I really don't. He's piqued my interest enough that my frustration over the interruption is gone.

"Don't worry about it, I have a minute. What's up?"

He hesitates, and I wait a few long seconds. So long that I'm almost concerned he's not there anymore. I would have heard those beeps that indicate the call ended, wouldn't I? But then he clears his throat, and my grip on my phone eases. I hadn't even realized I'd been holding it so tightly.

"I was going to ask if you wanted to hang out or something? Catch up," he clarifies.

"Really?"

Usually my doubt is just an intrusive thought, but that one slipped out.

"Yeah, really."

"I'd love to," I say quickly. A small alarm goes off in my mind, telling me I shouldn't seem so eager. That it might make him change his mind.

Shut up, Autumn. Who hurt you?

I ignore the answer that pops up in my mind.

"What are you doing tomorrow?" he asks. "I have a shorter work day, we could get dinner."

Short notice on anything usually makes me panic, but my reaction now is different and unfamiliar. Most of the time when someone wants to catch up, it's followed up with months of messages about things coming up, life being busy, having to reschedule for… never.

It never happens.

I'm relieved there are no such hoops to jump through here. I want to see him.

I snap my fingers as if he could see or hear it.

"Oh no, I actually have plans with a bottle of wine and a good book tomorrow night."

They're plans I rarely cancel, despite my joking.

"Can you ask them to reschedule? I don't get a lot of nights off, I'm sure they'll understand."

I sigh loudly. "They can be a bit volatile, but I'll see what I can do."

The sound of his chuckle on the other end sends a shiver down my spine.

"Anywhere in particular you want to go?"

There's a smile in his voice, and it puts one on my own face. I know he's not intentionally charming me, but I am definitely feeling charmed.

I have to pause for a second, watching the bubbles in my bath twinkle with every minuscule pop before I have to ask a dumb question. My heart pounds a little harder.

"At the risk of sounding like an idiot, you're not asking me..."
I can't finish the sentence, because the idea of Miles wanting anything to do with me as more than friends is absurd. Even *that* in
itself is a bit unbelievable to me. I'm just in uncharted territory
here. Miles and I don't know each other at all anymore. I know that
logically, morally speaking, he'd never ask me on a date. Not only
because of Justin, although that reason is a big one, but because he
probably still sees me as an immature teenager. "Like, it's not..."

"A date?" He laughs.

My cheeks suddenly feel warmer than my bath water and I wish
I hadn't bothered. Now we both know how absurd I am.

I fumble, trying to think up a denial, or a joke, but nothing
comes to me.

He continues before I can respond. "No. Just two friends.
Catching up. Over dinner. That's not weird, is it?"

I don't know what qualifies as weird anymore, but I shake my
head, aware he can't see it.

"Not at all. That sounds great. You can just tell me when and
where, and I'll be there."

We go over details, and it's surprisingly easy. I almost feel like I'm
waiting for someone to jump out and tell me I'm being pranked.
It's hard to believe he wasn't just saying what I wanted to hear
when we bumped into each other that day.

Long after the call ends and all of the bubbles in my bath have
popped, I can't stop my racing mind. I never thought Miles would
be in my life again.

So much for unwinding before bed.

6

AUTUMN

The restaurant is one I've been to before, which eases my nerves the slightest amount. A small, locally owned Italian place with vibrant decor and comfortable booths. Vic had a phase where she made us eat here at least once a week, and by the time it was over I thought I'd never want to see another piece of garlic bread as long as I lived.

It's about a year later, and my mouth is currently watering over the thought of it.

Overthinking situations is what I do best, which leaves me sitting in my car staring at the front entrance of Capria's Kitchen. What if he isn't here? What if he isn't coming? Worse– what if he *is* here? I'm reminded of a time where just the thought of this man would have my heart beating unevenly. It's actually doing so right now, the years had me fooled into thinking that might change.

I shake the thoughts from my head, and see one option before me. I have to get a grip and get inside before I stress out about it anymore.

My keys catch on my emergency brake as I attempt to step out of my car, causing a slightly embarrassing scene where my ass lurches back into the seat it had just left.

Please don't be watching me through the window.

As if sitting in my car for a solid few minutes to psych myself up isn't embarrassing enough.

I make it inside the nearly empty place, and immediately my eyes shoot to him. He has a view of the windows in front, and I try not to get in my head about that fact.

Try and fail.

He stands as I approach, a warm smile on his face. I'm not sure if I should hug him. I *want* to hug him, but suddenly I can't remember if I put on deodorant today. I'm definitely starting to sweat, and it would be a tragedy if he got a whiff of my armpits.

I shouldn't be as nervous as I am, but there's no easing it. This might as well be a date. By the time I reach the table I've subconsciously decided I *am* going to hug him, and I'm grateful that he goes right in and hugs me back. It's probably the best hug I've had all year, thanks to the familiarity of him. Something I've really missed.

He even smells the same: slightly citrusy, fresh, and clean.

I'm seventy-five percent sure I have deodorant on.

"Hey! You look great," he says as he pulls away. I blush at the small compliment, and hope the makeup I'm wearing is enough to hide the evidence.

"Oh," I start. "Thanks, so do you."

We sit on opposite ends of the booth, and I notice waters are already on the table. His is half empty, and mine is covered in condensation.

"I hope you weren't waiting long."

"Not at all, a couple minutes maybe," he says with a wave of his hand. I know he's lying, being courteous. I spent more than a couple minutes in the parking lot, and I wouldn't have missed him walking inside.

When the waitress appears and asks if we want anything else to drink, I barely glance at the menu before deciding on one of the fruity cocktails pictured at the top of the page. I think reconciling with your ex-boyfriend's brother calls for a drink.

I'm surprised when I hear him say he'll have the same.

"I wouldn't have guessed that's your thing."

He laughs, and the sound alone makes me feel more at ease. "It's not. I'm sort of," he pauses briefly, searching for the words. "I'm trying new things lately."

Right, like leaving the house to go to the grocery store.

"Mid-life crisis already?" I joke.

"Not quite. I— well." He shoots me a strained smile, conveying how uncomfortable whatever he's about to say makes him. "I'm actually.... newly divorced. From Kara."

My jaw drops before I can stop it, and I immediately feel like an idiot. I close my mouth and try my best to give him a sympathetic look.

He sees right through it and shakes his head. "You don't have to feel sorry for me. It's been a really good thing."

I'm not sorry for him, I'm more relieved than anything. I've thought getting away from her would be what's best for him for *years*. He's always been too good for her. Too kind when she was too cruel.

"I'm still sorry you had to go through a divorce. I'm sure the details have been stressful."

"You have no idea." He sighs. "But let's talk about something less depressing. What have you been up to all this time?"

I've never been good at talking about myself, so I'm grateful when our drinks are placed in front of us. I take a sip to kill a second while I think of where to start. It's great, the perfect combination of sweet and strong. A glance back up at Miles and his facial expression tells me that he disagrees. I hold back a snort as I watch him continue drinking with a grimace.

"I don't know where to start. Some of it hasn't been too great either," I admit. I keep my tone light, and give him a shrug.

"What's the best thing that's happened to you since the last time we saw each other?" he asks with genuine interest.

"Probably the birthday party I went to this weekend. Not a lot going on since last Friday," I say with a smirk, surprising myself. I know what he means.

Miles chuckles.

I pause for a moment, still not used to talking about my accomplishments.

"I published a book."

His eyes widen at that small sentence.

"You mean you *wrote* an entire book?"

I nod, knowing that my makeup is definitely not saving me from how red my face and chest have become this time.

"I'd love to hear about it," he says.

Actually, if you happened to notice any similarities between yourself and my main character you'd love *to run the other way.*

"It's just a silly, little romance. Not that big of a deal."

He's shaking his head before I even finish talking. "I'd say that's a big deal. How long did it take you to write?"

"Over a year," I admit, almost embarrassed by that.

I know I shouldn't be, it takes a lot of people a lot longer. Once I tried to join an online writer's group, I couldn't help the shame I felt when all of their writing journey's took months at the most. It didn't matter that none of them had day jobs like I did, I beat myself up about it.

"I was working full time for most of it," I explain. If I had more time to write, I could've done it much quicker. Which is the exact reason I quit my job right after leaving that group.

Writing *is* my job, my dream job, even though it hasn't given me much of an income.

Yet.

"I'm impressed. It must take a lot to actually finish something like that and put it out into the world. More people probably give up than actually go through with it."

"I was almost one of those," I confess. "I have a lot more abandoned ideas than completed ones."

"Don't we all." It's not a question, but a statement.

And I like it. It makes me feel more like I'm just another human, instead of the failure my mind makes me out to be. Rationally speaking, I know that's not what I am. I have my proud moments, but I have a lot of doubtful ones too.

Plus, it's nice to feel like I have a small piece in common with Miles. I've always thought of him as someone who has their shit together in a way I only wish I was capable of. I can't even say I've gotten all that much closer in the last few years. I don't plan on telling him that the book has been a flop so far, and I've still spent way more on the process than I've made in the last few months since publishing. I'm not great at social media or putting myself out there, and it shows in my sales.

By the time we're both in the middle of our meal and at the end of our second drink, the conversation steers back to the serious stuff. Like his ex-wife.

Ex. Wife.

Still wrapping my head around that one.

"You really didn't like her, did you?" he asks me, but he looks amused rather than insulted.

"Not as much as she didn't like me!" I raise my voice a little louder than I should in a restaurant that's now full of people, but he's unfazed. "And *I* had good reason! I was always nice to her, and she despised me just for existing."

"Yeah," he says. "She was kind of a bitch."

I burst out laughing at that. The drinks must be getting to the both of us.

"That probably doesn't make me seem like a great guy," he adds shyly. "But I'm not just saying that because we're not together anymore. There were definitely things I loved about her, but I was always aware that she wasn't the nicest person behind it all."

I don't know what to say to that so I give him a sympathetic frown. I'm glad he knew it at least. I always hoped he'd realize it before they ever got married, but better late than never.

"I think she was jealous of you."

"If I had just taken a drink, I'd be tempted to spit it out right now." I keep my facial expression serious, and he smiles wide at that.

"I'm serious," he says. "My family liked you—" *Not by the end they didn't.* I keep quiet as he goes on. "They didn't care for her at all. And she always got frustrated when she couldn't get her eyeliner to look like yours."

"That second reason is solid."

"I know you're being sarcastic, but I really did wake up to her crying once because she had to leave for work and '*Autumn said it only takes her five minutes.*'" I notice his face drop as soon as the words are out.

It's obvious he feels guilty talking poorly about her, despite it being the truth. I know exactly what it's like to have respect for someone that has none for you. I also know that it can feel really good to let go of it for a few seconds and say how you really feel.

I like that I'm the person he's letting go in front of. He has to know that *I get it*. I can't count the times I blurted out an insult about his brother, just for him to laugh with me about it instead of taking his side.

What a full circle this feels like.

7

AUTUMN

I 'm feeling on top of the world after dinner. There's something so refreshing about opening up to someone outside of the usual people in my circle. My friends are just as invested in my life as I am in theirs, but they've experienced things with me *as* I go through them. I wouldn't trade them for the world, but it's not the same as updating someone with fresh eyes. Someone with an outside perspective. They're interested in a different way.

I refuse to let myself consider that I'm excited because I might possibly be swooning a bit.

Nope.

No, he's just a shiny new friend. He'll feel like one of the girls in no time.

I'm so lost in my thoughts that I almost jump out of my skin when I notice Reya is leaning against my front door. Her face is red and she looks flustered. I realize in that moment that I haven't checked my phone since I walked in the restaurant over a couple hours ago. We sat there talking for so much longer than I expected to, but by the time we switched to drinking water, we had to wait before driving home. Neither of us cared at all, the conversation flowing so easily.

"Where have you been?" Reya's voice is raspy, like she's been crying or yelling. I wrap her in a hug without hesitation.

"I went to dinner," I mumble into her hair. I hope she can hear me, muffled as I am. "What's going on?"

She pulls away, and based on her expression, I think it's because she'll burst into tears if we stand here a few more seconds. As soon as the door is unlocked, I rush in and scoop Elaine into my arms before she can dart past us. She's always waiting right by the door, hoping for her chance. I've honestly lost count of how many times I've had to chase her down. Once the door is shut, I kiss the top of her head and let her continue on her way. Probably to scratch at said door like a puppy who's eager for a walk.

Reya pulls her coat off, mindlessly dropping it on the floor. I have to hold back the urge to say anything, because there's a coat closet *right* behind her. She knows this, but now is not the time for me to worry about it.

"I really suck at relationships," she says.

Then my friend starts sobbing.

We sit on the couch and I wrap her in my arms without saying a word. This isn't a normal occurrence, she doesn't cry in front of me often. Even after years of dealing with her ex-husband and separately raising their daughter, she's always held it together. She acted like it was a blessing she got to do so.

I wouldn't have been so strong in her situation. Being away from her daughter half the time, not being able to control *half* of her life. It would drive me crazy with worry, especially if the father of my child was hers.

Caleb never really learned how to grow up, or communicate, or compromise.

I don't pry, because I know she'll talk when she's ready. I just hold her, and gently run my fingers through her bright pink pixie cut.

A few minutes pass before her tears dry up and she pulls away from me. When I see how red her face is, and how her eyes still glisten under damp eyelashes, I want to pull her right back. Reya deserves the world, and it breaks my heart that she doesn't have it.

"I'm sorry, love. I guess I've been keeping that in for a while."

"If you think about all the times I've cried on you, I'd say this was way overdue."

That makes her laugh, thankfully. I jump up and grab a couple of sodas out of the fridge, still being patient as ever. She drinks Pepsi like it's water so I usually have some on hand. She takes the can so eagerly, you'd think she was dying if she didn't.

"I broke up with Olivia."

I inhale a harsh breath. That wasn't what I expected her to say.

"I thought things were going well. I thought you liked her."

She groans and throws her head back. "I thought so too, but my standards are so messed up. I've been *asking* for the bare minimum, and that's not what I want for myself. I shouldn't have to ask!"

I nod in agreement. "It's not what I want Dahlia to grow up thinking is acceptable, either. I want her to have zero doubts about what she'll deserve from someone someday."

"But that doesn't change how much you liked her?"

Her eyes well up again, but she shuts her eyes tight to fight them off. "Not even a little bit. It's been six hours and I miss her."

"What is it you miss about her?"

"She was funny. Really funny," she says.

I don't know how anyone could take Reya's laughter for grant-ed. If she thinks you're funny and you can coax a laugh out of her, you usually want to do everything you can to keep it coming.

"If you want someone funny, what are you doing here?" It's a fact we all know well, I am not the one with the jokes in our group.

Reya smiles. "I didn't want to laugh, I wanted to cry."

That *is* my strong suit. Whether crying or comforting, I think I'm pretty good with the emotional stuff.

"You made the right move. You and Dahlia deserve better than the bare minimum."

"I know." She makes eye contact with me, and they shine with even more unshed tears. "I wish it hadn't taken months for it to hit me. What if it doesn't next time, and I end up married and unhappy again?"

"Well, I think you're better prepared now. This happening for the first time since your divorce might have been exactly what you needed to make sure it won't happen again."

She nods slowly a couple times before standing and heading towards my living room window. I don't follow, but I admire the view when she opens up the blinds to gaze outside. It's so perfectly yellow out there, the leaves remaining on the trees make me smile.

How could you not feel optimistic during the season of change?

Reya does what she does best, and decides to change the subject. Feeling vulnerable is not her favorite thing, but I'm grateful for the moments she does give me.

"What's new with you? Catch me up on all things Autumn."

"I just had dinner with Miles."

She turns so fast it's a blur and suddenly she's back to sitting beside me. "He asked you to dinner?" I nod. "You went to dinner?" I nod again. "How was it?"

I can't help the smile that spreads across my face, even if she's going to make assumptions about it. "It was really nice. We got to catch up, talk about life. He's still just as great as I remember."

"Just as hot as you remember, too?" When I don't answer, she presses. "I don't believe you were *too flustered to notice* that first time. Come on! Spill the tea!"

I cover my face with my hands in an attempt to keep her from reading me, but it shows my cards anyway.

"I'm going to start planning your wedding," she blurts out. "Look at you right now! I see you blushing under there!"

I'm laughing, appreciative of the way she knows me. I love her enthusiastic self, but I can't get caught up in her attempts to find me a husband right now.

"You stop that! That's absolutely not going to happen," I tell her. "Even if he wasn't Justin's *brother*, he just got a divorce."

"I don't see the problem." She holds up her fingers to count on them. "Justin is so far in the past that it's irrelevant." She points the next finger. "He's *divorced*. Not married, not complicated. *Available.*"

"You of all people should know that just because someone is divorced, it doesn't mean they're available," I point out. " And it definitely doesn't mean things aren't complicated."

"Well fine," she concedes. "Maybe it'll take a few months, but you can still flirt. Build this thing up now, so you're ready to act on it later."

I shake my head, as much as a part of me wishes that was realistic. "It's not happening, Reya. I think we're going to be good friends."

She seems to think on my words for a few seconds. "I think it's time for us to meet him. Vic and I can tell you right away if he's interested, and then you can stop pretending you're not." She's fully confident in her words, as if she hasn't been wrong before.

About her own love life *or* mine. I don't question her.

"I guess we'll see."

Miles and I talk every night for a week. It's nice to know that our dinner wasn't a fluke, and our conversations don't lose momentum. One of us usually ends up falling asleep on the other, but we pick up where we left off in the mornings. Every time he responds to me is a bit of a surprise, going against my insecurities that try hard to convince me he won't.

I have him on speaker as I put my clean laundry away. He laughs every time I have to tell Elaine to stop eating my socks. He thought that was only something that dogs do, just like I did before I found her. I had to give him the entire list of traits she has that make me think she was a dog in a past life.

"So being an author is your only job?" he asks me. "That must be nice, getting to choose your schedule every day."

I hold back a sigh. That's what I thought too, before I realized I wasn't destined to become a bestseller after publishing my first book. It's an expensive path to take.

"It *shouldn't* be my only job, to be honest. I've been looking for something, but I'm being picky," I admit.

"What are you being picky about?"

"I just want something that isn't going to get in the way of my writing too much. With hours, or with how much brain power it takes. The type of jobs I'm used to doing typically do."

"What are you used to?"

"Mostly administrative stuff, but..." I trail off, thinking about how much my last job sucked the life out of me. I can't go back to something like that.

"Unless you're about to say that it's the worst job in the world and you'll never do it again, I might have an idea."

Despite the fact that it just *might* be the worst job in the world, my interest is piqued.

"Okay, what do you got?"

"My mom is looking for an extra person around her office right now," he says. "Part-time."

If I could physically deflate like a balloon, that's what I'd be doing right now.

"Oh. Um..." Words fail me for a few seconds. "Thanks for throwing that out there, but that's probably not the best idea."

Before he can respond, Elaine leaps from the floor and lands right onto my phone. I watch it happen in slow motion and reach out to catch her a second too late. Her toe beans manage to land right on the big, red button that ends the phone call. I sigh as I pick her up, and hope Miles didn't think I ended the call over his suggestion.

I wouldn't want him to think I'm upset and overreacting over something so small. I still don't know what Justin told his family about me back then, but I know how emotional I was. I know what they saw.

I cradle Elaine in one arm, surprisingly easily, and pick up my phone with my free hand. It's around her dinnertime so I switch my multitasking to calling Miles back, and scooping some food into her bowl. Hopefully that distracts her for a while.

"Why not?" he asks instead of a greeting. His question sounds genuine, like he can't think of a single reason.

"Hello to you, too. Sorry, my cat hung up on you."

"No hard feelings. She'll have to meet me in person. Won't happen again after that."

"Is that so?"

"It is so. She's going to love me so much, she'll start fighting you over who gets to talk to me. We might even have to start video calling for her sake."

I laugh at that, but I definitely don't agree to anything. I'm nervous enough about phone calls, I don't need to add my face into the mix. "Confident with cats, are you?"

"I've never met a pet that didn't love me."

I don't doubt it for a second.

"So, why don't you think it's a good idea to work for my mom?" he persists.

I groan at his inability to let it drop.

"So. Many. Reasons." I wish after all this time, I wasn't so awkward whenever the past got brought up.

"Justin sized reasons?"

My grip tightens around the shirt I'd just picked up. We've done a good job of pretending he doesn't exist so far. I'm surprised to hear the name come out of Miles' mouth.

"Pretty much," I admit through clenched teeth.

"I don't look at you and think of him anymore," he confesses. Hearing it makes my heart skip a beat, although I can't explain why. "She probably doesn't either. A lot of time has passed."

"I would hope so," I mumble.

"I'm serious," he says eagerly. "She has a nice office downtown. It's pretty simple work, I help her out every once in a while."

"What does she do?"

"Interior design. She picked it up a couple years ago and she's *good*. She's got a solid client base."

"Hmmm." I draw out the sound so he knows I'm thinking.

Am I thinking about it, though?

Would I consider this? I guess it wouldn't hurt too much to interview, but the idea of being around Amelia all day freaks me out. She was too good at making me feel like I was an issue when things got bad with Justin. Like if I never came around again, her family would be perfect.

"I can feel her out first before saying anything," he offers. "Just mention you and see what her reaction is."

That seems like a safe option.

"It would be nice to start over with her..."

"So, you'll consider it? At least talk to her?"

"Sure," I concede. "Let me know what she says, and I'll... I'm willing to interview."

"Awesome. I'll give her your number if that's okay." He keeps talking but I'm zoned out now. I give some half hearted response, and just hope Amelia has changed over the years as much as I have.

8

Autumn

Seven Years Ago

"I don't want to go," Justin tells his mom as we're all seated around the table for dinner. Myself and the three members of their household. Amelia's new boyfriend is here too, along with his son that's a few years younger than we are. The two of them are so quiet, it's easy to forget they're in the room.

My shoulders drop, and I'm instantly so disappointed I could cry. I've really been looking forward to this trip, and he just ruined it for me with five words.

"Why on earth not?" she asks him.

He shrugs, pushing food around his plate but not eating any of it. Looking uninterested and uncomfortable has been his thing lately, and it's starting to really wear on me. I don't know how to get through to him, he hardly talks to me.

"You don't want to spend time with your family?"

"I don't want to be stuck in a car for hours," is his only response. It is a long road trip, so it would make sense if that was the issue. I just have a feeling it isn't.

They go back and forth a few times, her trying to convince him, and him not saying much at all. Even her boyfriend tries, which is a surprise to all of us, but Justin ignores him. It makes me feel second-hand guilty. I almost want to respond for him, but I wouldn't know where to begin. Speaking up isn't really my thing.

Everyone at the table looks as defeated as I feel. He's set on staying home, and since he's eighteen, Amelia reluctantly gives in. She's not happy about it, her mouth stays a thin line throughout the rest of dinner. I've listened to her excitedly go on about these plans for months, and I know she's put a lot of time and money into it. I feel bad for her even more than I do for myself.

When Justin gets up from the table, way before anyone else does, he still hasn't eaten any of the food on his plate. I think he's not going to acknowledge me when he walks it to the kitchen, but he turns at the last minute.

"You should still go," he says. His eyes don't linger, he never looks at me for very long these days. Then he drops the plate into the sink, and escapes to his room.

He doesn't want me in there very often anymore either.

I miss him a lot. It sucks to miss someone right next to you. I just keep hoping that whatever rough patch he's going through will end soon.

I don't realize I'm crying until Miles nudges my arm. It's subtle enough to not pull any attention to me, but I know that's his way of comforting me, telling me it'll be okay. He doesn't know that though, Justin doesn't treat him or Amelia any better. We're all equally as worried and frustrated.

I sit there with my head down, pretending to focus on my plate, but I'm not eating it anymore. I'm using Justin's tactic of pushing it around.

It's not uncomfortable to be at the table with my boyfriend's family without him here. I've been having dinner here for years. I hang out with his mom as much as I wish I could hang out with my own.

My parents live right down the road, and they don't even call to check in anymore.

I don't realize when Miles and I are the last one's left sitting at the table until he nudges my arm again. "You should still come with us."

"I don't know." I search for a reason other than feeling like I was only invited as an extension of him. "I'm worried about him being alone for that long."

"Maybe it'll be good for him." Miles shrugs. "He wants to shut everyone out, and we haven't really let him. Maybe if we do, he'll be back to normal by the time the week is up."

Wouldn't that be nice.

"I guess I didn't look at it that way."

"That's because you're a good girlfriend, and I'm a crappy brother." I crack a smile at that, although it's so far from the truth. "You know mom won't let him go a couple hours without calling and checking in."

I like when he doesn't specify that Amelia is *his* mom. It's a small way of making me feel like I am a part of this family, and not just the girlfriend Justin brought around.

Amelia appears, standing by the table next to my chair. "He's right, I won't."

"I really do want to go," I tell them.

"Then it's settled," Miles says with a big smile.

I can't help but smile right back at him.

ele

Kara doesn't go with us, but she was invited. She blames it on work, but even Miles doesn't seem to believe that. They've been together for almost a year now and she doesn't spend a lot of time with his family.

The rest of us have a fun time on the road, being tourists. I see lots of new things, considering this is the first time I've left the town I was born in. We stay at a few different hotels, some of the rooms fancier than anywhere I've ever stayed. It's nice to feel included, and I can tell Amelia is going out of her way to do so.

I'm still so aware that I'm the outsider here.

I don't think I'd feel any different if Justin had come. He doesn't text me back or answer my phone calls the entire week we're gone. I can't help but notice that he answers every time his mom calls. I stay quiet about it because the last thing this trip needs is for me to share the dark cloud hanging over my head.

I think Miles can see it, he's definitely more intuitive than his brother is. He's been my favorite part of the entire trip, and I find myself thrilled that we become better friends than we were.

Although, I think a big piece that's played a role in our bonding is that Kara isn't answering her phone most of the time either.

He got up one night to answer a call after the lights were off and everyone except myself was fast asleep. Before he stepped into the hallway, I could hear her raised voice through the phone. I pretended to be asleep, just to save him the embarrassment. That is, until I heard him groan on the other side of the door. I instantly knew he hadn't grabbed a key card, and would be too polite to knock, not wanting to wake any of us. I quietly slipped out of the bed, conveniently closest to the door, and let him in.

His eyes were red, and his hair was messy which told me he'd been aggressively running his hand through it. He did look embarrassed to see me, but I offered him a small smile. Then, without a single word, I stepped away and went back to bed.

I can't help but feel like Justin wanted me to stay gone even if I'm not the only one. His entire household did come back along with me. He talks to all of us even less than he was, and I prefer his silence to all the snapping and yelling. Amelia has had to step in a couple times when he lost his patience, and send me home. She doesn't blame me as far as I can tell, but she doesn't realize how much it makes me feel like I'm being punished. I love my best friend, and living with her isn't so bad, but it doesn't feel like my home. I don't know what that does feel like, but Justin's must come close.

Only a week after we've returned, he lets me into his room with no intention of talking anything through. I'm hesitant, but I want to try anyway. Maybe *this* time he won't freak out if I pry a little. I don't think he can keep things bottled up forever. Everyone has a limit, don't they?

I look around the room, taking in the space that's starting to look less familiar to me. An ache builds in my chest at the reminder of what's become of our relationship. This distant and cold person is not who he is, and I want the old version back.

He grabs my wrist and tries to pull me towards his bed at the same moment my eyes land on a pair of earrings on his nightstand. Dainty things with a blue stone.

I subconsciously tug on my unpierced ear, and feel some things click into place about the last few months. Things that should have clicked a long time ago. He doesn't see where my gaze has landed, or understand why I'm frozen, so he pulls me again.

"What is your deal?" he asks.

A name plays in my head on repeat, one that I thought was done haunting my life.

I harshly tug out of his grip, and run straight out of the house with tears streaming down my face. He doesn't follow me, not this time.

I'm as relieved as I am devastated.

9

AUTUMN

I'm nervous for more reasons than one as I take in the small office building. From the sidewalk, you can see everything going on inside the brightly lit space. The walls are painted a sage green, and every piece of furniture is a dark shade of brown. There are so many plants placed around the open room that I don't bother counting them. From this image in front of me alone, I'd trust her to make over my apartment.

I don't notice anyone inside from out here, which makes me question what I put in my calendar. I'm almost positive she told me to be here at eleven, and it's currently two minutes until then. I could run back to my car until the second I'm on time, but that feels like a bit much.

With a deep breath, I push the glass door open and hope there's a bell to alert someone of my presence. Mostly, I just hope there's someone here to *be* alerted. I imagine there must be since the door wasn't locked.

There's no sound other than some soft radio music, and there's definitely no one in the main room. I take a deep breath, and approach the large desk closest to the door. What other option do I have other than to wait? I've never been good at situations like this. How long is too long to stand here? Should I try to message her? Should I call out in case someone is hiding behind one of the two doors I see in the back?

"Hello?" I decide on the last option without realizing I even made it.

A squeak comes from behind one of the doors, followed by some shuffling, and what sounds like someone kicking something. Sure enough I hear some quiet exclamation in a voice that's definitely not Amelia's.

"Sorry, just one second!" the voice calls.

I'm waiting there for a couple more awkward minutes, before a bright eyed, red-haired girl comes bouncing out. She doesn't look any older than twenty.

"You must be Autumn!" She shakes my hand when she reaches me, and it's a surprisingly firm grip. "Sorry about that, I was trying to get some food in me and lost track of the time. I'm Kaitlyn! I run the show around here when Amelia is out. I'll just look over your resume and ask you some basic questions if that sounds good to you!" Kaitlyn is *very* bubbly, it reminds me of Reya.

"Sure, sounds great," I say with my best smile. "Amelia isn't here?"

"She's running late at an appointment, it's hard to say when she'll be back. Do you want to have a seat?" She points towards one of the smaller desks with two cushioned chairs in front of it. "Can I get you anything? Coffee, tea, juice, water?"

"No, I'm okay. Thank you."

I walk over and drop down into one of the chairs, which is much deeper than it looks. I sink right in, and struggle to sit up and look professional. My purse falls to the ground in the process, some of my things spilling out onto the floor. I *have* had plenty of interviews before, I *know* how to do this. It's frustrating me that I'm failing to look like it within the first few seconds of this thing.

Once I've managed to scoot myself to the edge of the seat, and collect my things, I realize Kaitlyn is laughing.

Upon eye contact she stops, and waves her hand. "I am so sorry, don't be embarrassed. Those chairs ruffle a lot of feathers, and it never gets less entertaining. I spilled an entire coffee down the front of my shirt the first time I sat in it. Think of it as an initiation! I'd say that was a pretty harmless one."

I smile at that. The explanation calms me down, knowing it could have been much worse. Her personality helps too, not what I was expecting. Especially because *Amelia* is what I was expecting. I think I'm relieved that's not the case.

"That's fair enough."

She reaches out for the folder in my hand. "Let's see that resume." I hand it over and watch as she reads it in its entirety. She doesn't look up or say anything until she's completely done.

"Pretty impressive," she says. "I do have to ask why there's a large gap here, that can be a red flag."

I gulp nervously, like I'm a cartoon character or something. I never know how someone will take it when I explain what I do, and what my goals are. Not a lot of people take it seriously, or want to hire someone that's not fully focused on the job they're applying for. Been there, had that go wrong.

"I'm an author. I used those gaps to focus on writing and publishing," I explain.

"An *author*?" She says it like it's the most exciting thing she's heard all day. "Why isn't that on here? That's incredible!"

I go with honesty, because she's given me no reason to think I should have to fake an answer. "It was on there once upon a time, but I got a couple of negative responses. It comes off as the equivalent of putting babysitting on your resume at sixteen. People think it's filler." I shrug in a way that says, *what can you do?*

"Wow. I can't say that surprises me, but how frustrating! You should be able to brag! What have you written? Have I heard of it? Will you sign one for me? I've never owned a book signed by the author before."

Her excited babbling lifts my mood significantly, and before I know it we're laughing and talking like a couple of old friends. She asks lots of questions, none of them pertaining to the job I'm here for. She's interested in *me*, in my writing. It makes me feel good.

After twenty minutes of explaining the plot of my book, how I got started with writing, what I'm working on now, and promising to sign a copy for her, I feel a gust of air hit my back.

The first words said are, "Amelia, you *have* to hire her!"

I think I love Kaitlyn.

I hear a chuckle from behind me, and I turn to see a ghost. Well, it feels like I'm looking at a ghost, because I never thought I'd willingly be in the same room as this woman again. She looks more or less the same as she used to with a short black bob, and her signature red lipstick.

I'm surprised to see her staring at me with endearment as she walks forward and holds her arms out. Luckily, I don't fumble getting out of my seat and giving her the hug she reached for.

"You're so grown up," she whispers. Then, gently grabbing my biceps, she holds me an arms length away and looks me over. "You're *so* grown up!"

I giggle nervously, not used to being examined like this. "Yeah, I guess I am."

"You two already know each other? So you're hiring her, right?" Kaitlyn asks from behind me.

"Did you take notes?"

"Notes?"

"Of her interview answers?"

"Oh," Kaitlyn says. "No, I didn't do that."

Amelia sighs, but it doesn't seem serious. Not with a smile still stuck on her face.

"How does a trial day sound?" she asks as she looks back to me. "Come in for a few hours, let you get a feel for how things go around here?"

I nod eagerly. "That would be perfect."

We work out the details, the three of us chatting at Kaitlyn's desk for another few minutes. I can't get over the way Amelia keeps looking at me, as if she's proud of what she sees. I wasn't expecting such a warm reaction considering how cold she was the last time we spoke.

When I finally walk out of the office with instructions to come back in a couple days, I can't restrain the smile on my face. I'm excited to tell Miles how well things went and I'm momentarily surprised that he's the first person that comes to mind. Maybe it's because he's the one that referred me, but I haven't even told the girls about the potential job.

I'm usually so quick to give them every detail, but I can't tell one of them something without telling the other. As much as I love Reya, she's been on overdrive with comments about my potential love life. She means well, but she's also trying hard to avoid any conversation about how she's doing with her breakup. That one day was all I got, and I'm not surprised, despite the messages I've sent to check in.

I send a message to our group chat, letting them know we're overdue to catch up. I refrain from adding that it has nothing to do with Miles, and hope it's not what either of them assume.

The three of us meet at Vic's house for lunch. She didn't get a chance to find a babysitter, which worked out great because we are a gushing mess over these babies.

Her daughter, Amira, who I can't believe is already three, hangs off of me the entire time. I'm not complaining about it for a second, I don't see her as much as I'd like to.

"So, what's the new job?" Reya asks with a mouth full of cheese. Lunch is an elaborate charcuterie board, filled with some things I don't even know the names of. Fruit, cheese, meats, crackers, cute little pieces of bread, and it's all arranged in a spiral pattern. I don't understand how Vic does it all. She has super powers.

"Another receptionist position, and it's not exactly official. I have a working interview on Monday." I pick up a grape, but stop myself from eating before I'm done talking. I like to think I have manners. "They do interior design and they work out of the office a lot, so it should be laid back."

"But your boss would be Justin and Miles' mother?" Vic asks right as I pop the grape into my mouth.

"Well, yeah," I say, chewing.

"How could that possibly be *laid back*?"

I shake my head, and readjust the toddler that's falling asleep in (and trying to fall out of) my arms. "She was happy to see me. It wasn't awkward or anything."

"How does she feel about you guys hanging out?"

"I don't know. He might not have told her. I didn't get details about that conversation." Vic and Reya both open their mouths to ask their next questions, but I stop them. "It doesn't matter anyway, because he and I are only friends and that isn't changing. Why wouldn't she be okay with that?"

I watch as they glance at each other with raised brows.

"The look on your face when you text him says you're full of it," Vic points out.

"That's true," Reya adds with her mouth full of food again. Okay, we all *clearly* have the best manners around each other. "The texting face says it all."

Vic mumbles some sort of agreement and looks at me like *I'm* the one being ridiculous right now. I roll my eyes, and look down at Amira's sleeping face. My arm has gone a little numb, but she's so worth it.

"You guys look at my face too closely," I mutter.

Reya comes around the counter to wrap her arms around my shoulders. "Why wouldn't we? There's always so much going on there."

"I'm sure it's going to go great," Miles tells me confidently.

Quite the assumption.

"You shouldn't be that sure. I've blown it with plenty of jobs before."

He's quiet for a second and I wonder what he's thinking about that. I find myself trying to imagine what I look like in his eyes, with the knowledge of who I used to be. I consider myself a completely different person, but that doesn't mean that's what he sees.

"Is that popcorn I hear?"

A laugh bursts out of me, not realizing he would be able to hear it.

"It absolutely is. I'm going to give myself a break tonight and watch a movie."

He gives a hum of approval. "What are you watching?"

"I haven't decided yet, but... " I trail off, getting an idea. Possibly a bad one. Better to rip the band-aid off, right? "I know you just got off work, but would you want to come over? Help me decide what to watch?"

As soon as the words fly out, I regret asking them. I'm sure he has better things to do than hang out with me. Like hanging out with actual friends that he didn't have a front row seat to years of their pity party for.

"I mean— sorry. Never mind, I don't know why I asked."

"You don't know why? You don't want to hang out with me?" He fakes a sound of offense.

"No, I just mean... you don't have to. You probably have stuff going on."

"I don't have anything going on. A movie night sounds like fun."

His response is casual enough that I physically relax. We've had lots of movie nights together in the past. There's no reason for this to be any different.

No pressure.

Unsurprisingly, my body doesn't listen to my mind, and I can feel myself begin to sweat at the idea of him being in my space.

"Okay, great!" I say, louder than necessary. "Bring microwave popcorn if you have it because this is my last bag and I *will* demolish it."

I text him my address and then spend fifteen minutes cleaning up my messy apartment. When he arrives with a bag full of snacks, I think I'm in love.

Not *actually* in love, obviously. That would be ridiculous. It's just that snacks are the way to my heart, and he just made sure that I will be keeping this friendship.

"How do you feel about horror movies?" I ask him.

He looks at me with a side eye that gives me his answer, and I burst out laughing.

"Not a fan? That's okay, I'm nothing if not reasonable. We could watch a romantic comedy instead," I give in my cheeriest voice. The corners of his mouth tilt up at that.

"You don't give a guy a lot of options."

"How about one of those depressing, but meant to be inspiring movies where the dog dies?" The look of horror on his face is exactly what I was hoping for. "Whew, you passed that test."

He leans towards me and snatches the remote from my hand. "Don't worry, I'm nothing if not reasonable," he mimics.

I can't even be irritated, because I'm still a little starstruck at having him here. How many times while writing, or reading back my novel did I wish I could see him again? Creating Cam, the love interest, was only so much of an outlet. There are just some things, some *people* you can't get out of your head that easily.

I blush just thinking about it, because of course my mind goes to the inappropriate scenes I wrote with him in mind. Not the thing to be doing when he's sitting a couple feet away, watching a movie with me. If I would have guessed we'd be here, I would've based the character on someone much more unreachable. There are plenty of hot, famous men I never stand a chance of meeting. Why couldn't my inspiration have been one of them?

If I'm being painfully honest, Miles is much better looking than any of the ones that come to mind.

I watch as his arm comes up to rest on the back of the couch, getting comfortable. He seems to zone out as he rubs the throw blanket that's draped there beneath his fingers. Whatever thought was in his head takes a few seconds to pass and give him the freedom to turn and look at it. I've never seen anyone stare at a blanket for so long, and I'm confused at first.

Until I'm not. It has multiple holes in it by now, lots of them from Elaine. It's yellow and knitted, and pilling *so* badly, but I just keep throwing it in the wash.

It's *his* blanket, or at least it used to be. He stuck it in a box for me on the day I officially moved out of his place. I'm embarrassed to still have it, especially given its current condition. It wouldn't have been difficult to replace the damn thing, but it comforted me. I might as well have received it as a toddler, the way I grew attached to it. It had to be with me everywhere I went, and then it found a home on this couch in this apartment a few years ago.

"I've kind of missed this blanket," he says quietly. "It's still so soft."

"Unfortunately for you, I am unwilling to part with it."

He smiles, but doesn't respond. I notice he doesn't stop touching it, though.

The remote is finally in play, and Miles starts to search, scrolling through all of the genres until he lands on horror. I keep my mouth shut, just smiling to myself. He's not an indecisive person, which I'm grateful for, and he lands on something pretty quickly. It looks like it's about a haunted house, but before I can finish reading the blurb, he's asking if I'm okay with it.

"One of our residents was watching this the other day. It didn't look so bad."

During one of our many phone calls, I learned that Miles manages a small retirement home, and he loves what he does. It's sweet, and it makes all kinds of sense to me. He's always been the type to take care of others.

"Looks decent enough."

Deciding there's enough here that I don't have to worry about eating it all in the first half of the movie, I investigate the snack situation. A box of microwaveable popcorn, a big bag of peanut M&M's, a bag of pretzels, and some hard ciders. It's a little random, but they're all things I enjoy so I choose the bag of pretzels.

"Oh, hold on," he orders as he grabs the bag from my hand. He grabs everything else too, and makes his way to my kitchen. I whine in protest, but he just smirks. "It'll be worth it, I promise."

I watch Miles make the popcorn in the microwave. He puts it on for too long, but I notice he's listening for the moment the popping slows down. What a skill.

He looks around my kitchen without asking for direction until he finds another big bowl to throw it into, but he doesn't stop there. He throws in the candy and the pretzels too, using his hands to mix everything together. I'm definitely intrigued.

He lifts his hands to show me a colorful, buttery, chocolate mess coating them. "This was always my favorite part."

I am not okay with how adorable that is.

I wonder how much this grown man would hate being called that to his face. Not that I'll ever do that, but someone *really* should, just to see.

Once he's done washing his hands, he plops down next to me and sets the bowl between us. I look at it curiously, not usually one for mixing sweet and salty.

"Don't tell me you've never had this before?"

I look at him like he's crazy. "Kind of a specific mixture for me to have tried before."

I go in, grabbing one of each of the ingredients. He smirks at me as he watches me pick them out. "Smart. And it's a family thing, I thought maybe Justin had shown you."

I shove the snack in my mouth, hoping to mask how uncomfortable it makes me to hear his brother's name. Thankfully he's too busy filling his own face to notice. It is pretty good, actually. It doesn't change my stance on sweet and salty, but he looks like it's the best thing he's ever had in his life.

"That's amazing," I exaggerate. "How did you keep this from me when we were younger?"

He shrugs, but it's not genuine nonchalance. "I didn't make it for a long time. My first date with Kara was at the movies, and she was miserable the whole time. Complaining that she couldn't stand the smell. It was so bad we ended up leaving before the movie was over, so I just stopped buying it after that. I didn't want her to think my apartment smelled bad."

Seconds pass while I wrap my head around that.

"Popcorn?"

He nods.

"Who doesn't like the smell of *popcorn*?"

"Kara, apparently."

I see it on his face that he's uncomfortable talking about her again, and I hate it. It makes me wish there was something I could do to reassure him.

Instead, I turn my attention back to the movie and we continue to watch in silence. It's not a bad movie, but it's cheesy. I've judged its cover a million times while searching for something to watch, and don't feel too disappointed that I've skipped it until now.

The only sounds in my living room for an hour and a half are the crunching of snacks and the opening of cans. I'm so used to doing this alone, but I find myself really enjoying his quiet company.

I'm disappointed when it ends, not ready to say goodbye for the night. I almost want to ask him what movie is next, but I don't know if that's too presumptuous. He might be tired, might have to work early tomorrow. I'd feel rejected despite his reason, so with that in mind, I decide not to say anything.

I'm nervous to look over at him, worried that he'll take that as his cue to go. To keep myself from doing so, I pretend to be interested in the credits that are now on the screen.

I am not reading a single word of it.

My beautiful, wonderful, amazing cat picks this exact second to jump into his lap and start kneading. That means in less than sixty seconds, she'll curl up into a big, fluffy ball and claim him as her bed. I know for a fact now that she is on my side, despite our struggles with her chewing on my phone chargers.

I'm *almost* willing to completely let go of the fact that she's ruined three of them.

"I guess Elaine doesn't want you to leave yet."

He runs his hand down her fur, from her head to her butt and continues to repeat the motion.

"I told you she'd love me," he says with a smirk. "I won't leave then, unless you want me to?"

I shake my head. "No. This is nice."

He smiles in agreement, and we pick out another movie.

10

Autumn

I can't even begin to imagine what the inside of Miles' house would look like. His old apartment had a hand-me-down couch and a couple posters on the walls. Does his mom help him decorate now? Does he decorate at all? Are any of Kara's things there? I don't even know if he bought it before or after the divorce.

These things keep me up at night. Well, they would if I had initially thought about them last night instead of this morning. I know it's his day off, because we stayed up late talking while I tried to get some chapters written.

He distracted me enough that I finished exactly *one*.

The first couple hours after I woke up were spent making up for it, and I'm very satisfied with my work by the time ten rolls around.

"Hey, A."

I make a face at that, and I am *well* aware he can't see me.

"Where'd that come from?"

"I'm not sure, it just came out." He chuckles. "I don't have to use it again."

"No, no, no. I liked it. Please use it again."

"Okay, then I will." I really enjoy being able to hear the smile in his voice. *Ugh.* "What's up?"

"I haven't met your dog."

"That's true. We should fix that."

"What are you doing today?"

I hear something drop in the background, a loud, metallic clatter.

"Shit. I'm trying to get my house cleaned before my mom comes over, but putting dishes away with one hand is harder than it looks. Hold on, one sec." I hear him put his phone down, and pick up whatever he dropped. "You're on speaker, it's just me and Freddy."

I'm confused for all of two seconds before I remember that's the name of the lucky pup.

"Good morning, Freddy."

"He perked up at hearing his name, that's probably the best you'll get out of him right now."

"I'll take it. What are you and Amelia up to?"

He groans. "What she's always up to: decorating. And it's one hundred percent against my will, but she won't take no for an answer now that I'm 'going to be dating again soon.'" He pauses. "Her words, not mine," he clarifies.

I like that he clarifies. I don't want to think any harder on why that is.

"You don't want your house to look nice?" I ask, not acknowledging the rest.

"It already looks nice. The problem is that my mother and I have different definitions."

I chuckle. "I've got to see this, I'm so curious."

He takes me very literally, because only a few seconds pass before a video call request comes through. I don't have a drop of makeup on my face, my hair is knotted and sticking up in weird places. There's no way I can answer him like this.

"Oh! Hold on!" I hang up on him completely as I jump off my bed and run over to my vanity. I rush, feeling a little bad. I settle for simply brushing through my hair and blending out some concealer under my eyes. It's not as great as I'd like to look, but it's an improvement.

I then go to the kitchen and start a cup of coffee to appear slightly more functional. I know it shouldn't matter, but I'm still working on myself. There will be a day when I care less about what people think of me, today just isn't it.

I call him back three minutes after hanging up on him. Not too bad, I think.

He's laughing when his beautiful face appears on my screen. "What was that about?"

"I was..." I blank, not finding any good excuse.

Where's my ability to think on the spot when I need it?

"Were you still in bed?"

I roll my eyes. "Technically."

"Hey, I'm not one to judge." He sets his phone leaning against something and puts his hands up in surrender. "I got up an hour ago, but I would've stayed there longer if I could've." He proves that further by letting out a yawn.

I point my cup of coffee to the wall behind him. "Let's see it then."

He picks his phone up once again and flips the camera. Miles is very thorough in his tour, showing me every room and every wall.

I'm actually quite impressed, and a little sad that Amelia is about to change it before I get to see it in person. His living room is perfectly color coordinated with tans and reds, but the winning piece is a massive wall of posters.

Across from his couch with its burgundy throw pillows, is a wall *covered* with red posters. There are all different shades, sizes and kinds. Some are of old bands, or video games, or movies. They fill the entire wall, in a big, red mosaic.

I make him keep the camera on it for a couple minutes, pointing out the ones I recognize. It's beautiful and I need one.

"Don't let her touch that wall," I say as he guides me back to the kitchen where we started our call. Now, *that's* a room that could use some work. I don't spot a single thing adorning the walls or counter tops.

"Not a chance," he assures. "She already knows it's not going anywhere."

I hear the sound of his phone vibrating with a message, and he lets out a loud exhale. "I've got roughly ten minutes until the chaos begins."

"Then I'll leave you to prepare for the chaos."

"Wish me luck," he says with a sigh. He doesn't seem genuinely upset, just like he has to give his mom a hard time. "Do you want to come over later and see the finished result? You can finally meet this guy, too." He flips the phone camera towards a pile of brown and white fur bundled up on the ground by his feet.

"Sounds like a plan."

The promise of seeing Miles gets more exciting every time it happens.

Freddy is an absolute angel that instantly adores me. I must say, the feeling is mutual when I sit down on the couch and he rests his head on my leg. I'm convinced I'll never move from this exact spot. Not until he does first, anyway.

Miles approaches with an extra drink in hand for me and shakes his head like he can't believe his eyes. Apparently the attention I'm receiving is a rare occurrence. I soak it up, enjoying feeling special.

His house is gorgeous, and has a yard to match. It's not too far away from town, but enough that the surrounding area is lightly wooded. I'm captivated by the log cabin exterior, and how you'd never guess how modern everything looks on the inside.

It doesn't seem like Amelia changed too much, though I'm sure there's plenty I didn't spot on our video call earlier. There's a couple of new rugs, some shiny bar stools in his kitchen. Simple things that do a lot for all of the open space.

He hands me a controller and starts up a video game I'd pointed out on a poster. Something I used to play when I had less going on.

I give him a giddy smile.

We talk while we play, or should I say, while he kicks my ass. I ask about his job, his favorite residents. He asks about when I started taking my writing seriously, and what my goals are. I don't know that I've ever felt so comfortable around anyone before.

When we're over the game, because winning must get *so* boring for him, we switch to some show we've both seen. Another thing we just end up talking over.

"Do you need water or anything?" he asks as he stands. It makes me stop and realize how the time has gotten away from me. My phone tells me it's not late, just after seven.

My growling stomach reminds me I haven't had anything to eat in hours.

"Water would be great. Do you have any popcorn?"

"Do you want some real food?"

I nod eagerly and enjoy his responding laugh. He pulls his phone out of his pocket and opens something I can't see before he hands it to me.

I have never felt so grateful for food delivery apps.

It's too warm when I wake up, and the first thing I notice is that I don't even have a blanket over me.

Weird.

The second thing I notice as I start to sit up is that there's an arm around me, and my head rests on a hard chest.

My entire body locks up in a panic. I have no memory of how I ended up in this position, but we must have fallen asleep after we ate dinner. We definitely didn't make the decision to cuddle while conscious.

Miles has one hand against my back, his other on my hip. I want to groan with embarrassment as I realize how completely draped over him I am. Fully pressed up against his body with a leg over his waist.

His breathing is slow and steady, so I'm fairly certain he's still asleep. I might as well stay put, and let him come to the same conclusion when he wakes up. Despite the heat radiating from his body, he *is* rather comfortable.

I carefully relax back into him, closing the centimeters I'd put between us. Holding back a contented sigh, I let the feel of his hard muscles overwhelm me. If it were anyone else, I wouldn't be sure I could fall asleep like this. I usually need my space to sprawl out, and stay cool.

Miles is different. Making me feel comfortable is a special ability of his.

That is until I hear him sigh, and feel his fingertips trace up my back and over my shoulder.

I try not to stiffen. I try not to alert him that I'm awake.

I fail.

"Is it too warm in here?" he whispers. "I can turn on the air."

I clear my throat but all I can do is nod. Still against his chest, and absolutely not changing that to look up at him. At least not until he gently lifts my arm off of him, and I quickly remove the rest of myself.

I couldn't be more embarrassed.

The couch is deep enough that I have a couple inches to scoot back. I keep my eyes closed, scared to meet his gaze. I'm not sure I could in the darkness of this room, but it's not worth the risk.

I don't want to know how he's feeling.

When he stands, my ability to think comes back to me. I'm warring with myself on whether or not I should just collect my things and head home.

I finally open my eyes to glance at the digital clock on his stove, which reads two in the morning. The sight of it is enough for me to know I'm too exhausted to pretend I could drive right now.

Tomorrow sounds like a great time to process all of this.

Or the next day. Or never.

Nestling into the throw pillow that's perfectly cold from being neglected, I start to close my eyes before I hear a thud. A whispered curse comes from Miles across the room, causing me to sit up.

"Are you okay?"

Another falls from his lips before he says, "I just kicked the wall, I'm okay." A cool breeze floats through the room then, making the urge to sink in this couch for a few hours of uninterrupted sleep impossible to resist.

Or it would be if I didn't feel like I was imposing on his space.

I can see his silhouette move through the darkness, and I feel the couch move with his weight when he sits down.

What if he's too nice to tell me to go home?

I open my mouth, about to ask, but quickly stop myself before any words come out.

He scoots closer to me until we're touching again, and then I feel his fingers brush lines up and down my arm. The movement pulls all the air from my lungs, and I fight it with a shaky inhale.

This can't be blamed on sleep, he's *choosing* to be touching me right now.

Butterflies are waging war in my chest, but I stay still and stare towards what I can see of his face. His eyes are open, and he's staring right back at me with a blank look. I get the feeling, even in the low visibility, that I'm missing something.

My limbs ache with the desire to wrap themselves around him. I'm hesitant. I'm nervous.

He breaks the silence with a whisper. "Can I?"

I'm not sure exactly what he means, but I think I would agree to anything he asked of me right now.

"Yes."

He slides into the space beside me and pulls me close. We almost end up back in the same position we started in.

I'm stunned by how well Miles fits in all the right places.

In addition to the lines my thoughts are crossing, we're surely crossing some physical ones.

I do cuddle with my friends occasionally, this doesn't really *have* to mean anything deeper than it does with them. We're both probably a little starved for human contact, and what better solution?

I dare to drape my leg over him again, and it skims over a *very* hard ridge. Every single thought I just had flies from my head quicker than I've ever experienced. A hot bolt of electricity shoots through me, telling my body that it has a problem to fix. I move my leg away from the issue, because I do *not* agree with it. I can't.

Miles doesn't react, despite how obvious I made my retreat.

His lack of action helps to ground me, and my heart rate slowly starts to even out.

"Good night, A." His whisper is hoarse.

"Good night, Miles."

11

AUTUMN

I'm finishing up my hair when I hear the doorbell ring. It's a rare occasion, but it's usually a delivery guy ditching a package at my door. I'm racking my brain to try and remember if I ordered anything, but I come up blank. I've been really good about saving my money lately.

I run the straightener through the last section quickly before investigating. When you live alone as a woman, you don't open your door without investigating.

My heart rate instantly spikes when I look through the peephole.

"What are you doing here?" I ask as I open the door.

It's not the most polite of greetings, but he doesn't seem to mind.

There's a shopping bag in Miles' hand, and he holds it out to me.

"You said you weren't feeling great earlier so I grabbed you a couple things."

His face turns a little pinker than usual and I gape. Miles Cress is standing in front of me with a gift, and *blushing* about it.

I mentioned that I had some cramps earlier, but I didn't explain any further. I suppose he did live with a woman for years, it would be concerning if he didn't know what period symptoms were.

I must be in shock because I don't grab the bag, not for an awkwardly long amount of time.

He went to the store for me.

"Autumn?" he says to snap me out of it.

I clear my throat and hope he doesn't notice how close I am to crying. I hate that I never have control over the water works.

"That's so nice, thank you. I–" I pause because there aren't any words that feel good enough. "You really shouldn't have."

He's looking at the bag like he's not sure why he did it either, but then he slightly shakes his head.

"It's no big deal. I wanted to."

I could melt on the floor right here, right now.

I could also get used to him being the kind of friend I can count on for cuddling and impromptu deliveries.

Moving to let him inside my apartment, I finally take the bag. It contains Midol, some bright pink vitamins, and a couple of my favorite snacks. The tears build up for a second, but he doesn't notice them right away.

"I don't know if you've heard of them, but Kara would swear by those vitamins. She said they—" He looks at my eyes then, sees the moisture gathering, and steps towards me with his arms open. I fall right into his embrace and more tears fall.

I'm grateful that fate decided our complicated history wouldn't stop us from being friends.

Even though hugging him like this with my face pressed against his sweater? The way his cologne transports me back to sleeping in his arms? It's temporarily fogging up my rational thinking, and I wonder what it'd be like to have more than a friendship.

I pull away, not wanting to reward my thoughts.

"Are you okay?" he asks.

I clear my throat again, because I know it'll crack if I don't.

"Physically? Yeah. Mentally? I'm pretty upset that I have to go fix my makeup now."

He laughs at that. "Well, don't let me keep you. I just wanted to drop that off."

"Actually," I say before thinking it through. All I know is I want to be around him right now. I doubt Reya and Vic will mind him crashing our night, but he might mind their incessant questions and comments. I cross my fingers behind my back, and take the chance anyway. "Would you want to come with us? We're going mini-golfing. Just a couple of my friends."

"Mini golf is always fun," he says with a small smile that gets to me more than it should.

I light up. "Perfect! I'm gonna go fix this." I motion to my face. "They'll be here to pick us up in like twenty minutes."

The girls freak out when I message them to say I invited him. Every response is in all capital letters and the two of them go back and forth with each other when I don't respond. I do not feel great about the fact that they keep referring to this as a first date, but my hands are too occupied to argue. I have a feeling this night is going to be chaotic.

"Okay, I have to warn you," I start as I walk out into the living room. I find him studying some of the artwork I have hanging on the wall, and something about that makes heat rise to my face.

Everything he does, even something so simple and small as looking at my home decor just feels so sincere.

"Warn me?" he asks after a moment, turning to face me.

"My friends like to meddle."

"What exactly will they be meddling with?" The smirk on his face is teasing. It makes me wonder what he's assuming, whether it's the truth or something much less awkward.

There's a part of me that doesn't really want to voice it, like it's wrong to acknowledge the idea of it at all. On the other hand, he might think I'm on the same page as they are. I don't want him to be under the impression that I've said something to encourage their ways.

"You and me. Getting those two to understand that a man and woman can just be friends is going to be an impossible task."

"Ah," is all he says before turning back to the wall.

I refuse to let myself overthink that response, despite how much it feels like an itch begging to be scratched.

The girls get here earlier than I expected, and instead of texting me to get my ass outside, they walk right through my front door. I can't say I'm all that surprised.

I catch the disappointment in Reya's eyes when she sees that she didn't interrupt anything juicy. Vic is a better actress, and she gives him an innocent smile.

"It's Miles, right?" She already knows the answer. "I'm Vic." Instead of shaking his hand, she goes right in and wraps him in a hug.

"Good to meet you," he replies. He doesn't look weary of the affection, and it's a relief. Then again, her hugs are amazing, *and* she wasn't the one I was worried about.

"I'm Reya," she practically yells. She's bouncing on her heels like a little kid. She probably overdid it on caffeine today, which isn't a rare occurrence. "You can call me Rey, though."

"Since when does anyone call you Rey?" Vic asks her, as confused as I am.

"Since now." She says it like it's obvious. "As Autumn's future husband, he gets special nickname privileges."

I place a palm to my forehead, hoping he picks up on my embarrassment.

"Let's not start this already. No one's getting married."

"You think that *now*," she replies.

I roll my eyes so hard it's a miracle they don't get stuck that way. Miles is quietly chuckling to himself.

This is going to be interesting.

I'm very pleased to discover that the place serves alcohol. The last time I'd been here I wasn't old enough to drink, because what adult suggests mini-golfing as a way to spend a week night? Yet, the second we arrive, I'm disappointed that it's been so long.

Reya continues to make comments that Miles and I attempt to ignore. We share wide eyed looks, and struggle to control our laughter at some of the wild things she says. He seems nothing but amused, which has kept me from completely freaking out.

"You're pretty tall," she points out as he hands me his drink. A bright red slushie with vodka in it. We go back and forth holding each other's cups when it's our turn.

"I guess I am."

"How tall are you?"

He takes his shot and doesn't make it very far. It doesn't seem like this is his game, but he doesn't mind. He's having fun, smiling, joking, getting along with my friends. They are eating up his every move.

I was really on to something when I invited him along.

"Six two, maybe?"

"Wow," she responds blankly. Turning to me she adds, "My poor daughter has two short parents, but you could give yours a fifty-fifty chance, Autumn."

"I'm going to pretend your head is a golf ball when we get up to the windmill." There's no bite behind my words, this is just Reya being Reya.

"Sounds exhilarating." She winks at me, *actually* winks, because she's the only person I know that can get away with it. It's impossible to be upset with her.

We give up on marking down our scores after a while, but it's obvious that Vic is kicking our butts. It's likely due to the fact that she hasn't had a single sip to drink, but has been rather encouraging when it comes to our own.

Sneaky little designated driver.

I wouldn't say I'm drunk, but I can't taste the cherry flavor in my drink anymore and I'm not slowing down. My focus has been everywhere other than the game itself.

It's been mostly on Miles, actually. The man clearly takes care of himself. I appreciate his body and the definition of the muscles that I can make out through his sweater. The urge to grab them, *feel* them, is a strong one.

Maybe I am drunk.

It's a miracle that he doesn't seem to notice my ogling, especially because Reya does. A fact she's being pretty obvious about with the pleased look on her face, and the way her eyes keep darting back and forth between us.

I am so perfectly exhausted by the time we're done and piling back into Vic's car. I almost don't even notice myself starting to lean against Miles' shoulder, but my body sure does. My heart rate instantly spikes in a way that tells me I'm in dangerous territory before my brain can catch up.

I mumble an apology as I scoot myself away from him and back into my own seat. I don't even know how I ended up sitting in the middle.

Reya's voice interrupts my embarrassment, and we make eye contact in the rear view mirror that she's clearly adjusted to get a good view of us.

"That was cozy! You two look so good next to each other." A hiccup gives her pause. She really should take it as a sign to stop talking, but that would be too easy. "You'd make the cutest babies."

Vic pulls the mirror back where she needs it with a chuckle.

I groan. "Reya, if you don't shut up I'm going to–"

"What are you gonna do, babe?" She turns to show me the innocent look on her face and I can't help but giggle. She twists a little further in her seat to peer at Miles. "I don't hear any complaints from you."

He puts his hands up in a surrender. "No comment."

"That's a comment in itself, my friend."

I don't let it be known, with my expression or with any words, but I'm thinking the exact same thing.

"Thanks for inviting me," Miles says as we walk through my front door. His words are slightly slurred, and I grin at that. I don't think I ever got to see him like this: drinking, letting loose. He knew how to have a good time, but years ago I would have thought he was too grown up for something like what we did tonight. It's ironic now that he's older, but my mind travels to how he said he was trying out new things. It makes me irrationally happy to be the person he's trying new things with.

"I'm glad I did. That was a lot of fun." I spin to face him, making myself dizzy. "You're more than welcome to stay over. The couch is really comfy."

I set my bag down on the floor, and then decide to sit down right there next to it. Partially out of laziness, partially because I'm gonna lose my mind if I don't get these boots off. My feet want to breathe.

"That would be great." He smiles in thanks.

"I'll grab you a pillow and some blankets."

As soon as I get these damned things off.

The boots aren't the easiest to untie, and I struggle for what feels like forever with the knotted laces. Autumn from a few hours ago did not have present Autumn's best interest in mind with the double knots.

Miles points towards the hallway with a question on his face, but I answer before he can ask. "Bathroom is the first door on the left."

I unsuccessfully work at these boots for long enough that Miles goes to the bathroom, washes his hands, and comes back to find that I've made zero progress. He doesn't hide the smirk from his face when he takes in the pathetic sight in front of him. He might be too nice to outright make fun of me, but the smirk gives away his urge.

"Do you need some help?" he asks with a hint of laughter in his voice.

I drop my hands and sigh defeatedly. "I sure do."

My breath hitches for a reason I can't identify as he lowers down on the floor in front of me. It takes him way less time to tackle the laces, and I find myself a little stunned. I *know* it shouldn't be impressive, but he's basically my hero right now. Who knows how long I would've been sitting here if it weren't for him?

Plus, he just looks so *good* doing it. That stray curl that likes to fall onto his forehead is doing its job, and his brown eyes are slightly scrunched in concentration. I don't realize how hard I'm staring until he looks up and his smooth voice snaps me out of it.

"All done."

"Thank you." I'm surprised when my words come out as more than a squeak.

"No problem," he replies. He doesn't back away despite being done, and it feels intimate. He's close enough that leaning a couple inches forward would have us kissing.

Just the passing thought of it makes the air between us feel electrically charged.

I think I must be imagining that his focus drops down to my mouth. I *must* be delusional to think I'm not the only one having a moment here.

A chill runs down my spine in a way that isn't uncomfortable, but thrilling. Like I'm sitting at the top of a rollercoaster, waiting for the drop to happen.

I try to reign in my thoughts. Try to figure out if I'm seeing what I want to see through my current haze. He doesn't move an inch while I silently assess every detail of his face. He doesn't say a word.

That probably tells me enough.

I'm not sure what to do with my conclusion, but there's no doubt that something burning in his expression makes me feel desired. I don't even care that it's likely because we're both drunk, I want to *soak it up*. I want to stay right here on this end of that look for as long as possible.

We both slightly lean into each other. I don't know if he even realizes he's doing it until one of his hands raises to the side of my face. The other steadies himself on the floor, and I like the idea of him bracing for something. For me.

Instinctively, my hand clutches onto his bicep. It's my way of bracing for *him* while also living my fantasy from earlier this evening.

He nods his head in a way that seems to be asking permission as his thumb brushes my cheek. I can feel his breath on my face, and I am so tempted that it feels like a knife in my side. It's sharp, and sobering, and it makes me want to feel that breath in other places.

I can't respond with words, nothing would come out if I tried. Instead, I close the short distance and softly press my lips to his.

My action flips a switch instantly, and he doesn't hesitate to kiss me back harder. His full lips roughly capture mine, and the hunger I feel from him makes my chest catch fire. His hand slides back into my hair, his grip tightens and makes me feel brave enough to let my tongue trace his bottom lip. He lets out a small, appreciative groan that quickly spreads the flames lower.

He still tastes like our cherry slushies, and I can't get enough. It tastes better on his tongue than it did in my cup.

With hands that are gentle and somehow possessive, Miles leans me back without breaking our kiss. Before I know it, I'm lying on my back with his body covering mine.

I feel his hard length against me and my heart rate spikes. Every thought that might have remained in my head is gone, but my body moves on instinct and my hips lift to move against his. Maybe it's too presumptuous of a move, but I don't have time to care because he pushes back against me.

I feel his moan more than I hear it, and I echo the sound. A little too loud maybe, but I'm unable to care. Nothing exists outside of how good this feels.

Neither of us can seem to get enough of this moment or each other, our tongues continue to explore, and our mouths don't stray. Not even as his hand slides down, over my breast, and to the bottom of my shirt, before it slips underneath.

I'm a panting mess when skin meets skin, and I have to pull back in order to take a proper breath. He mercifully trails his lips down, along my jaw, to the sensitive line of my neck. I'm shivering with need when his hand, now resting over my rib cage, slips under my bra and his thumb grazes the pebbled skin underneath.

"Fuck," I whisper, almost inaudibly. I know he hears it when a chuckle shakes his chest.

I closed my eyes at some point, and our gazes lock onto each other when I open them. I don't know what it is about it that brings me back down to earth, but it does.

I'm suddenly completely aware that this is a terrible idea.

With his intense attention on me, I scoot backwards a microscopic amount and let out a nervous giggle. He doesn't move for a few seconds of hesitation, looking as worked up as I feel. Eventually he sighs, giving me his usual, charming grin, and slowly shuffles back.

I hate the absence of his body heat.

"We're so bad," I try to say jokingly, but it comes out in a whisper.

"Yeah, we are." His voice is gravelly. His eyes won't leave mine, making me wonder what he's looking for.

My familiar, insecure thoughts creep in. I should be doing anything other than wondering what's going through his head. I don't even want to talk about it. I want to pretend this didn't just happen.

I clear my throat. "Do you need anything to drink? Or a snack? I've got lots of stuff."

I'm still on the floor, still breathing heavily.

I still can't decipher the look on his face, but I'm too tired to try. I don't even trust myself to stand, unsure of how capable my legs currently are.

"Water sounds great, but I'm sure I can get it." He jumps to his feet, and extends a hand out to me. My legs do what they're supposed to, but my lungs don't, because he ends up pulling me too close to his face again.

When he's the one to step back, I can't help the sinking feeling of disappointment in my gut. I've been trying so hard not to think of us as more than friends, but now? Now I'm completely screwed, because there is no chance I'll ever get this off my mind. There's no chance I'm not going to want to do that again.

Kissing has never felt like that in my entire life.

"There's filtered water in the fridge. Unless you're a weirdo that likes sink water, in which case I think you can find it on your own." The words fly out nervously, an attempt to avoid an awkward silence.

"Why would that make me a weirdo?"

"It tastes like pool water."

"I think it tastes like drinking water."

"You've obviously never done a side by side taste test."

I sound so drunk right now.

"And I'm not going to, I'll just take your word for it."

I look away when I notice his sight drop lower again.

Nope, nope, nope.

It's time for bed.

I head for my hall closet, containing all the extra pillows and blankets a person could need. When they're dumped on the couch and Miles appears next to me, glass of water in hand, I quickly put space between us.

"Good night, Miles."

"Good night, A."

His tone tells me there are words in his head that he doesn't voice.

I rush to my room before he can change his mind, and lock the door behind me. Not out of mistrust for him, but myself. It's the equivalent of putting up a big sign. Something to make me stop and think.

Caution: hazardous material.

Going out there again tonight would be extremely hazardous. I'm not even going to attempt a bedtime routine, not with the way my hands are still shaking. I'm somehow wide awake and dead tired all at once. Skin care can wait for a better time.

A glance at my bed tells me that the two things I need to survive tonight are thankfully trapped in this room with me. A sleepy Elaine, and my good, old laptop. I do what I do best when my emotions are high, I put them into my writing.

I walk out into my living room the next morning after a quick shower and some concealer, to find it empty. It's a bit of a relief, but I can't deny a bigger part of me wanted to see him. I want to know how his curly hair sticks up in the mornings, having missed the chance the last time we woke up in the same place.

I can't help but feel like his absence means he wanted to avoid me, too.

I think about sending him a text, but I wouldn't know what to say. There isn't a single thought in my racing mind that's casual enough to put into words. I check my phone to see that it's already ten, which makes my shoulders relax slightly. I'm content for now with the fact that most people start their days before this time. After all, I was up until three, writing some scenes I feel very happy with.

Scenes filled with *a lot* of tension.

12

AUTUMN

Halfway through my trial day at Amelia's office, I'm feeling very confident. This is a cakewalk compared to my last office job. Filing, updating info, answering emails. I'll occasionally get to do some research, and looking at pretty houses all day sounds like heaven.

I wasn't expecting there to be enough work to keep me busy, but there are so many clients that it makes me wonder how the two of them have been getting everything done.

I'm filing forms away when my phone vibrates on the desk. I wince at the sound, momentarily forgetting that Amelia doesn't mind if I have it out. She doesn't have the mindset that it would ruin appearances, everyone needs their phone for everything these days.

I pick mine up and see a text from Miles. I pretend my heart isn't thundering when memories of last night flash in my mind. He wants to know if I'm getting a lunch break today.

I go back to my filing without responding. Instead I do what I do best and overthink my current situation. If that's his lead up to asking if we can talk, I'm not at all ready. I don't want to talk.

I want to be in control, and right now control feels like ignoring what we did.

I'm too familiar with rejection. I decided years ago that I'd never let Miles be someone that makes me feel that way. It was a big part of why I'd removed myself from his life, it was easier to hurt myself than to let him eventually do it.

I really dig myself into a mental hole as I embrace this mindless task, until Amelia walks over to show me something new. Scheduling the clients is basic, but she takes extra care in building their style profiles. If it's even possible, she's over prepared by the time she walks into someone's home and gets to work her magic.

I like to think of myself as creative in more ways than one, and I find everyone's preferences fascinating. I'm hoping this trial day turns into a sure thing, as long as nothing's already ruined with the son of my potential boss. He told me that he occasionally helps out around here, and that would be too much to handle.

I'm lost in thought, scrolling through the client profiles when a familiar head of curly brown hair walks through the front door.

I do a double take.

And then I beam at him, instantly forgetting any reason I might have not to.

Amelia's voice intercepts him as he makes his way towards the desk I'm sitting at. "To what do we owe the pleasure, son?"

She's smiling at him, but it doesn't look quite right. Maybe it's the way her eyes are shifting from the coffee in his hand and back to his face.

"I thought Autumn could use some caffeine." He says it as he holds up the drink in his hand.

He lifts an eyebrow at me as if to say, *Tell me I'm wrong after the night we just had.*

My cheeks heat, but I try my hardest to look calm. The last thing I want right now is for Amelia to think that we're acting odd.

Miles brings the drink over and sets it on my desk. I glance at the cup suspiciously, wishing I wasn't cursed by my inability to drink milk. It's quite the problem when, for example, someone wants to surprise you with a coffee.

"It's almond milk, I'm not trying to poison you."

I stop breathing.

I haven't mentioned it anytime recently which means he must have remembered that fact from *years* ago.

I am swooning.

I grab it and take a sip. I have to hold back a moan when the pumpkin spice hits my tongue. "Oh, you really shouldn't have."

"That's what friends are for, right?" It almost sounds like he emphasizes the word *friends,* but it was subtle enough to make me question if I imagined it.

I meet his eyes and see something mischievous hidden there. A glint that tells me he's panicking a lot less than I am.

"We're friends?" I pretend to look confused, and he rolls his eyes exaggeratedly.

"If you don't think so, I can just take this back," he teases. He goes to swipe it out of my hands, but I have wheels on my chair and I back away too quickly for him.

"I'm a simple girl, I'll be your friend for some coffee."

He laughs loudly at that, and it feels out of place in the quiet office. I remember who else is in the room and glance over at his mom. My stomach drops when my eyes lock onto her glare.

Her tight expression falls quickly when Miles begins to walk over to her. The insincere smile is back, and I'm curious if he sees it for what it is, too.

"Can I steal her for a lunch break?" he asks her. "I have to be at work in thirty."

I try to ignore my body's reaction to his question. I don't think I should be flattered by this drop by, assuming there's a less flattering reason. He looks happy to see me, but that doesn't mean he's *flirting* with me, right? It doesn't mean he enjoyed himself last night and wants to kiss me again or anything.

Right?

Amelia quickly stands and gives him an apologetic frown. "I'm sorry honey, I have a lunch appointment I need to leave for." She looks to me. "You'll be alright until Kaitlyn gets back?"

Not only do I have her calendar right in front of my face and there are no appointments today, but I don't even officially work here yet. If Kaitlyn is gone longer than five minutes I am *going* to panic. I'm way under qualified to be left alone after only a couple hours of training.

I smile regardless, my people pleasing tendencies taking the reins.

"Yeah, I should be fine," I lie.

At least I know how to take a message if the phone rings.

She nods in thanks. "I'll walk you out, Miles."

He doesn't protest and I don't show either of them just how much she's unsettled me in only a few seconds.

"Thanks again," I call out to him before they reach the door.

"Anytime," comes his response.

He doesn't look back at me, and I think it has to do with the tight grip his mother has on his arm.

Shit.

By the time Amelia comes back to the office, I've already taken a little lunch break, *and* gone through every single profile in the system. There are so many of them, and each one inspired me more than the last. Maybe the main character in my next book will be an interior designer. If this works out, I'll have plenty of time and inspiration to make that happen.

I'm thinking only of that, and *not* her reaction earlier when she leans against my desk next to me and smiles. I still don't buy it.

"How has it been?"

"Great. Much easier than my last office job," I tell her truthfully.

"I'm glad to hear that. We can nail down your schedule before you leave today, if you feel like you want to do this."

I'm so appreciative of having a choice that I can't mask my enthusiasm. "I do, definitely. Thank you for giving me a chance to feel it out first."

"Of course. I was happy to." As paranoid as I am that this woman is holding the past against me, I believe her. Maybe I've let my overthinking get the best of me. Wouldn't be the first time.

"I have to ask," she adds, but pauses briefly. "Well, I have to ask if you and Miles are..." Her sentence trails off as if she wants me to fill in the blank. I stiffen in my chair, guessing that our interaction *did* seem odd to her.

I don't fill in the blank, I just look at her as I wait for her to find the words.

"Are the two of you together?" she finally asks.

I quickly shake my head. "No, we aren't."

I'm glad that was the question she chose so I didn't have to lie.

I try not to feel offended when she breathes a sigh of relief. It's no use.

"Good. It's nothing against you," she clarifies, putting a hand on my shoulder. Something tells me that's not fully the truth, but I refrain from reacting. "My family is going through a lot right now. I'm sure you know his divorce hasn't been finalized for very long. I worry about him so much, and I just want him to take time to do things for himself."

She gives me a look filled with so much emotion that I suddenly want to hug her. Watching your son be trapped with someone like he was... it must have been torture. I'm sure I only felt a fraction of it all those years ago.

When she sees my sympathetic look, she goes on. "And Justin... don't get me started there." I didn't, but I stay quiet as she goes on. "He's been holding onto his own marriage by a thread, and we all know it's going to snap any day now. It's a vulnerable time for all of us."

My eyes widen, hopefully imperceptibly, because I was not expecting that. Not for her to tell me anything about him, but especially not *that*. I'm not sure how to feel, knowing his marriage to the woman he cheated on me with is failing.

Karma took so long to do her thing that I don't even feel satisfaction over it.

"I'm happy to welcome you here, I just don't want anything from the past to complicate the present. Okay?"

Complicate.

She doesn't notice the way her word choice hits me. It yanks me back to a time where that's all I felt like I was. A complication.

Such a simple word, and yet it makes me feel like I'm no longer this woman who's put in the work to know I'm more than that.

"Okay. I understand," I force out.

"I'm glad you do." If she notices how I've gone pale and shaky, she doesn't mention it. "So, shall we go over that schedule?"

We decide that I'll work three days a week. Not too short of a day that it's a waste of time to drive down there, but not long enough to put a large strain on my writing time.

The pay is a few dollars more than I've ever made in an hour. I know it's not an appropriate amount for the job, but I wasn't going to question her on it. I'm excited about everything I'll be able to get done in the next few months.

13

MILES

I can't stop thinking about her.

Her smile. Her laugh. Her mouth.

I don't know what spell has been cast on me, but I went from being a somewhat happily divorced man, to a boy with a crush on a girl overnight.

I walk through my front door with a pizza box in hand, thinking about how badly I want to kiss her again, and worrying that I won't get to. I didn't miss her stricken expression when she pulled away from me last night. I understand it, how conflicted she must have felt. This is scary territory.

Her face lit up as soon as she saw me this morning, but I couldn't let that get my hopes up. No, not when I keep picturing the way she ran to her room to get away from me.

For good reason. I have to remind myself every five minutes that she used to be Justin's girlfriend.

I set the box down and give my dog his usual greeting of scratches behind his ears. He's thrilled to have me home, showing me so with a wagging tail and a drooling mouth.

"If only I could share this with you, buddy."

I scoop his own food into his bowl, always making sure he's fed before I am. A knock on my door makes me jump, and I spill some of the kibble to the floor beside his bowl. At least I know he'll take care of the clean up.

The door opens before I even move to answer it.

"You should really lock that."

"I do, Mom. I just walked in the door and my hands were full."

"You just got home? I thought you got off twenty minutes ago." As if normal people are home within twenty minutes of getting off work.

To be fair, I usually am. It's not like I have a lot going on in my life. I wave a hand towards the pizza on the counter.

She accepts the answer, and then crosses her arms. That's never a good sign. I don't wait for whatever she's going to reprimand me on, diving into the dinner I should have eaten hours ago.

"Have you absolutely lost your mind?" she asks me right as I'm about to take a bite of my pizza.

I feel betrayed by the timing of her question.

"What are you talking about?"

"Autumn," is all she says.

"What about her?" I ask cautiously. I don't think she'd tell my mom what went down between us, but I could be surprised. They sat in a quiet office for a few hours. People talk.

I start eating the food that my stomach has been dying for, but it's also an attempt to appear casual. Nothing says casual like a mouth full of cheese and bread.

"You walk into my office with coffee, and a flirty grin, and you expect me to be ignorant?"

There's a pause because I'm still chewing. I'm tempted to fill it by rolling my eyes at her like I'm seventeen again. "Is that why you were so upset earlier? It's not like that, we're just friends."

"Does she know that? She had heart eyes the second you walked through the door."

Okay, I can't help but roll my eyes this time.

"Yeah, she knows that." There's no reason for me to think that's not the truth.

Unless you count her breathy moans as my hand slid up her shirt as a reason.

Fuck. Not the thing to be thinking right now.

"We're just friends," I repeat. "It's nice to talk to someone who doesn't act like going through a hard time makes me contagious."

When I go back in for another bite, she's quiet. I know she's thinking, probably glaring at me while doing so.

By the time I look up at her, she doesn't look angry at all. She feels sorry for me, which is worse. Way worse. I'm the only one who's allowed to feel sorry for me.

"Live life for yourself right now, honey. Don't let some girl get in the way again."

"I'm not, I promise." I know it's the truth because regardless of what happens, I know I'll be fine. Autumn isn't getting in the way. If anything, she makes me feel like I'm making progress.

"Good. I worry about you so much." She pulls me into a side hug and kisses the top of my head. "You and your brother. You both deserve better than what you've got."

I know she genuinely worries, but her words feel like an intentional reminder of his place in my situation. It frustrates me for a total of five seconds, until it hits its target.

I'm being selfish. I haven't been blind to it, but I've been thinking that Justin's reaction would be an inconvenience instead of
warranted.

Who am I to say it wouldn't be?

— ele —

Justin's kids have just been put to bed, to my dismay. They're my
favorite part of visiting my brother's house. When I ask about
Isabelle, he has nothing to say. It's been months since I've seen her
face, despite her living here, which confirms that she's been hiding.
Not just from me, but her husband, too.

I know for that reason, he counts on me to stop by like this. He
gets even less social interaction than I do.

He gives me a funny look as I approach the couch he's slumped
on.

"Since when do you drink those?" he asks, and nods towards the
hard seltzer in my hand.

I shrug. "It's all you have."

He squints his eyes. "So you're going to drink it anyway? Who
are you, and what have you done to my brother?" I laugh as I
sit down next to him, but he doesn't drop his suspicion. "Something's wrong."

I consider for a split second telling him everything. That I've
been talking to Autumn, what mom had to say to me about it.
I want to ask him what he really thinks about that. The thought

vanishes quickly, knowing it won't lead to any good. She's trying to protect him after all, it's the reason she was upset in the first place.

I give him a partial truth. "Mom just stresses me out sometimes."

He nods in understanding and the topic drops like that. I know he knows the feeling.

My mind never wanders far from the kiss. I can't remember the last time it felt like that with anyone. Granted, I'd been with Kara for so long that it's no wonder everything before her is a blur. I don't think she, in the eight years we were together, ever made me feel like I needed to kiss her in order to survive.

Which makes no sense really, because Autumn stole the air right out of my lungs.

I look over at Justin, lost in some show he's watching. The bags under his eyes are dark, and he's clearly lost weight. I wish there was something I could do to help him.

I wish everything wasn't so complicated.

I wish I could go back in time to the day the two of them met, and introduce her to *any* other guy. One that isn't related to me.

I want to know what he thinks when he hears her name. If there's guilt or regret, maybe nothing at all.

Hopefully someday I'll have the courage to ask.

14

AUTUMN

EIGHT YEARS AGO

I'm not feeling good.

I'm on my period.

Even after four years of dealing with it, I always forget to take painkillers before the cramps get this bad. I was supposed to work tonight, but that lack of foresight meant I couldn't handle standing at the cash register for hours.

Does that mean I should have stayed home, and not gone to my boyfriend's house? Probably, but I know his mom has a heating pad around here somewhere.

I walk into the house without knocking, something Amelia has repeatedly told me to do. It doesn't look like anyone is home other than him, so I hope he can help me find the things I need to feel better. I'm not quite comfortable enough to go rooting around the place on my own.

I hear his voice through the door before I open it and I pause. I can't help my nosey instincts, and I press my ear to it, amplifying the words inside.

"I wish you were here, babe…" There's a pause. "Maybe tomorrow, when everyone is at work."

My brows furrow. Is he leaving me a voicemail?

I try to listen further, but he's speaking quietly. Maybe opening the door would be a good idea, seeing the look of surprise on his face when he realizes he doesn't have to wait until tomorrow.

I start to reach for the knob and then freeze with a thought that makes my head spin.

He knows I have to work tomorrow night.

"Really?" he asks someone that isn't me.

I gasp, realization hitting me like a brick.

"My mom would love you, it's not that."

What the hell?

I'm frozen in place, listening to more of his unintelligible words. My thoughts race, trying to put together a puzzle without any pieces.

"No, you're so beautiful," he tells them. "I really can't wait to see you."

Now the bricks are piling up on my chest. I don't want to believe what I'm hearing.

Mentally cutting whatever rope was holding me back, I barge into the room.

He looks like he got caught, the way he throws his phone out of his hand so quickly. It hits the edge of his bed frame with a crack and drops to the floor. His eyes are wide as his head jerks in my direction.

I hate the sight. Instead of acknowledging him, I glance at the phone. There's a call still going. The name Isabelle sits on the screen. I try to recall if there's a face in my memory bank to match, but I come up blank.

"Hello? Justin?" Her voice is so quiet coming from the small speaker, but I'm on high alert. I could hear a pin drop.

He's breathing hard as he walks over to end the call. That's what he does first. He doesn't say a word, doesn't attempt to comfort me in any way until Isabelle can't hear it. Then he approaches me slowly, like I'm a wounded animal ready to pounce with one wrong move.

"I thought you were at work. Why are you here?" His voice is so calm, as if there's nothing important going on.

"Who were you talking to?" I ask him. My own words come out eerily quiet.

He shrugs, doing his best to feign innocence. "A friend from school."

"Who?"

"Tony," he says without hesitation.

The bold lie is such a shock, that a cold wave washes through me. He has to know I saw the screen, that I heard part of the conversation. I'm feeling like I might pass out if I don't get out of this room. I ignore him when he calls my name, and I run away.

I'm mortified when I see his brother is now standing in the kitchen. I want to pass him without a word being said, but the concerned look on Miles' face makes me pause. "Are you—"

I shake my head before he finishes the question, and I keep going.

I don't know how those two are related.

I just barely make it outside, before Justin grabs my arm and pulls me around to face him. The door slams behind us, giving us a small amount of privacy, but the front porch still isn't the place I want to have this conversation.

We have to break up. I can't believe what's happening right now. I'm going to lose the people I've come to depend on. This house that's felt more like a home to me than anywhere has.

"I didn't know you were coming over," is what he has to say to me.

I laugh harshly in response. I can't get out of his grip, although I try. He just grips tighter, to the point that it should hurt, but I can't feel anything other than the pain of his betrayal.

"I'm sorry, Autumn. I'm so fucking stupid. You're just not always here, and I get so—"

"Stop talking."

He doesn't.

"I'm really so sorry, please babe," he pleads with me.

Babe. All I hear is the way he just called her that, too.

"She asked me out, and I said no at first, I swear. I can show you the messages, I tried to say no! She just kept confronting me at school, and sending me pictures, and I was—"

He goes quiet for an entire second, taking in the disbelieving look on my face.

"I said stop, Justin."

"I can't, I'm freaking out. I don't want to lose you." He just goes on and on, and I have no choice but to mentally check out for a minute. "I only want to be with you, you're everything to me. Please say you'll forgive me."

He doesn't wait for me to speak, he doesn't give me a chance to forgive him at all. He just keeps going. He puts his arms around me, wipes tears from my face, begs for forgiveness.

I stand there and feel like I'm watching this happen from a bird's eye view. I think I believe he's sorry, but sorry doesn't fix anything. I've never been in a situation like this before. I've never had anyone tell me what I'm supposed to do. What if he's telling the truth and this isn't going to happen again?

I want to believe him, I want our relationship to be okay. Losing him would probably hurt more than this does.

"Please, babe."

There is some comfort in his presence, in the fact that he's fighting for me to forgive him. I don't think I want him to stop fighting for me.

"It meant literally nothing. I'll never talk to her again, I'll block her right now." He pulls his phone out to show me, but when he gets the block button pulled up on the screen, he hesitates. "Do you want me to? Will that help?"

I shrug, because I don't know. She goes to our school. He'll still see her there every day. They probably have classes together. Will blocking her make any difference? Would it be overreacting on my part if I told him he had to?

He puts his phone away, without blocking her, and continues pleading with me. I'm not really aware of anything else until my phone starts buzzing in my back pocket. It goes off at least five times in a row. I'd think it was a phone call if there was a pattern to it.

I pull it out, ignoring his protest.

There are message requests, meaning I don't have the person as a friend.

From Isabelle Larson.

He must see the look on my face change as I stare down at it, contemplating if I want to know what she has to say. She could be assuming I'm the reason he hung up on her and lashing out. Do I want to be attacked by a girl that's trying to pursue my boyfriend? I've never been good at confrontation.

Suddenly my phone is pulled from my hands and Justin is reading the screen with his jaw clenched. He clicks on the notifications and opens the messages. I lean forward to look, but he turns it away from my view.

I don't even have the energy to argue. There's a good chance I'm not strong enough to face them anyway. Possibly later, when I'm alone and have had time to calm down.

Possibly.

"See, she's crazy, Autumn. Harassing me isn't enough, she has to harass you too. I should've blocked her from the start."

You still haven't blocked her, I think to myself.

"What did she say?" I ask, my voice so small and weak.

"Just a bunch of bullshit you don't need to hear. I'm sorry, babe." He taps a few things on my phone, and pulls away from my feeble attempt to stop him.

When he finally hands it back, the messages are gone and he's blocked her from my account. "Let's not give her any more time of day, what's done is done. I'll do whatever you need."

I nod, but it feels like I'm lying. The pain of the cramps I was experiencing is nothing in comparison to what this day has turned into. I don't know how we're supposed to move forward.

When he begs me to go back inside with him, it takes a lot to convince him that we'll be fine if I leave. I tell him I'll see him at school tomorrow.

With some distance and a head that's slowly clearing, I re-member school is where Isabelle will be. I wonder if she'll try to confront me with what those messages said, and feel even more sick at the thought. Maybe I lied to him, maybe I won't be there tomorrow.

15

AUTUMN

Sometimes I wonder if I'm cut out to do what I want with my life. Most of the time it's a no-brainer, I can't even contain all of my ideas and creativity. I look at the world with a lens that picks up every small, inspiring detail, and I want to make use of it. I *want* to do this.

The first time I held my book in my hands, I knew all the struggling was worth it. I knew I'd do it all again, over and over, even if it meant I'd spend every last penny on the process. There was no amount of money spent or tears shed that weren't worth it to experience that final result. I had never been so proud of myself, so full of excitement.

I've had many doubts since then. I know where I'm lacking, I know I need to put myself out there more. It's just that every time I try, I crumble. I never know where to start, there's too much out there.

Vic tries to help occasionally, but she has even less time to worry about these things than I do. And she really doesn't most of the time. I think she posts on Instagram once a month, but that still makes her far more experienced than I am.

Don't get me started on Reya. She thinks she's qualified, but she works her phone like an eighty year old woman that's upset with how far technology has come.

Today is a tough one, filling me with doubt. My laptop sits open in front of me, my brain yells at me to get a move on. All I've done for hours is stare at the screen and contemplate my life choices. My mind is a tangled, anxious mess.

Even Elaine must sense it, because she's being extra sweet as she nuzzles against my shoulder. Her little trick perks me up most of the time, but I don't have it in me now. I give her chin scratches in thanks, and her purring makes me want to give up and go to bed.

So I do. I slam my laptop shut for the night, hoping tomorrow can be a more productive day.

I do need help. I can't ask Vic, and I can't afford to pay someone, but somehow I'm going to figure it out. Trying to tackle too much on your own never works well for anyone.

My phone begins to vibrate with a call, and breaks through my thoughts.

I wasn't expecting to hear from Miles anytime soon. We've both clearly taken a step away from our friendship since that day Amelia spoke to me. At least, I know that's my reason, but I don't know if Amelia would have been as blunt with him. He's smart, though. It doesn't take a rocket scientist to tell what she was thinking. It was probably the reminder he needed, too.

That this is far too complicated for us to acknowledge.

I hate what he must think of me now. I don't even like what I think of myself in this situation. I used to feel guilty enough when I realized how much I was crushing on him.

I don't answer the call, letting it ring and ring until it doesn't anymore. Elaine looks up at me as if she can tell it was him. Maybe I'm imagining her disappointment, maybe I'm projecting, but she squints her eyes.

It feels terrible to ignore him, but he's good at reading me. I am not in the right headspace for him to figure me out.

My phone starts up again, another phone call. Elaine looks down at it first, then back up at me.

She is so much smarter than she pretends to be.

"Stop looking at me like that," I mumble.

And I answer it.

One second of silence. Two seconds. Three.

"Hey?" My voice is soft and unsure.

"Autumn! How's it going?" He sounds cheery enough, but I notice that he doesn't call me A.

Not that he was *strictly* going by that nickname, I just think I've started to prefer it.

"It's... going okay. How are you?"

"Yeah, same here," he says.

Three more seconds without either of us saying a word.

"So, hey," he continues. "I was calling to see if you were still doing that Halloween party?"

Shit. I almost forgot about it. I haven't put much into planning other than sending out a few text messages. I almost wish I could pass the torch to one of the girls this year, but my apartment is the easiest place to make it happen. Vic has a nice house, but I'd never even consider asking because her children deserve to sleep in their own beds without being woken up by a bunch of loud, drunk, adults.

And Reya's place is half the size of mine.

Our party has always been at my apartment anyway, ever since I first moved in. It started out with the three of us playing board games and making fancy drinks while we waited for trick-or-treaters to come around.

It's changed a lot over the years. We made more friends, included more people. We take their kids out on the actual holiday now, so I aim for the closest Saturday that doesn't interfere with their fun.

There's something so special about how excited little ones get about costumes and candy. Reya's daughter was barely walking and talking last year, but we had a blast. She held her hand as they walked up to every door. Vic had her baby boy strapped to her chest, and I got to carry Amira while she was dressed up as a little ladybug.

She got the most candy. You could see every face light up when they saw her.

"Yeah, I'm still doing it. You totally don't have to be there, it's not anything exciting."

I can't think of a single reason he'd want to.

"I want to," he says quickly.

I breathe a sigh of relief that I hope he doesn't notice.

"Okay."

"I put together a costume. It's also not *anything exciting*, so that's good."

"What is it?"

"I guess you'll see next week." I hear his smile, and want to throw my phone across the room. "Really, don't get excited. It's simple."

"It's okay. I can't expect everyone to put as much effort into these things as I do."

I guess I have something to do while I'm not writing. I could clean this place up, get it decorated.

"Do I get to know what *your* costume is?"

"How would that be fair? Absolutely not."

He laughs, and I hear Freddy whimper in the background.

"You better put me on speaker. I don't want him to feel left out."

"He's never left out. We're playing fetch as we speak, he just hates when it takes me more than two seconds to throw the ball."

I look down at my cat who looks perfectly content in my lap. Eyes almost closed, but not quite. Paws crossed. It's like she wants me to see how much she enjoys his voice. Enjoys him.

I'm still projecting, probably.

We chat for a couple more minutes, keeping the conversation light. No one mentions the kiss, or does any flirting, and I don't know how to feel. Relieved that I don't have to pull my thoughts together after my conversation with Amelia? Disappointed that I don't know how he's feeling?

I really shouldn't want to know.

I walk into the brightly lit office, and almost stop in my tracks when I see Miles instead of Amelia sitting at the large desk. He doesn't notice me right away while he studies the computer screen. His fingers fly across the keyboard impressively fast and I hate that I find it attractive. I hate that I find everything he does attractive.

Only when I place my bag on my desk does he stop and look up at me. I try not to melt on the other end of his smile, it's a relief that he looks pleased to see me.

"Good morning, Autumn."

Again, not A.

"Good morning, Miles. What brings you to the boss's chair?"

"She has a cold. Wrote me a list of things I could do to help out today. There's a list for you, too. On your keyboard."

Sure enough I pull it out and there's a small list printed out on her fancy, lavender letterhead paper.

"You offered to come in? On your day off?" As if he's not always working his ass off, it's a wonder how he looks so well rested all the time. I can't say I'd do the same in his position, I appreciate my downtime.

Although, most of my downtime is still filled with work. I guess it doesn't really count.

"A couple hours won't kill me. Unless you take longer than that, we can head out whenever we're done." He's got his signature smirk on.

The next hour is spent in silence, and I check off my tasks faster than anticipated. Responding to emails, scheduling appointments, scanning some paperwork. The phone doesn't ring at all, so I'd say Amelia picked a good time to be out sick.

I'm overly aware of the other person in the room while I work. It makes it hard to think clearly about what to do with him. I have no clue what to say and how to say it. I spend the hour changing my mind on every single thought that crosses through it.

"Well, I guess I'm done," I tell him as I log off my computer and start to collect my things. It takes a handful of seconds before

I'm standing and ready to go home. Considering I've had no luck figuring out how to approach a conversation with Miles, I don't think I'll try.

I know I'll regret it when he doesn't text me later. Things haven't really gone back to normal. The other night on the phone was a fluke.

I hate how much it upsets me. I don't like going from one-hundred to one the way we have. I let myself get used to it. I let myself get attached.

He speaks before I start to walk away.

"I can be done. I just have to finish up this email." He points down at his keyboard. "Do you want to grab lunch?"

The breath of relief that flies out of me is too loud to ignore, but he graciously does.

"Yeah, I could eat."

"Perfect."

It's a lovely, rainy day, but the cafe he chose is a few minutes away on foot. I didn't bring an umbrella because I'm not sure I own one. I've always loved the rain enough to sacrifice my hair and makeup just to feel it on my face.

He has one, because when isn't he prepared for anything? I'm nervous when he offers to share it with me, but grateful. Nervous, because my shoulder brushes his arm as we walk under it together. Grateful, because I don't want to look like a drenched mess when I sit across from him for the duration of lunch.

The busy downtown street is noisy enough that we don't really talk on our way there. It's not an awkward lack of conversation either, it's calm. Peaceful. Our walk is filled with music from the shops we pass, and tires on wet pavement.

I'm grateful that I'm kept from having to look at him, because something tells me I'd be tempted to kiss him again.

Only because the rain makes everything romantic, *not* because I want to complicate things any further than they are. Obviously.

I've never been to this place he takes me, and I think it's fairly new. The small building is warm and inviting, and the smells of coffee and bacon invade my nose as soon as we step inside. It's a little too crowded for my taste, but he doesn't seem to mind as much as I do. He leads the way past the sign that tells us to seat ourselves. We weave through the packed tables to a single empty booth that I hadn't noticed in my initial scan of the room.

Fresh cut marigolds sit in a small vase on our table. Fairy lights hang down like icicles above us. I think I love this place already.

Things start out easily enough. I ask him about his week, he asks about mine. It helps me put my guard down, and hope that maybe we can just move forward without looking back.

Until he sighs.

I fidget with the strap of my purse, a small way to ground myself in preparation of this conversation.

"Can I make this awkward for a minute?"

I hold my menu up with my free hand. "Already? Before food?"

His responding smile is gorgeous.

"Yeah. I'd rather get it out of the way."

He props his elbow up on the table, and it gives him the reach he needs to scratch the back of his neck. As if he's nervous, which is a *fantastic* sign.

"We should talk about the other night." He can't meet my eyes and I don't blame him. I'm doing a pretty good job of faking confidence by being able to look at him right now. "About the kiss." Those three words come out on an exhale, like it took too much for him to say them.

But he glances at my lips once they're out, and I don't even think he realizes it. My pulse begins to thrum loudly in my ears.

What I wouldn't give to be in his mind right now.

"Okay, yeah. We should."

Our adorable waitress— her name tag says Naomi— has terrible timing. She drops off a couple of waters and takes our drink orders. Of course, I get a coffee. Considering we haven't looked at the menu yet, we have an excuse to think about what we want to say for a couple of minutes.

I deserve an award for staying calm.

Only when Naomi cheerily jots down what we're having to eat and takes our menus, does Miles look at me again. His smile seems sad, strained.

I really hope this doesn't hurt.

"I like that we're friends, A. I don't want anything to be messed up between us."

I nod a couple too many times.

"Of course. Me too."

"This week has been weird. I kept my distance because I was figuring out how to say this."

I keep nodding.

"You're..." He pauses, choosing his words carefully. "I think it's obvious there's attraction here. It could be easy for something like that to... accidentally happen again. Maybe we should come up with some ground rules."

His words bounce around my head.

I'm not a fan of the word *accidentally* in his sentence, but I don't let myself dwell. The fact that he wants to come up with rules means he wants to stay friends. That's a good thing.

It's a good thing, Autumn. Calm down.

I shake it off with more of that false confidence.

"Okay. No flirting, no cuddling, or the other person has to remove themselves from the situation?" I can't believe how easily it flies out of me, especially because the memories of my body wrapped around his choose this moment to flash through my mind. I don't know how capable I'd be of removing myself if that happened again.

"Yeah, basically." He nods. "Maybe no hanging out past ten o'clock. That seems to be when we act up."

"*Act up,*" I repeat, and laugh.

Equally amused, he laughs with me.

But then he reaches out and puts his hand on mine. It's so unexpected that I startle a little in my seat.

"For the record, you're kind of my best friend."

If hearts could spontaneously explode, mine would do it right now. I want to tell him how adorable he is, and tell him that rules are overrated, but I don't.

I point to his hand on mine.

"That's probably against the rules." I joke to distract from the emotion that his words overwhelm me with.

He smirks before he pulls his hand away.

"You're one of mine, too. I can't call you *the* best one, or my girls would try to take you out. They're not fans of competition."

16

AUTUMN

"What are you reading?" Miles asks, standing a few feet away in my living room.

"Some romance novel." I show him the cover of the book in my hand.

Definitely something I should put down now that you're here.

He nods and looks around my apartment, studying every little inch, just like the last time he was here. It's like he's never here long enough to take in all of the details. Like my living room is a museum he could spend all day walking around.

Now I'm thinking of the last time he was here, and I hope he doesn't notice how red my cheeks suddenly are. I hate how much my blushing gives away.

His eyes linger on a photo frame, going down the line. I watch as he goes over all of them, getting a glimpse of who I've been while we were strangers.

"Who's that?" He points to a particular photo, and I get up from my spot on the couch so I can see which one he's talking about. I ask what he means, because it's clearly a picture of me. I don't look all that different, my hair was just a little shorter than it is now. I'm standing on the beach, with a huge smile on my face. It's a great picture, and that was a great day.

A great day that still hurts my heart a little. With that thought, I realize what he noticed. There's an arm wrapped around my waist, which belongs to someone that's cropped from the picture. There's just a shoulder, covered in a grey sweatshirt.

I felt beautiful, and happy, and *that* is what I wanted to remember.

Not Lucas.

It feels like so long ago that I actually stopped noticing him there at all. I stopped thinking about who else shared that day with me whenever I glanced at it.

I don't know how I feel about it being the first thing Miles sees.

"Oh. Nobody important."

I almost start to explain myself some more, but instead I get in his way and pull the whole frame down. Maybe it's an overreaction, but now seems like as great a time as any.

The frame is heavier than I remember and starts to slip out of my grasp for a second before Miles' hand is there assisting me.

"Thanks."

I settle for placing it on the floor against the wall for now. It'll work as a reminder for me to replace that picture sooner rather than later.

He gives me a look I can't decipher and moves on to my bookshelf, reading the titles as if he hasn't seen them before.

"Alright, I give. Which one should I read?"

I squeal and hop to him so fast, I almost trip over the frame. He's laughing and shaking his head as I do.

"Oh my gosh, so much pressure," I groan. "How do you feel about fantasy? Dragons?"

I pull the first book in one of my favorite series off the shelf. "It's better to go in blind, but know that it's heavy on the romance. Hope that's not a deal-breaker."

"Not a problem at all," he tells me as he turns the book over to read the back.

I lightly swat at his hand. "That's not going in blind!"

He just laughs as he lowers the book. "What about yours?" he asks while directing his attention back to the shelves. "It's got to be on here somewhere, right?"

My eyes try to pop out of my skull with the look I give him.

"I don't think you'll like it," I say, trying to quickly diverge from that idea.

"Why's that? Not enough faith in your own work?" He continues, still searching. "You'd think it would be on one of these top shelves..."

"It's probably not your thing. It's pretty cheesy."

"I like cheese. Despite what I may have led you to believe, I do watch the occasional romcom. Wait a minute." He stops, turning to me with squinted eyes. "You don't use a pen name, do you?"

Save me now, this man is too smart for his own good.

"Maybe," I admit. It's not too different from my actual name, and won't take him long—

"Ah, here we go!" His smile is victorious as he pulls my book off the shelf. He takes one look at the cover and says, "Yep, this is the one I'm borrowing. You don't mind, right?" I know it's a question that my answer will not affect. Even if I said no and snatched it out of his hands, he could find a way. He could pull out his phone and order it now that he has the title.

"The occasional romcom, really? Of your own volition?"

He gives me a knowing look. I'm not going to distract him that easily.

With a roll of my eyes, I accept defeat.

"You can read the book, but just know I'm not happy about it."

And I don't think you will be either.

"Why?" he asks with a laugh. "Why can everyone else in the world read it, but you don't want me to?"

"It's a little embarrassing," I admit.

A lot embarrassing.

"How so?"

There is no way I'm explaining that to him out loud. Not when there's a chance he might not pick up on it, or he'll give up after a couple of pages. A girl can hope, right?

"Better start reading and find out, huh?"

We sit on opposite ends of the couch with our current reads, the only sound in the room is the rain hitting the windows. It's coming down hard out there, and there's no better weather than this to enjoy a good book. I try to let it soothe me, hoping I can distract myself from the inevitable discomfort coming our way.

The book I'm reading *does* manage to distract me, to the point I'm forgetting to hide my smiles and laughter. Romance always does it to me, it's a miracle I haven't started squealing.

I'm biting my lip in anticipation of the love interest's next move when I feel a set of eyes on me. My face drops when I look up and lock onto Miles' piercing stare.

I don't want to ask. If he has something to say about the book, or a suspiciously familiar character, he'll have to offer it up himself.

I just keep looking at him. Maybe he won't say anything if he can read my face well enough, and then I can pretend he's not judging me. I could live with pretending.

He finally speaks when I don't. "I see why you didn't want me to read it."

"Oh."

His mouth widens into a grin. "Oh?"

I resort to looking back down at the page I was reading.

I'm definitely not able to focus on any of these words now. I can't tell if he's gone back to his book or not, and I'm too nervous to check. Minutes pass and I turn pages before I'm ready to. I'll just have to go back and find the last paragraph I can remember, because I'm determined to make it look like I'm not freaking out.

Miles makes things even more difficult on me when he turns in his seated position and puts his feet up on the couch. It's not a very long one, so he's close to me. If I need to stretch out my legs, we'll be touching.

It is absolutely ridiculous how much I want to, even if all I'll feel is his jeans on my knee.

I should have known better. They weren't lying when they said you want something more when you know you can't have it.

I wonder if reading my book, that's *clearly* inspired by him, is considered crossing our boundaries. I wish I'd had the foresight to use that on him before he picked it out, because it's far too late now.

"Autumn?"

I still don't think it's safe for me to look at him, so I don't.

"Yeah?"

"You don't look like you're reading."

"What else would I be doing?"

"I don't know. You haven't turned the page in awhile. It's kind of suspicious," he points out.

"How would you know I haven't turned the page if you were focused on your book?" I demand.

"Touché," is all he says before his focus leaves me again.

Ugh.

"Miles?"

He slowly lifts his head again. He's smirking, of course. "What's up?"

"Is there something you want to say?"

"There's plenty I want to say, but that doesn't mean I'm going to." His words feel heavy in the air, being the closest we've come to acknowledging our boundaries today.

I set my book down, completely giving up on it for the moment "That's not fair."

"Lots of things aren't fair."

I start to slide off the couch but he sticks out his foot to block me. I'm so caught off guard by it that I don't even have the ability to glare at him as I shove it away from me. "Don't touch me with your feet!"

Little does he need to know that my reaction has very little to do with not liking feet.

An amused laugh flies out of him, and I don't get what's funny.

"I have clean socks on. You're more than welcome to check."

"I've never wanted to do something less in my life."

I go to stand again but he puts his foot out again.

"Can I say one thing about your book?"

I think about it.

"Is it going to make me cry?"

"Possibly."

"Ugh." But I don't say no, and he catches it.

"This is really fucking good."

I gape at him.

"What?" he asks, as if that's not ridiculous.

It takes a few seconds for me to pick my jaw up off the floor.

"You're just saying that," I say while shaking my head. "You're just trying to make me feel better."

"I'm not," he insists. "I've never read romance before, so I don't have anything to compare it to... but I know I really don't want to put it down right now."

"I never thought I'd hear a grown man say that."

"I'm happy to be the grown man that said it. You know what else?"

I fix him with a look that implores him to get it over with.

"I'm so *eager* to find out more about this guy." He points at the brunette on the front of the cartoon cover. "He seems great, makes me wonder what inspired you to write him."

I groan as I throw my head back against the couch. "Shut up, Miles. I'll take the book away."

He grabs his phone from the nearby table and waves it at me. "Two day shipping, and you'd never even know."

"Something tells me I would, I doubt you'd be able to keep your mouth shut about it."

"Do you think he looks like me?" he questions, looking back down at it. "I think he kinda looks like me."

He's baiting me, waiting for me to admit what he's already figured out. Maybe knowing that I know that he knows that I know isn't good enough for him.

But it's more than enough for me.

"*Miles.*"

It's a good thing I love his laugh, because it isn't annoying me as much as it should be right now. I might actually find it a little reassuring that he's pressing my buttons, instead of bolting for the door. He still could at any point, but a glance down at where the book is open tells me that he's pretty far past all the incriminating details and introductions.

"My idea for this book came to me when I was still a teenager." I point a thumb over my shoulder, gesturing to the past. "She thought of it, I just wrote it. Okay?" I divulge that much with the hope it'll be enough to dismiss the topic.

But that only appears to confuse him, and I watch the lines form between his brows as he thinks. What I wouldn't give to know what was running through his head.

"I have even more questions now," he admits.

Well, I'm going to make him wait a minute before he gets to ask them. I grab my water, guzzling it down as if it'll make my stomach stop churning.

It must be nice to live life without anxiety that makes you feel physically sick.

"Okay," I begin with a nod. "Ask what's on your mind, *but* I can refuse to answer if I think it might... cross a boundary. It's been two days, hardly enough time to risk messing that up now, don't you think?"

I surprise myself with how believable I sound.

"Agreed." He looks away for a second, hand on his chin in contemplation. I reluctantly admit to myself that he looks like he belongs in a museum, as some perfectly sculpted statue for everyone to admire. It would be such a win that I'm the only one that gets to admire him right now, if I was actually allowed to.

"Why'd you give me green eyes?"

"Girls love green eyes. Next."

"Well that makes me feel adequate," he mumbles sarcastically. I want to add that I'm not one of those girls, that I could stare into his deep brown eyes all day, but that's definitely on the inappropriate list. "What made you do it?"

Well that went from zero to one hundred really fast.

"I think I'm not allowed to answer that."

"You said you were a teenager, that doesn't count." The intense look in his eyes tells me that's bullshit. He knows a fraction of what I'm going to say, that much is obvious.

"If you repeat any of this, or give me any crap for it..." I don't finish the thought because I don't know how to. I hide my face in my hands, not wanting his reaction, and hope he can hear me through them. Though it wouldn't be so bad if he couldn't. "I used to have a crush on you. You were nice to me after everything that happened... and I was young, and naive, and I didn't have any friends. You were the only person that didn't let me push you away, so I romanticized the crap out of it." I don't move my hands. I stare down at my lap waiting for him to say something, which unfortunately takes a while.

I have plenty of time to let my mind wander to negative places.

I hear rustling from his end of the couch, which causes me to finally lift my head. He's standing now, but not looking at me. I realize I'm slightly shaking as he makes his way towards my front door and starts slipping on his shoes.

Fuck. I should have refused to answer that one. It definitely feels like I broke a rule.

I shouldn't be so hurt that he's following them, but *he asked.* He told me it didn't count.

He pauses with a hand on the doorknob. "Can I call you when I get home? I need a minute."

I slowly nod in response, even though the eye contact is still nonexistent. All I get as a goodbye is a clipped smile.

17

AUTUMN

I know I *should* be fine, it's not like I'm his girlfriend or anything, but I'm not fine. I feel so dumb.

"Autumn Owens, you need to get it together," I tell my reflection in the mirror. I don't think she's hearing me very well. "He might have a good reason for all you know! Stop jumping!"

Still nothing. I've jumped to all kinds of conclusions since I first woke up twenty minutes ago.

I have to get ready for work with absolutely no energy to do so. The only thing that gets me through my makeup routine is more yelling into the mirror.

I still feel like a zombie when I eventually drag myself out of my apartment and into my car.

One bright side of the ice covering my windows on this freezing morning is that none of my neighbors can see the mini-meltdown I might have in my driver's seat. I have at least a couple minutes to sit here while everything defrosts, and I spend it with my forehead against the steering wheel.

I wish I could have the same mindset he does right now. I wish I could stop thinking about him. I wish I didn't have the urge to message him and beg for an explanation every five seconds.

I know why none of that is possible, and it makes my chest hurt.

A flick of my windshield wipers reveals that my time is up, and I'm not excited. How does one play it cool while sitting across from the mother of the man who has you feeling this conflicted?

I'm going to figure it out, or die of embarrassment while trying.

Amelia picks up on my mood the second I walk in the building. "Why the long face?"

I give her my best fake smile.

"Didn't sleep very well, still trying to wake up," I lie. While I couldn't fall asleep until after midnight because I was waiting on someone's call, I slept in late enough to make up for it.

Then I woke up with the worst sinking feeling.

"Do you want to go on a coffee run? I'm having the same issue this morning, I could use a caramel macchiato" she says with a sleepy smile for emphasis.

"Sure, that'd be great." A little walk to the nearest coffee stand will be a pleasant distraction.

"Kaitlyn will be here in between meetings, would you mind grabbing her a coffee? Black." I raise a brow and she gives me an agreeing nod. "I thought she was a green tea smoothie girl at first. *That* was an awkward day."

I fish my wallet out of my bag, not wanting to carry the whole thing down the street.

"Oh, put that back." She laughs a little, and my cheeks heat. "Here." She pulls what looks to be spare change from her back pocket, except the bill she hands me isn't spare change. It's a hundred dollar bill.

It's always so odd for me to see people be so casual about their money.

And that's *why I'm not the one paying for coffee.*

"If they can't make change, you can grab some muffins or something. Thanks, dear." She looks back down at the color swatches on her desk, and I take that as my dismissal. Without grabbing my phone, I head out.

I love the days where the sun stays hidden behind the clouds, and everything's left in a comfortable shade. It makes me feel capable of anything. Right now for instance, it's making me feel like it doesn't matter that Miles didn't call me last night. I can get over it, even if we never talk again. I've gotten over much worse.

A couple passes me, walking the biggest golden retriever I've ever seen. The dog couldn't be more different than my small pal Freddy, but that's where my mind goes. I picture him and Miles snuggled up on his couch, playing games.

It takes more than a day to lose a habit.

All the buildings downtown are old, and they remind me of a small town in a Hallmark movie. Green vines trailing up walls, and string lights wrapped around lamp posts. It feels like they skipped all of the coming holidays and went straight to Christmas.

Even the coffee stand I approach has frosted windows that are begging to be covered in drawings of snowmen and candy canes. It makes me smile to myself.

As I wait, I eavesdrop. There's one person ahead of me at the walk up window. They're clearly flirting, it's evident in every giggle that comes from the girl working inside. I glance at the back of the stranger, and he seems good looking. Broad shoulders, smooth black hair. I've never been good at flirting, but I imagine it must be freeing. To walk around with charisma, and confidence, and use it on unsuspecting baristas. I have none of those things, and even if I did, there's only one person that I feel like flirting with.

The way my mind keeps traveling back to him is really inconvenient.

And by inconvenient, I mean it makes me nauseous.

I realize as the guy grabs his coffee and leaves, that I recognize the girl in the window. It takes me the couple steps towards her to put it together, but I want to run when it hits me. If I thought I felt sick before, that was nothing.

It's Justin's wife. Isabelle.

The Isabelle. The one that bullied me at school because it took him too long to break up with me.

She doesn't seem to recognize me, her face stuck in customer service mode. It doesn't surprise me, I couldn't look more different than I used to.

"Good morning! What can we get you?" Her voice is disgustingly cheery.

I hesitate, gawking like the awkward human I am, before blurting out the drinks I need. She's good at her job, giving no reaction to my quivering voice. She keeps that smile on.

"Do you have change for this?" I ask her.

"Oh no, I just had a drawer pickup. I'm afraid I don't."

I'm quick to tell her it's not a problem, and order a few random treats from the menu. It does the trick, and she's carefully loading everything, including a cup holder with my drinks, into a large, handled, paper bag within a minute.

"Okay hun! I arranged it so nothing is likely to spill, but be careful." She hands it to me with both hands, and I take it from her the same way. I'm careful not to jostle it around, even though I'd watched her put stoppers in all of the lids.

"Thank you." I look up at her as I say it, and we make eye contact. Her face falls for a single second, and I can tell it hits her. She knows who I am.

Awesome.

Her farewell smile is now strained, and I want the ground to open up and swallow me whole. Small towns are not as cute as the movies make them out to be, considering how high the odds are that you'll run into people you don't care to see.

As if I wasn't feeling scattered enough, Miles is standing at his mothers desk when I walk back into the office. I have to resist the urge to drop the bag and turn around, because I don't know how to do this. I'm not great at pretending to be unaffected, the fact proven by my increased heart rate and sweaty palms.

I intentionally avoid looking at him out of petty anger, and a little bit of fear. I bring the goods to my desk, pulling out the coffees and treats. Kaitlyn appears out of blue, with grabby hands, and only sticks around long enough for me to hand hers over. She gives me a very appreciative thank you, and apologizes for having to leave again.

Amelia groans when I hand over hers.

"You're saving my life this morning."

"That's what I'm here for," I chirp. It's the fakest voice I've got, reminding me of Isabelle standing in her walk-up window again.

"Anything that could save my life in there?" Miles asks. There's obviously a hidden meaning, he needs saving from the fact that he let me worry all night.

As if he hadn't seen the panic on my face when he left my apartment.

"Muffins and scones," I reply. It sounds short, so I'm sure to look up and smile at him. I hope he knows it's only a show for Amelia. "Plenty of extra."

He comes up to stand way too close to me as he peeks in the bag. "Ooh, orange cranberry?"

I have to keep myself from swatting it out of his hand. "Actually, that one is for your mom. She's usually the only person that eats them."

"Ah!" She exclaims from her desk. "Good looking out." She reaches her hand out towards him, and closes it a couple times in a grabbing motion. He chuckles before handing it over.

"I should've known."

I focus on my computer, coffee in hand. Amelia always has a folder full of random notes about the recent clients she's met with, things they loved, things they hated. I add it all to their profiles for future reference. It gives me inspiration for my own apartment. Not that it's big enough, or luxurious enough for most of the things I see around here. I'd just like to play around if I ever have the extra money to do so. Maybe add a fake tree, or a large area rug.

Then I imagine Elaine getting her claws into all of it, and change my mind.

I feel Miles' eyes on me as I work.

Doesn't he know that's making it difficult for me to concentrate?

There are some scans where I can't read Amelia's handwriting. It happens every so often, because she has to jot these things down so quickly. When I look to her to ask, her focus is on her son.

And that *wonderful* scowl is back on her face, because she's watching him stare at me.

Where is your self awareness, Miles?

"Don't you have to get going?" she asks him before I can figure out my next move. I look at him just in time to miss the eye contact. He slightly shakes his head, like he's trying to snap out of something.

Took him long enough.

"Yeah, I have to get to work. Thanks for the scone." Then he hugs his mother goodbye, and leaves without another glance at me.

I'm totally fine with that, and not at all frustrated. Obviously.

Amelia seems to be back to normal when I ask about her notes. I'm grateful when the rest of the day flies by without any more discomfort. I could not handle it if it did.

"Oh! Here," I tell her as I pull her change from my back pocket. Instead of grabbing it, she shakes her head at me.

"Keep it."

I'm confused. "What? No, it's your money from the—"

"I know, darling. I'm telling you to keep it. Consider it a small thank you."

My mind refuses to wrap around this. "B-but, no, it's—"

She sighs like I'm a child that doesn't understand, which to be fair, is exactly what I feel like. "Don't worry about it. Think of it as a tip for all of your hard work." She gives me a once-over. "Maybe you could use it to buy some new jeans?"

I know she didn't mean it harshly, but it feels like a punch to the face. I look down at my jeans that were once a solid black, but have faded to a splotchy gray. I do wear them often, but that's because they're comfortable. I didn't think anyone would notice.

"Uh, sure," I mumble, feeling flustered.

"Good. Great," she corrects. "Now have a good weekend, and we'll see you Tuesday."

18

AUTUMN

It's finally the day of the party. I delegated some tasks to the girls to help me put things together, and it's all looking good. I should be excited, but I'm annoyed. Annoyed that I was *so* excited for Miles to come, and now I don't even know if he is. I wish I didn't care, considering I haven't heard a word from him since that day at the office.

If he does show up, at least I'll look incredible in my little blue dress. I shouldn't want him to notice, but I do. I want him to see me looking good, having a great time with my friends, and I want him to regret his radio silence.

Of course the romance writer in me is hoping for that outcome.

Ten people doesn't seem like very many until they're all sitting in my living room. Something I seem to forget every time I host. No one really seems to mind, they're all chatting away, helping themselves to snacks and drinks. Opening all the windows has helped, the cold air from outside negating all of the body heat in here.

I dressed up as a fairy, with a million blue details and wings to match. There's so much glitter on my face it would blind anyone that dared to shine a light on me.

It's perfect.

Reya and Vic show up looking like a picture straight out of a costume catalog. Reya is the cutest pink crayon I've ever seen, she doesn't even need to use the hat that comes with hers thanks to her vibrant hair. Vic is beautiful as ever with a tight, black dress, and bunny ears.

If there was a costume contest, one of us would win it.

Miles is here and still not talking to me. He arrived late and now he sits the farthest from me across the table. It's probably for the best, knowing if I got the urge to lean into him I wouldn't stop myself. Not when I'm a couple of drinks in and my mind is already laser focused on his every breath.

He did go simple with his costume, throwing a lab coat and a stethoscope over his usual work scrubs. I like it a lot more than I should.

Warm breath on my ear interrupts my thoughts before I hear my neighbor, Ben, whisper to me.

Yeah, *the* neighbor.

He's closer than he needs to be, but I don't have any room on my other side to scoot away.

"You totally just flashed me your cards, and if you don't put this one down next," he points to one in my hand, "I'll be very disappointed."

I can't help but let a laugh slip out at that. If I'd been paying better attention, that *was* the card I'd play, so I'm slightly glad he noticed. My next move in this card game is not where my thoughts lie.

I go through the rest of it on autopilot. He occasionally leans in to whisper to me, even asking me about his own moves. I think he just wants the excuse to talk to me, and everyone seems to have picked up on it too. His sister whines at him to stop cheating, and she's backed by Reya.

Miles looks a bit uncomfortable but he stays quiet the entire time.

I wish he wouldn't. I want to hear his voice more than anyone else's.

Miles

I don't realize I'm clenching my hands until it starts to hurt. I try to shake the tension from them, but it's pointless.

A look around tells me no one is aware of the state I'm in, and I'm grateful.

For the most part. I wish she would notice.

Instead, she's looking at that guy and laughing. Their knees are touching. She looks so at ease, which I don't think I've seen when it's just the two of us.

I have no idea who he is, and he doesn't seem to care who I am. He didn't introduce himself, and hasn't looked my way since I got here.

It rubs me the wrong way in combination with the fact that he's been hogging her attention. I try to think back to the photo that was on her wall, the one that felt like a gut punch. If this is that same guy—

I think someone's saying my name, and I'm pulled away from my thoughts.

"Miles? Where'd you go?" It's Autumn, amusement in her voice. "It's your turn."

It is so good to see her smile in my direction, even for a second. I know she's mad at me. I know I fucked up.

I grab a card, and continue to play the rest of this game without a single thought about it.

She eventually wrangles everyone to take photos, until it feels like there are hundreds of polaroid pictures floating around the place. I watch her go around, joking, laughing, telling people where to stand as she clicks away. She's having a great time, and I'm glad I get to watch her while she's distracted.

That bright smile of hers turns and walks towards me, and my eyes widen in surprise.

"Get over here." She playfully grabs my arm, and my instinct is to joke that she's breaking a rule.

I don't. I don't want her to let go.

I follow after her, but instead of going where she points me, I reach for the camera.

"You haven't been in a single one of these photos."

"Neither have you!" she protests. "Get over there."

"I have an idea!" The voice comes from behind us, and it's her friend, Reya. "Since neither of you have been in any photos, you can both get your butts over there and take some together." She snatches the camera with a large smile, not allowing room for arguments. I can't think of a reason to argue with that, especially when Autumn puts her hand on my arm to walk us over.

She bounces over to stand in front of the decorated wall, and I follow without a word. Black and orange streamers create a curtain behind us, surrounded by orange lights, and paper bats.

"Say cheese!"

I do not say cheese when the flash goes off, which warrants a glare from the fairy next to me. I can't help but smile wider at the sight of it, and then she can't help it either. It's an image I don't want to look away from, with her cheeks flushed a perfect pink. The flash goes off again, and we both face Reya. She takes a picture of that, too.

"Okay, I'm done!" she squeaks from behind the camera. Autumn moves to grab it from her, right in time for her cat to dart past her feet.

"Elaine!" She yells as she loses her balance. Luckily, she falls in my direction and I steady her with a laugh. A laugh I can not, for the life of me, stop once it starts. The beers I drank while feeling sorry for myself are really doing their job.

I can't even remember what I was feeling sorry about when I look down at the most beautiful woman I've ever seen to find her giggling back up at me. If there was ever a perfect moment to kiss someone, this would be it right here.

If our lives were normal, if things were simpler. This would be a dream.

I don't really care when the flash goes off again, but it seems to snap Autumn out of her giddy state. She quickly backs away from me, the smile on her face becoming a thin, polite line. I want to do whatever I can to change that again, to make her face light up.

I reach for her arm, but she jerks away so fast that she bumps into the counter. Two glass bottles meet the back of her elbow and go crashing to her kitchen floor. She gasps, rushing towards the shattered pieces to reach her broom. I do grab her this time, my arm wrapping around her front to pull her back.

A sharp inhale of her breath tells me I'm not the only one appreciating the way she feels against me, but then she's pushing my arm away.

"Please don't touch me," she whispers, soft enough that it reaches my ears only.

My heart plummets, crashing like the bottles did, but I remove my arm.

I pretend those four words didn't just manage to sober me up in the worst way.

"I'm not letting you walk near that mess with bare feet. I've got it." I find the broom tucked in a corner of her small kitchen and start to sweep the mess together.

"I can do it," she protests, reaching for the handle.

"I said I've got it," I snap, pulling it out of her reach.

She looks so heart-wrenchingly sad for a split second, but then it's gone. As if I completely imagined it. The tone of my voice must work because she's turning back towards her friends. I notice how hard half of them are staring, like they just witnessed something they're going to talk about later. All I did was keep her from cutting open her foot.

When the glass is in the garbage, I know I have to get out of here. She's back to chatting and drinking, and standing way too close to that guy.

Please don't touch me, her soft voice plays in my mind again. Now it's obvious that she's avoiding looking in my direction.

I snatch my car keys off of a hook and head out the door.

"I don't think so," comes Vic's voice from behind me. I turn to see her hand held out expectantly. "I'm not letting anyone drink and drive tonight, buddy. Hand them over."

I shake my head, not having planned on driving anytime soon.

"I was just going to sit in my car and wait it out for a bit."

"Can't wait it out inside?" She gives me a knowing smile.

"No," is all I say. I manage to get the door open, but I don't get it closed behind me before she's got a hold on it. I let go and keep walking, my sour mood making me lack any patience.

"Then I'll wait with you for a while, just to make sure." She skips towards me, looking accomplished when she's by my side.

"I swear I'm not going to drive. I just want to be alone."

She gives me an assessing look, up and down. "I believe you. Doesn't matter, because I'm still following you. You and I should get to know each other better." There's something in her tone that makes me feel uneasy.

"I'm not looking to get to *know* anyone."

"Oh, dude." She shakes her head, and holds up her hand to show off a huge diamond ring. My shoulders sag a little in relief, and we continue towards the parking lot.

Vic talks the entire way.

"Autumn doesn't let a lot of people in, but it's usually a good pick when she does. She brought us together, Reya and I." She sighs. "I couldn't stand that girl at first, and now she's one of my favorite people on the planet. Maybe I'll be able to say the same about you someday."

"You can't stand me?"

She laughs warmly. "You're pretty tolerable, actually. We're already halfway there."

I raise my brows at her when she walks around to the passenger side of my car and tries the handle.

"It's cold out here." She motions toward the door as if I don't realize I'm leaving us to stand out here. I'd love to get in my car and turn the heat on considering I can see my breath in front of my face.

"Am I signing up for an interrogation if I unlock that door?"

"Possibly." She shrugs like she hasn't decided yet.

I don't know why I accept that as good enough, but the locks click and she looks pleased. It's almost colder in my car, and I waste no time turning it on so I can get the heater going.

"So, you left without saying goodbye."

I nod.

"Because you want to wrap your arms around her and keep her away from Ben, but you can't."

I hold back an eye roll at the guy's name.

"Where'd you get that idea?"

"You're easy to read. Staring all night, looking like a wounded puppy. She thinks it's for her own good to pretend she doesn't notice."

I don't respond, and the car is silent for long stretch.

"Do you think that's true?" Vic asks.

"That it's for her own good?" I shrug. "It's complicated."

"Is it? I mean it's not ideal that your brother is..." She cringes and I fail to hold in my snort of amusement. "But you're both big kids now. You should make decisions that make you happy."

Maybe she reads the hesitation on my face, because she adds, "You make her happy."

"It doesn't seem like that's true right now."

"You really are clueless."

I shrug.

"It could be so simple."

"Anything else?" I know I sound like a jerk, but there's only one person I wish was in my car telling me about Autumn's feelings and it's *Autumn*.

But it will never be simple. Even if Autumn still liked me, if she thought of me the way I was trying not to think of her, it wouldn't matter. There are other parts of this equation.

Vic studies me as if something on my face will tell her which magic words will break through.

"Yeah, actually," she finally says. "If you think I'm wrong, why would she leave her own party to see where you went?"

"What do you—" I'm interrupted by a knock on my window that makes me jump. "Autumn?" I start to roll my window down, but decide against it and get out of the car. It's obviously not my first time seeing her in that little dress, but my breath leaves my lungs at the sight of her in the moonlight.

"What are you guys doing?" She tries to sound casual but I can see the concern on her face. I just can't tell if it's because I left or because she's overthinking the reason her friend is currently sitting in my car. Said friend has decided not to move from the passenger seat, but she's not acknowledging that we're out here.

"She followed me out as I was leaving," I explain. "We talked."

She nods her head slowly.

"Why are you leaving?"

I shrug. I'm great at that tonight.

"What's wrong?"

It's obvious that Vic is within earshot even with the car door closed so I shrug again. It feels like I have stage fright over talking to someone I love talking to.

She rolls her eyes when I don't respond.

She reaches past me and bangs on the window behind me.

"Will you go inside, please?"

Without a word, Vic gets out of my car and makes her way back towards the apartment. She gives us a little wave before she disappears.

I like Vic, I think she's a good friend to Autumn. I just wish she was right.

It could be so simple.

"Now? What is it?" Autumn presses.

"You were having a good time, you should go back inside."

"You're right. I *was* having a good time, until I realized you had disappeared."

"Don't let me ruin anything. I'll see you at the office."

She shakes her head adamantly.

"No, you don't get to just leave again. I'm still pissed off that I haven't heard from you all week, you're not doing that to me again." She grabs my arm. "Make it up to me. Let's go back inside."

I plant my feet firmly. "Autumn."

"Unless there's another reason you're so desperate to leave." She must see something switch on my face because she starts to nod. "Talk to me, Miles. Come on," she pleads.

"I probably shouldn't," I whisper, silently begging her to understand why and let it drop.

She briefly pauses, inspecting me thoughtfully.

"You can *say* anything."

I hesitate for a while. She stands there and waits. I can't say anything, but I can start somewhere.

"I know it's not fair..." I start. "I'm just having a hard time with our dynamic in there. You seem really close with that guy all night, and then you tell me not to touch you. It's too much right now."

I'm worried it's always going to be too much, but I don't say that.

"I'm sorry. That wasn't okay." She looks down, but not before I notice the blush on her chest and neck. "I'm not interested in him. You know what the problem really is, right? I don't have to explain it?"

I look at her with as much astonishment as I can express. How could she think that I know *anything* when it comes to her? I've never been this clueless in my life.

"No," I say with a shake of my head. "I don't. All I know right now is that I thought we had a moment, and then you shut down. You shut *me* down when I tried to help you."

Before I realize what she's doing, her arms are around me and I'm melting into her. I rest my cheek against the top of her head, and I feel sane for the first time tonight. No one in the world could deny how perfectly we fit together.

"I like this too much," she confesses. Her voice is muffled into my shoulder, and she tilts her head slightly so that the next words come out clearer. "I'm not allowed to, but I do. When you grabbed me in the kitchen I felt like I had two options. The one I didn't choose was to throw myself at you and make a fool of myself."

I scoff. "You wouldn't have made a fool of yourself. You think you're not allowed to hug me? Friends hug."

She squeezes me tighter for a split second.

"That isn't what I meant," she whispers.

There it is. An admission that should make me feel on top of the world, but somehow it makes me feel worse. It changes everything and nothing.

This woman is going to be the death of me.

I don't respond, knowing that this is what she didn't want to do. She didn't want me to feel like this, but we're so far past that point now. I've felt this trapped since before she even told me why she wrote the book.

I can't get over how much space I must have been occupying in her head back then, and I had no idea. Things would be so much different if I had, there's no chance we'd be here. Whether they'd be better or worse, I don't know, but a small part of me is glad for the way things are. In a weird way, it feels like pining over her is the right thing to do.

I'd rather have it than nothing.

We hold onto each other for longer than friends would. I don't let myself care, I enjoy the moment. I hug her like I have no idea when I'll get to hug her next, because I don't.

"You wouldn't have made a fool of yourself," I say again with ten times as much meaning.

I feel her muscles tense, but neither of us pull away.

"I wish we could just stay out here."

"Me too," I say, and I mean it more than she knows.

"But my feet are freezing."

I back away from her to look down at her feet. She is wearing the smallest, thinnest pair of slippers I've ever seen.

"Shit, Autumn. You have to get inside."

"I don't want to without you," she says, and her eyes lock with mine. I love the way her head has to tilt back to do so.

I can't say no to her.

Neither of us move for at least a minute. We just stand there watching each other like we know we're not supposed to.

The reminder of her freezing feet is the only reason I look away first, and walk her back inside.

19

AUTUMN

There are some really impolite clients that exhaust me more than most things about this office. Not that there aren't sweet ones. Some already remember me when they call, and even ask how I'm doing. I had a woman bring me flowers the other day because she noticed my desk looked empty. I cried when she left.

But some of them can't seem to be bothered with talking to me at all, even when I'm their only option. I've dealt with the dehumanizing reality of customer service before, but this feels different. Personal. I try to shrug it off, but I can't help but wonder if they know more about me than they should. Does Amelia kill time with clients by telling them about her son's ex-girlfriend? I don't want to know.

The only thing that exhausts me more is trying to act normal around Amelia. I feel like someone has written *I have feelings for Miles Cress* on my forehead, and I'm constantly trying to cover it up.

I'm nervous whenever he texts me throughout the day, that she'll somehow sense the guilt I'm feeling. Or see it on my face, I guess. I've never been a good actor, what you see is what you get. No matter how hard I try.

"I read your book," Kaitlyn's voice suddenly comes from behind me. I'm not awake enough to react.

At least not right away, but it only takes a few seconds for panic to set in. The only people I know in real life that have read my book are the girls, and they already knew every incriminating detail. They had no connections to him, or his family, and therefore I had every reason to trust them with that information.

Kaitlyn on the other hand? I have no idea what she'll do with it. I'm terrified.

"Yeah?" It comes out raspy, and betrays just how exhausted I am. I clear my throat.

She giggles as she walks around to face me.

"Don't freak out, I fucking *loved* it. I might lose my mind if I never get to read more about those two."

The world around us disappears.

"Wait, what?" I must be hearing things, because it sounded like she just said she loved my book. I shut my eyes, giving my sleepy brain a moment to catch up and...

She actually did say that, didn't she?

"Really?"

"Yes, really! Oh, don't do that!" She leans over the desk and hands me a tissue. I hadn't even noticed there were tears welling up in my eyes. "Your makeup is too cute. What are you writing now? Is there more Cam? I'm not exaggerating when I say I *need* more of him."

I don't know how, but it feels like I'm wide awake now. Her excitement feels like a shot of espresso.

"I think I'm in shock."

With some more prying, I explain a little about what I'm currently working on, and watch her face drop and pick back up, over and over again. I've never met anyone so expressive, and I love it. I love feeling like I'm not the only one that cares what I'm writing.

Well, the only one other than a whopping thirty Goodreads reviewers.

"I have a confession," she says once I've gotten all the fun details out of my system.

That's always scary. I narrow my eyes at her.

"I may have posted a video recommending your book, and my thousands of followers may have blown it up a bit." The smile on her face as she finishes speaking is sneaky. Pleased.

"I— You have thousands of followers?" For how chatty this girl is, you think she might have mentioned it before. "How many thousands?"

"Ninety." She lifts a shoulder like it's not a big deal. "I just talk about things I like. A couple years ago I did a makeup tutorial that went viral. There were articles about it everywhere."

Not one ounce of surprise fills me at that, her personality tends to pull people in.

"What does 'blown up' mean to you?" I ask skeptically.

She pulls out her phone and opens up an app I've never heard of, something about a clock? Yet another factor in my failure of a debut, I'm sure.

The wind completely knocks out of me when she shows me the screen and one number stands out among the rest of what I'm looking at. *Two million views*, sitting on top of a thumbnail where she's holding up my book.

My book.

"How? What? I don't..." Full sentences are too much for me to handle right now.

The smile on her face grows.

"Isn't that amazing? I have the best followers." I take in her appearance, and she looks genuinely happy for me. It's a lot to wrap my head around.

"Wow," I breathe.

"Do you want to see it?"

"I don't know," I say.

Then I grab the phone from her before I can think better of it, and play the fifteen second video.

I blink a couple times when it restarts and I hit pause. It was so short. So simple. She barely touches on the plot. She didn't mention knowing me personally. She didn't even say it was a five star book, she just asked for their thoughts on it.

I decide to look through a few of the comments, although I'm nervous about what I'll find.

How'd you know I needed a new book rec???

omg this looks adorable!

add to cart

People just trust her opinion. Just like that.

Kaitlyn looks at me expectantly.

"What do you think?"

"I think I love you."

After an exhilarating conversation, where I admit my social media flaws to my coworker, she agrees to help me out. She wants nothing in return but signed copies of *every book I ever publish*.

I'm on cloud nine.

Miles

"I am ready for this thing to be done," I grumble, attempting conversation. The office is quiet with the other two out at an appointment. While things have been good between Autumn and I, the tension is noticeably thicker. I'd rather be talking than letting my imagination run wild with it.

"Thing?" she asks without looking up from the book she's reading.

"Yeah, the office anniversary thing. It's already next weekend."

"Oh, sounds fun." Her words are quiet, distracted. I turn in my seat to face her.

"You'll be there too, right?"

She looks up and blinks a couple times before shaking her head.

I frown. "Why not?"

"Uh, Amelia hasn't mentioned it to me?"

A weird oversight, considering how particular my mom is about these things.

I stand and approach her desk. "She probably forgot, there's been a lot on her plate."

She puts the book face down, and turns her chair to face me.

"I don't think that's it. I mean, why should she want me to be there?"

"Why wouldn't she? It's a work party. You work here..." I let the words trail off, studying her face.

She's closed off, I can see it in her eyes. It's not the first time I've noticed she does this, but I wish it could be the last.

She shakes her head. "I've only been here for a few weeks. I think she would've mentioned it if she wanted me to be there." I don't miss that her voice sounds more hoarse than it did a second ago.

"Why do you do that?" I ask quietly, and without thinking.

"Do what?"

It's probably a bad idea, but I put my hand over hers, and trace a couple of soothing lines with my thumb. I don't think about that either.

"You assume you're not wanted anywhere, even with me. Your instinct is to question why someone would want to be around you." I see moisture build in her eyes, but she blinks it away and looks down at her desk. I feel like I'm failing. "You're my favorite person, Autumn. I always want to be around you."

Even when I shouldn't.

I lean in closer, pushing for her answer. If there was anyone she needed to hide from, it's not me.

"Why," I say again.

It's obvious she's battling herself. A few seconds pass, and I almost ask again, but then she shifts her focus to my hand that's still on top of hers.

And she pulls it away so quickly, I'm stunned.

"I feel like you're trying to make this impossible."

"What? What did I do?"

"Your hugs, and your eyes, and your compliments, and your hand holding. You're driving me crazy." I watch as she buries her face in her hand and groans.

"I'm sorry, I didn't mean to—" To what, comfort her? Care about her? Of course I did.

I think the line we've drawn is too fuzzy. It's even fuzzier for me after our moment in her parking lot the other night. I can't stop thinking of those gold and green eyes piercing through me, holding me upright.

I hate that they're being hidden from me right now.

"I don't know what to do. I'm not trying to—"

"I know you're not trying to. You don't have to try anything, because you're *you*."

The way she says it makes me feel like it's an insult.

"Ouch."

When she lifts her head, the response I get is an eye roll. I think it's directed more at the situation, the lack of options than towards me. I could be wrong.

Sick of dancing around what we're both thinking, I motion between us.

"Is this that bad?"

She flinches at the words, like they physically hurt her. It didn't feel great to say them either.

"Yeah."

Blowing out a shaky breath, it hits me that I agree with her.

As if emphasizing just how bad it is, my mother chooses that moment to blow into the building like a windstorm. Her hands full of shopping bags, her cell phone pressed between her cheek and shoulder. She's trying her best to politely disagree with whoever's on the other end of the call, when she stops midsentence at the sight of us.

I straighten and step away from Autumn's desk so fast that it has to look suspicious. We might as well have been making out, given her reaction. She lets the phone drop, landing on the hard floor with a dramatic clatter.

It's good she has a phone case that could keep it alive in the midst of a tornado.

"What are you doing?" Her tone is accusatory.

"Talking."

She doesn't even hide how pissed off she is, and practically throws the bags onto the floor before grabbing her phone.

"Sorry, *Justin*. I'll have to give you a call back, honey."

I attempt to hide my cringe at her emphasis on his name. The two people that make the woman I care about so anxious. The reasons we're struggling so hard to be friends, but can't be more.

The look on my mother's face makes me get it, now *I'm* fucking anxious.

"You can close up," she says tightly to Autumn. "Doesn't look like there's much going on."

"Sure," she responds shakily. Then, standing, she avoids looking at either of us and goes to pull the blinds down over the front windows.

The glare I'm met with when my attention lands back on my mother makes me want to scream. It makes no sense to me that she's this angry, not when she adores Autumn most of the time. I don't believe that she thinks she's trying to protect her sons. She can't actually think *we* need protecting from *her*? Autumn is the one that needed protecting all those years ago.

"You forgot to tell her about the party."

"What are you talking about?"

"She didn't get an invite."

"Correct."

That's all she says. She doesn't elaborate.

"Why?"

"It's okay." I hear from the other voice in the room.

My mother gives her a smile that doesn't fully reach her eyes.

"I didn't think you'd want to hang out with our clients outside of your work day."

Autumn barely shrugs, looking like a deer in the headlights.

"You didn't think to ask?" I press.

Another lethal glare.

"I should have. My mistake."

"It's okay," Autumn says again.

We make eye contact, and I don't want to look away. I want it to just be us in the room again so we can finish talking.

Then my mother lets out a sudden, delighted sound and I turn to see her smile widen.

"Truly, I am sorry that it got away from me. I'd *love* it if you were there. I'll text you the details."

Her change in demeanor makes me suspicious, but I accept the win. *If* that's what it is.

Autumn doesn't look like she thinks so.

I watch as she finishes closing up. She sanitizes the front door, vacuums the rug at the entrance, and flicks lights off once she's put everything away in the back. My mom pretends to be focused on the bags she brought in, but I can feel her attention on me.

I don't care.

I want to wrap my arms around Autumn the second we step outside, but her words linger. I'm making it hard for us to be friends. I have to stop touching her.

She won't even look at me. Following her all the way to her car, I'm silent. What else is there to say? We both know how difficult this is, but I can't be the one to let it go. I can't let *her* go.

"I don't think I'm capable of staying away from you," she says, as if reading my mind. "Regardless of how bad it is."

We're on the same page there.

"It's not *bad* though, is it?" She looks up at me, confused, and I continue. "I want to be around you because it's... great. It feels great. I smile so much when we're together that my face hurts."

A soft smile pulls at her lips, because I know she gets that.

"I guess it's everything else that's bad."

Everything else includes the woman still inside the building.

"Are you okay?"

She still seems a little shaken, but I can tell she's calming down. I lift my hand to place it on her shoulder, but I pull back before I do. Her eyes track my movements, almost seeming disappointed when they fall to the ground again.

"I'm okay. I think I get why she's like that."

"Care to share?"

Autumn shrugs. "Everything used to be so complicated, you know? I'm trying to see it through her eyes, and I'd probably not be my biggest fan."

"But you haven't done anything wrong."

She doesn't respond. I'm filled with so much sadness over what she carries around, how she sees herself.

"Come with me next weekend."

She turns and puts her hand on her car door handle. I wait for her to pull, but she doesn't. Her head falls against it, and she lets out an exhausted sigh.

"I can't do that. I can't go."

"Yes, you can."

Autumn turns her head to the side.

"We both saw that inside, right? We both know she doesn't actually want me to be there."

"So? I'll be there. We can drink and snack and hide in the storage room, away from everyone." I want her to look at me. "I might have to socialize a little, but it'll be more bearable if you're with me."

She hums in response. "We could get drunk in any storage closet."

"Sometimes you have to get drunk in a mandatory storage closet to enjoy all of the optional ones. Once this is over with, it's your pick."

I am ecstatic to hear the laugh that flies past her lips.

"I just... I don't know. It's hard for me to walk into a room where I know I'm not wanted."

She finally meets my eyes, and I try my best to convey how much I mean my next words.

"You're wanted in every room I'm in."

She almost looks like she believes it.

She will, I'll get her there. Whatever it takes.

20

AUTUMN

The days fly by. I focus on writing and work. I fail at any attempt to get Miles off my mind, or to stop stressing over my interactions with Amelia. I haven't received any of the harsh reactions I got from her that day at the office, but I'm always on alert. I'm always waiting for the next one.

I hate the way I made Miles feel, so I've been trying to make up for it. I've been pretending I'm not struggling with our close friendship. I might even fool someone with an outside look in, they would think we're just two besties. No romantic or sexual tension here, no sir.

But there's *so* much of it on my end.

As a single woman, pretending the way I am, I'm grateful for vibrating toys.

I really don't know what I would do without them sometimes, but today it feels like I don't know what to do *with* them. Nothing is enough fuel for this fire I'm trying to start. Not even the smutty book on my nightstand is doing the trick.

My racing mind knows exactly why I'm struggling, and it feels like an internal tug-of-war to keep avoiding it. The last thing I need is for my body to react to him more than it already does.

A knock on my front door interrupts my hopeless attempts. I sigh and stop what I'm doing. Not that there was much going on for someone to interrupt, but I'm still annoyed they showed up unannounced.

The knock happens again, sounding like someone with a purpose. I groan as I pull my favorite vibrator away, switch it off, and toss it on top of my comforter.

I guess we'll just have to try again later.

I pull my pajama pants on as I exit my room and make my way to peer through the peephole in my front door.

"Sorry!" I say, pulling it open. "What are you doing here?"

I should've known it was him.

Miles gives me a shy smile.

"I can't find my wallet. I think I might have left it here the other night."

A laugh bursts out of me as I let him inside.

"You've been driving without a license all week? You're so bad." I start helping him search, pulling pillows off my couch and feeling in between the cushions. I haven't seen it anywhere, so I assume if it's here that it's got to be in some random, hidden place.

"It was pretty embarrassing when I pulled up to the gas station after waiting in line for twenty minutes only to find I had no way to pay for it."

My attention is so focused on what I'm doing, that I don't think about where he's looking. I hear things being moved on my dining table, then the kitchen counter. I'm positive he won't find it there, but I let him continue.

Unfortunately, his next stop doesn't register as a problem until it's too late. He's stepped into the hallway, probably going to check the bathroom. In order to get there he has to pass an open door that—

"Wait, no! No!" I practically leap towards him, hoping to distract him before he looks to his right.

But that's exactly where his eyes land on their way to me. Through the doorway, into my brightly lit bedroom.

There's no way in that second he would miss the bright purple vibrator sitting in the middle of my white comforter.

There is nothing in the world that could ease this tidal wave of embarrassment flowing through me.

His body stiffens for a moment, so quickly it would've been easy to miss if my eyes weren't so intently focused on him.

"I don't think it's here," he says with a gravelly voice.

"I'm sorry," I blurt out. "I'm so embarrassed." I'm not going to let this be one of those times where I refuse to say anything in the moment and overthink it later.

He shakes his head slightly. His jaw is clenched so tight, I can only assume he's frustrated. How many boundaries does that cross? Where do toys fall on the list?

Fuck. What I wouldn't give to rewind the last couple of minutes.

"No, don't be. I'm sorry I—" He clears his throat. "I interrupted."

That word somehow makes my embarrassment soar even higher and I start rambling.

"I wasn't expecting anyone, and when I heard the door I should have just put it—"

Something flashes on his face, like the confirmation that I was just using it is too much for him.

"It's okay," he reassures, taking a step closer to me. His eyes drop to my chest to watch how quickly it's rising and falling. "Calm down."

All I can do is give him a small, hesitant nod. He's one to talk, looking the opposite of calm right now. He takes another step right in front of me, and I'm still wound so tight that it's an effort not to grab him. His cologne smells irresistible, and it is not helping.

His hand reaches up for a split second, but he drops it before touching me. I hate that I snapped at him for it the other day.

"I should go," he says.

I try not to look as deflated as I feel. "Right. Yeah."

"Work," he explains.

"Right," I say again.

I'm staring at his mouth now, but despite his words he doesn't move away from me.

"It's not because of you." I tilt my head up to meet his eyes and catch that they move up from my lips too. I feel like I could burst into flames right here. "I mean, you didn't do anything wrong. It's just..."

"Rules?"

He nods once.

If only I had the courage to tell him I don't care about the fucking rules right now.

"Tell me what you're thinking," I ask instead. It's not me talking, it's my desperately horny alter ego. She's going to start some problems that I'm not sure I'm ready for.

He shakes his head, but I think it's an answer to his own internal argument.

This time when he reaches up, he cups the side of my face and he laces his fingers into my hair. His mouth is so close, I'm overwhelmed by his spearmint breath. I want to taste it.

"I'm jealous," he admits. My eyes widen as his fingers tighten their grip before he continues. "Of an inanimate object, because it doesn't have any rules to follow. It's not going to piss anyone off by touching you."

I have to close my eyes. I have to catch my breath. It's not going to happen while I'm looking at him. I'm not actually sure I still have functioning lungs at all.

This is too much. I know without thinking that I won't be the one that pulls away from this. I breathe his name, softer than he might have heard. It's a plea, but it could be directed at either one of us. For him to take this further, or for me to stop it completely. I couldn't tell you.

I know he hears it when his lips graze mine, so softly that it's torture. I somehow manage to remain still, to not pull him closer and deepen it the way I crave to.

I feel him shudder, and I wonder if it's for the same reason. If he's testing his restraint as much as I am.

"I have to go," he whispers against my lips.

I nod more times than is casual. I don't open my eyes, but I feel the absence of him when he steps away.

"I'll see you soon?" he asks.

"See you soon."

My front door opens and closes a moment later. I fall back against the wall and sink down to the floor.

No vibrator in the world could help rid me of this feeling.

21

MILES

"Why are you looking at me like that?" I ask Patty.

I've been working with her for a few years. She's one of the grouchiest residents we have here, but she tolerates me more than anyone else. It works out most of the time, and I try to stop by at least once a day. It doesn't work out so well when I have interviews, or tours, or scheduling issues, and she refuses to let anyone else into her room.

I'm cleaning up her kitchen after she forced one of the new caregivers to leave. She was crying when she got to me, and I had to give her the warning she should've received from the person training her. If you can't check in on Patty without interrupting whatever show she's watching, you have to send someone else.

She's lucky today was on the slower side, or she'd have to sit and look at the mess all day. Instead, she's sitting and looking at me from her place in her chair.

"What is with you, boy? It's making me sad just looking at ya." Her voice has the remnants of a southern accent, and it makes me want to smile at every serious thing she says.

I thought I was hiding my emotions better than that, but I should've known. Patty is too intuitive. She somehow knew the day my divorce was finalized without me saying a word about it. She knew Kara didn't treat me very well, even though I never said a bad word about her.

"That ex-wife giving you trouble?"

"No, nothing like that. I haven't talked to her in months." Almost a year, actually. The second divorce was on the table, we forgot how to talk to each other. It was easier to avoid the other person, and she moved in with her parents when that became too difficult.

It's been radio silence since everything was settled, and I don't have any urge to reach out. It makes me feel like an asshole, like I should at least care how she's doing, but I don't. I know for a fact that she's happier without hearing from me.

"Glad for that, at least. What's got you all shook up?"

Patty's a persistent one too. I don't want to admit what really has me shaken up. I also don't want to use her as a therapist, because that's definitely not how this dynamic is supposed to work.

"Ella will be here in an hour, are you going to let her take you down to dinner?"

"That's not going to work on me."

"It's lasagna tonight, isn't it? You like lasagna."

"Stop deflecting, boy."

I drop the towel I was holding with a sigh.

"There isn't enough time left in the day for me to explain."

"Try and shorten it for me. This show is pissin' me off anyway." She throws a hand towards the television where Family Feud is playing.

I scratch the back of my neck as I stop what I'm doing to turn around to face her. If looks could kill, she'd be a serial killer. I don't think she knows how to relax the muscles in her face, even when she's in a good mood.

I don't know how the fuck to word this. It felt like my heart jumped right out of my chest when I saw the bed, white sheets thrown to the side. I only knew it was still where it belonged because the image of her lying there, taking care of herself, had my blood aggressively pumping downwards.

"I guess you could say I have a crush," I start. That seems like a safe enough statement. It's an *understatement*, but that's not important.

"That's a bread crumb, I want the whole slice. A crush doesn't leave your eyes looking that tired."

"No, but this job does," I joke. "You can't send all of our new hires running, Patty."

"She was nervous, and chatty, and I wasn't in the mood."

I hold back on telling her that she's always chatty with me. I have no idea what I did to deserve it.

"I know you love your job. Try again."

"You are relentless," I tell her and turn back to the towel on the counter.

The sound to her show is suddenly muted.

"If you know that about me already, why are you dragging this out? What's this girl doing to you?"

"How do you know it's a girl?"

I know that she's rolling her eyes without even having to look at her.

"Because I've never seen my grandson flirt until the day he met you. Only a straight man would've pretended not to notice the way you did. He's too handsome." She says it so matter-of-factly that I chuckle.

"Fair enough. I just..." I search for the right words. The less intense version of what I'm feeling. "I'm not supposed to like her. It's complicated."

"Everything is complicated. Who cares?"

"My mom, apparently."

"Oh no, not your mother." She says sarcastically. "What does she have to do with anything? I know you're not still living under her roof."

I've never met any of my grandparents, but Patty feels like a grandmother to me. I know the feeling is mutual or she wouldn't pry into my life as much as she does.

It's why I know I shouldn't, but I keep answering her.

"There's more. There's... history." I pause, dreading the revelation. "With my brother."

It's silent for five uncomfortable seconds until Patty surprises me by slapping her knee and shouting a laugh.

"She—" Patty pauses to catch her breath, but just keeps on laughing. "She switched brothers? I'd hate her too, you idiot. Any mama would."

"It's not like that."

Autumn hasn't done anything but exist, and I'm tired of being the only one that believes that. She's the one that got hurt, she's the one that's still struggling thanks to her time as Justin's girlfriend.

I hate that Patty isn't the only one that's made assumptions about her.

"Doesn't matter. It's messy, mama's want their boys to avoid messy." She is speaking from experience, she has five of them.

"It's not like that," I say again, but I know my voice sounds weak. "It wasn't on purpose, it just kind of happened. It didn't even *really* happen."

She shakes her head, decided on her opinion. "My advice is to not let it. Stop before it's too late."

I don't answer that part, because if I did, I'd have to admit that it's already too late.

Suddenly the sink full of dishes looks way more interesting than it did before. I'm grateful when she doesn't call me out on avoiding the conversation further.

"Taking them to the vet!" She screams at her television. I smile to myself. "These stupid people."

22

AUTUMN

S pace is exactly what we need, I know that. I freak out every time we're in close proximity. I make this thing between us even more complicated, and I always feel like an idiot for not saying more.

Or for not saying *less*.

I should take this back and forth as proof that we should stop trying to make a friendship work, but I can't bear the thought of losing him.

I've tried texting. I typed up fifty different messages, going about it in every way I could think, and none of them felt right.

Hey, how's it going?

Do you want to grab lunch tomorrow?

Can you erase the other day from your memory so we can pretend everything is normal and fine and not *sexually tense?*

I couldn't get myself to press send on any of them. So here I am, on a Saturday night, drinking wine out of the bottle and feeling sorry for myself. Elaine is sitting on my lap, feeling pretty sorry for me too. Her paw rests on my arm, which is her best attempt to comfort me while she sleeps. Her constant purring keeps me calmer than I should be.

She really is special.

I keep hoping I'll hear a knock on my door and open it to his gorgeous face. His stupid, gorgeous face that I can't do anything with. Of all the times he's shown up at my door unannounced, why can't he do it right now?

I know why. I know we're on the edge of a cliff, and I know we're starting to slip.

I need to get it through my head that this isn't some romance novel I'm writing. If he did miraculously show up, it wouldn't change our circumstances. It wouldn't erase the past.

I'm not sure when I start crying, but one swipe at my wet cheeks tells me it's going to be a long night.

I've been putting off my friends, because they want updates I don't have to give. They still think this is cute and exciting, instead of a complete disaster.

I know they care. I know they want to hear what's going on, even if it disappoints them. I know I can rely on them when I don't want to be alone with my thoughts, and right now I really don't.

"I'm so fucked," I cry into the phone the second they answer and greet me.

They both speak at once with their concern, or in Reya's case, excitement.

"What's wrong?"

"What did you and Miles do?"

Hearing his name come out of her mouth makes the tears fall faster, and soon enough I'm crying so hard that words aren't possible.

"Shit. I'll be right there, okay?"

"Me too! Hang in there, babe."

"Wine always makes you cry," is the first thing Vic says when she sees the bottle.

"That's so true," I admit. Maybe even my subconscious knew I needed to let it out.

My friend sits down next to me and starts rubbing my shoulder. I sink into my seat further, feeling soothed. "Babies asleep?"

"They were when I left."

"I don't feel too bad about stealing you away then."

She frowns. "You should never. Julian loves you too, you know. They could have been running around, screaming at the top of their lungs and he still would have insisted I come to your rescue."

"I'm glad you have him," I say.

"And we're both glad I have you. It's nothing you haven't done for me a million times."

I'd literally help her bury a body if she needed it. I'm flooded with another extreme emotion: gratefulness. Knowing that I can always count on my friends is overwhelming to say the least. I still feel like I'm getting used to it.

Elaine gets half of Vic's attention, and we sit there like that in comfortable silence until Reya arrives. I didn't even have to tell her that I'd rather wait until they were both here to talk. I probably don't look like a girl that wants to repeat herself.

She, like Vic, lets herself in and pouts when she sees me.

"This is what happens when you don't tell your friends what's going on."

I shrug. "I've been arguing with myself this whole time, I didn't want to have to argue with you guys too."

"Haven't you been arguing with me anyway?" Reya asks. "You fight me every time I bring up your potential future babies."

"There are no potential future babies. We're doomed to be friends forever." My voice cracks on the last word. "If we can even manage that."

Reya takes the seat on my other side. "That's enough of that, what happened?"

And I tell them. Everything.

About the cuddling, the kiss, the conversations with his mom. Setting boundaries and then coming close to breaking them more than once. Everything that leads up to the vibrator incident.

Including my stupid feelings that get stronger by the day, and the way I can't pretend they aren't there anymore.

"Yeah, that never works out for anyone," Vic says.

"I want to be so mad at you for not telling us." Reya grabs the almost empty bottle of wine, and starts sipping.

"You really should have, that wasn't doing you any favors."

"I couldn't have said any of this out loud a week ago!"

"What are you going to do?"

"I have no idea. I was hoping you two would have some advice."

"I think you should stop worrying about everyone else and go for it already. What do you really have to lose?" Vic asks.

"My job? Did you miss the part where his mom can't stand for him to even look at me? It's so weird, she's polite until she sees us within ten feet of each other."

The more I think about it, I'd only consider her polite half of the time. The other half might be her attempt at politeness, but it always feels so condescending. I still haven't spent that change she told me to keep, it just doesn't feel right.

"I don't think she could really fire you over that. It might just be tense."

"I'd rather be fired! You haven't seen that glare." I shudder, remembering the last occurrence.

"You could get a job anywhere, first of all. But if you're not willing to risk it, you've got to get over him," Reya says, like it's the most obvious thing in the world. "Shut this thing down."

I squint at my pink-haired friend.

"Don't you think I would have already done that if I knew how? That's the problem here."

"You need a rebound or something. Someone to remind you that the world doesn't end and begin with Miles," Vic suggests. "It's been a few months, right?"

I feel my face heat with embarrassment. I know they're not judging me for that fact, but they're both far from having that problem.

Reya beams over at her.

"I am so excited that you and I are on the same page!"

"Says the girl that wanted her to have Miles' babies ten minutes ago!"

I pout. "I don't know how to find a rebound. That sounds exhausting."

"You don't have to find one, you've got easy access to the guy upstairs."

"God?" Vic asks, confused.

"Ben! You can save yourselves the awkward convo, and ride that train again."

She's right, but we stopped sleeping together for a reason.

"I wouldn't call it a train."

They both snicker, already knowing the details.

I guess that *was* back before I felt this desperately unsatisfied.

I roll my eyes at myself, hating that I'm even considering the idea.

There should be nothing stopping me. I'm single. Available. And yet I can't quite ignore the nagging feeling in my gut that seems a lot like guilt.

"Proceed with caution," Vic says. "But I don't think it's the worst idea."

I am not sold on it.

I wake up with my breathing heavy and my skin feeling like it's on fire. The cliffhanger to the dream I just had should be illegal. The fact that it was only a dream should be illegal.

The image of Miles trailing kisses down my body continues to linger in my mind, and I groan in frustration. My conversation with my girls did not have the right effect on my subconscious. It's torture.

I glance over to my bedside drawer where my favorite vibrator is kept. Grabbing it doesn't even sound like a good time.

Especially because all that makes me think about is how Miles knows what my favorite one looks like. He knows it's purple. He knows that I use it.

I wonder how much he's thought about that today.

I throw myself out of my bed and grab my phone, staggering out into the hallway. Elaine rubs against my leg as I go, causing me to stumble and almost trip over her. She's really good at that.

I go straight to my coffee machine, ready to toss a coffee pod in before pausing.

How long did I even sleep?

Another furry brush against my leg, followed by a howl of a meow reminds me before I even glance at the window. It's dark outside, and my cat wants dinner. I must have only dozed off a couple hours ago.

I bend down to scratch the top of her head.

"What a good, patient girl. You didn't even wake mommy up," I murmur in a baby voice that's reserved strictly for her.

I feed her, give her fresh water, and sit right on the floor next to her while she goes to town. She ignores my pets and praises, but I respect it. A girl's got to eat.

My phone buzzes in my pajama pockets and I pull it out with a sigh. I am too worked up over that dream, and I can't guarantee it wouldn't lead to dangerous territory if Miles were to reach out right now.

Thankfully, I get to stay in the safe zone.

Kind of.

Reya: *You better not be in bed feeling sorry for yourself...*

Me: *I'm not! I'm sitting on my kitchen floor feeling sorry for myself.*

Reya: *GET YOUR BUTT UP THOSE STAIRS AND GET SOME*

I roll my eyes. That's my initial reaction anyway, but then I stop and think for a second.

Why shouldn't I?

Maybe that really would be good for me. He could help me get rid of some of this built up tension that I can't take care of on my own. The kind of tension that someone's hands and mouth could take care of.

It's been a few months, *maybe* Ben has gotten better at using them. I quickly shoot him a message and ask what he's up to, knowing I very well may regret it.

Only minutes later, when my neighbor is standing at my door looking a little too eager, I give him zero bullshit.

"I just need a distraction, okay?"

"Consider yourself distracted," he says with a grin.

I'm already regretting my life choices.

23

MILES

I don't know what I'm doing here. I went on autopilot and all of a sudden I was staring at her front door from across the parking lot.

I'm not my own biggest fan at the moment. I've already done this once, didn't talk to her for days and then wanted to show up again like everything was fine.

As much as I know I should stay away, I can't. I didn't even make the conscious decision to be here, and I ended up here anyway.

If I was a better person, I would know how to stay away for good. It would suck, and I'm not stupid enough to think she'd be okay with that. We'd both be miserable, but eventually we wouldn't be, right? It would hit her that I *am* Justin's brother. She'd look at our family with more than just the hurt she held before, but disdain.

I'd never get to see that smile, or hear that laugh, but she would get to move on. She'd find out what it's like to want someone and have it be easy. Their family would love her. Their mom would have no reason to treat her like she's everything wrong with their lives.

The door opens. I stiffen like I've been caught, even though I'm far enough away to not draw attention to myself. I turn my car off, but I don't know if it's because I'm hiding or because I'm going to go up to her. I don't have a game plan.

But it's not Autumn that walks out, and I immediately feel sick to my stomach.

That guy that wouldn't leave her alone the other night. The one she told me she wasn't interested in.

Even from all the way over here, I know enough to feel complete dread. They're in pajamas. Her hair is messy, like it's been slept on, or...

She laughs, big and wide at something he says. I don't think. I don't know what I'm doing. One second I'm in my car, and the next I'm on foot.

I don't worry until I'm a few feet away. I have zero clue what to say to her. Ruining her night wasn't on the agenda, but I didn't imagine *this* being how she was spending it.

They hug each other, and my steps slow. Ben looks up for a second of eye contact, but it's long enough to catch the satisfaction there.

I'm irrationally angry.

"Oh, hey man." When he lets go of her, it's slow. His hand lingers on her shoulder possessively.

I see her head tilt to the side in confusion, but it hits her quickly. She spins, fast enough that her shoulder hits his chest. I'm annoyed when he doesn't back away.

She's so fucking beautiful.

Even as pissed off as I can tell she is, it's a relief to have her attention on me.

"Hey." It's technically a response to him, but my eyes are glued to her.

She turns back to him, whispering something I can't make out. He smirks and responds in a voice just as quiet, but I read his lips. *Happy to be of service.*

My mind is reeling. Instead of acknowledging me further, the two of them move. He heads to the stairs leading up to his place, and she marches for her front door.

I do the only thing I can think to do, and I follow her. It's the only thing I've been able to think for as long as I've been away from her. I want to be wherever she is.

The door is left open when I reach it. It gives me a small sliver of hope knowing she could've slammed it behind her and locked me out.

I stare inside for a moment, studying details that impressed me since the first time I saw it. The huge wall of bookshelves that are covered in books. My eyes dial in on the exact space I know her own book sits, although I can't read the spine from out here.

I have my own copy sitting on my nightstand. I bought it as soon as I got home that night.

"You're going to let bugs in," Autumn says from her kitchen, out of sight. Like she knows I'm standing here without hearing or seeing any evidence of it.

I quickly step in and close the door behind me.

Everything around me goes out of focus when she's in view again.

"Service?" I ask, and immediately regret it.

As I enter the kitchen, she's keeping her hands busy, pulling dishes from the dishwasher. She's trying her best not to look at me, and I understand why.

"That's what you have to say?"

I rub the back of my neck, searching for some better way to direct the conversation.

"No. It's not," I say before clearing my throat. "I'm sorry."

"Is that why you showed up? To say sorry?" The irritation in her voice is thick.

"It's one of the reasons."

She finally glances up to give me a look that tells me she's waiting for the other reasons.

"I just fucking missed you, A. I always miss you."

I breathe easier when her expression begins to soften.

"I missed you, too."

When her eyes linger, studying my expression, I move. Three small steps and I'm pulling her into me for a hug. Of course, I *want* to hug her, but I also don't need her reading anything in my expression that I've chosen not to voice.

"I feel worse when I'm not around you," I explain. "I keep thinking it might help, but it doesn't. At all."

"Yeah, I know the feeling."

She's the one to pull away and put space between us.

"I should have let you know I was coming..." I take a second to imagine what it would have been like if I'd knocked on her door ten minutes earlier and I wince. "It was a spontaneous decision."

Her face grows bright red. "I'm sorry that he— I mean, I didn't want—" She huffs out a breath.

"You don't have to apologize or explain anything to me."

Her eyes move back and forth between mine.

"Okay."

The line of her jaw is begging to be kissed, so I look away. But I smile, hoping to convince her I'm fine. That I'm not jealous, or frustrated, or hopeless.

I'm not a better man. I'm not strong enough to quit her. As much as I want a magical solution to fall into my lap, I'd still take this any day. The longing, the tension, the torment. If I could have anyone else in the world, without any obstacles, I wouldn't choose them.

Even if it means she has to move on for her own sanity. If she needs to blow off some steam with that douchebag upstairs.

She'll never be nothing to me. I can't let that happen.

I'd rather have her as just a friend than remember her as the one that got away. I want to see her life play out up close, not get small glimpses from accidental meetings around town or the occasional picture she posts online.

"I'm not like *with* him," she adds anyway. "It wasn't anything serious."

I nod slowly.

"Good. You can do better."

"I know," she whispers.

Her eyes are filled with an emotion that makes me feel more vulnerable and exposed than any words could.

Then to my relief, she suddenly pulls out that smile I love so much. "Want to watch a movie?"

I take the subject change for what it is.

24

AUTUMN

NINE YEARS AGO

I didn't want my first job to be at a grocery store, but I need a job more than I need to be happy with it. When my parents gave up on me and I moved in with Jade, they promised to pay my rent until I was eighteen. That was our deal. I'm not allowed to get my parents in trouble for abandoning me because they'll give me money while I try to figure out how to be an adult.

I'm a couple years away from that point, but they didn't take a lot of other things into account. Like the fact that I have to pay for food and clothes.

Jade and her mom take care of me, they do. Between them and Justin's family, I never go without and I'm grateful as can be. I just don't enjoy depending on other people. Probably a side effect of my parents making me feel like I couldn't even depend on them.

I go straight to Justin's house after my interview, holding a packet full of paperwork to fill out before my first day. I practically skip through the front door, I'm so excited to break the news. This means I can start saving for a car and soon enough I won't have to ask his brother for rides anymore. In the meantime, it means I can give him some gas money too, and even that makes me feel better.

Both of them are in the kitchen when I arrive and I spend a few minutes catching them up. The woman who had interviewed me was just as awkward as I am, and that's saying a lot. She made me feel like I'll fit right in every time she dropped her pen on the ground or hit her knee on her desk. To be fair, it was a cramped space.

I finish by opening up the packet I'm supposed to complete and looking everything over. I've never done this before, but it seems pretty self explanatory.

"But... why do you want a job?" Justin asks, as if he didn't know I was looking for one since the second I turned sixteen. His confusion confuses me.

"I've told you." I then list off all the reasons I can think of.

His stare is blank. "But Miles gives you rides."

"Yeah, but I feel bad." I turn to Miles. "Which is why I want to start giving you gas money until I don't need you to anymore."

He starts to respond, but Justin goes again. "Why? I don't give him gas money."

I refrain from rolling my eyes. "You're his brother."

"And?"

"You know what?" Miles interrupts. "You should start giving me gas money, Justin. You have me running you around town way more than she does, anyway. Maybe *you* should look for a job."

"I don't want a job. I'm in high school," he argues.

"So is she," Miles argues back.

"She shouldn't get a job either." He turns his attention back to me. "You barely have free time as it is, if you take this job I'll never get to see you."

Of course I had thought about that, and it did make me sad. Knowing that I'll have to run to work after school instead of here to hang out with him. It just isn't an option for me right now like he thinks it is. I don't have the luxury of expecting anyone to do anything for me. Regardless of what Miles said, he's not going to stop giving Justin rides. That's how it's supposed to go when you're family. You do things for each other without needing anything in return.

Unless you're mine.

"It'll take some getting used to," is all I say.

Justin and Miles go back and forth, pushing each other's buttons. I like that Miles isn't a pushover when it comes to his younger brother. Justin gets away with a lot in life. I don't resent him for it, it's just nice to see him receive a little resistance every once in a while.

I flip through the pages, skimming the words and signing where needed. Dress code, harassment policy, etcetera. When I get to the emergency contact portion, I freeze. Who do you put as your emergency contact when you don't have parents?

The guys must notice the look on my face because they both move their attention to the form in front of me.

"Can't you use Jade's mom?" Justin asks.

"She works like all day every day. I don't think that's a good idea."

"I don't think it matters really, they probably only call them if you die on the job or something."

Jade's mom is a delivery nurse, and I wouldn't want her to get a call about me in the middle of something much more important.

"And how would you know?" Miles chimes in.

"I'm assuming," he snaps.

I'm running through options in my mind when I blurt out, "What about your mom?"

Justin looks at me like I'm joking and then he scoffs.

"No. That's weird."

"How is that weird?" Miles and I ask at the same time. I say jinx before he can. He just chuckles before our attention goes back to Justin.

"She's not your mom."

"Neither is Linda."

"She's more your mom than mine is."

I don't know why that stings so bad, but it feels like a physical blow. I love Amelia, and we've been spending a lot of time together. She includes me in family things I've never done before, like cooking dinner, or going grocery shopping.

I like to think about what my life would be like if I'd had a mom like Amelia instead of my own. To hear Justin undermine it... even if it's just because he's possessive of her in some infantile way, it hurts.

"Are you really crying because I said that?" he moans. I don't bother to answer, afraid my voice will crack. He waits for a few seconds before sighing and heading off to his room.

I don't follow, I stare down at the paper that's making me feel way crappier than I could have imagined.

Miles leans in like he's reading it, but I know he already looked it over.

"You could put me on there. I don't mind."

My head snaps up. "What? Are you sure?"

He nods.

"Yeah, just maybe don't say anything to Justin about it. He's being weird."

I agree with that statement. "Thank you. That's really nice."

He grabs it from me and fills in his contact information. "Put that number in your phone, too. Don't be worried about asking me for rides to work or anything. It really doesn't bother me."

25

MILES

Autumn: *Am I riding with you?*

I told her she was. I don't regret it, but I'd be lying if I said I wasn't worried about the close proximity.

It's too late now, because I'm already on my way.

This party is supposed to be a thank you to the shop's clients, but my mom always gets carried away. There are always people she wants to impress. It's more stressful than it's worth in my opinion, but I don't have the option to skip it. As of now, neither does Autumn.

Keeping my eyes on the road, I tap her contact and call her instead of texting back.

She picks up within seconds. "Yeah?"

"Do you *want* to ride with me?"

She hesitates, not for very long, but I'm getting used to looking for these small details when it comes to her.

"I thought that was the plan, I just wanted to double check. You're one of the only people that I know going to this thing and the idea of going alone absolutely terrifies me." The way she says it so quickly, like the words are foregoing any filter, gives credence to what she says.

"Yeah, that's the plan." I'm already in the parking lot and stepping out of my car. "Just checking."

When she opens her front door, the air escapes my lungs. She's still in pajamas, which contrasts with her styled hair and makeup.

"You could have given me a heads up, I'm not even dressed yet!"

I give her a pointed once-over and watch the blush creep up her cheeks.

"You mean that's not what you're wearing?"

She grabs the center of her shirt, which happens to be a large red bobble on a cartoon Rudolph's face. "You know, maybe it should be. Amelia might appreciate the festive look."

If only.

Autumn

It takes me a lot longer than it should to get dressed. My hands shake as a result of how much I am completely freaking out. I can't get a grip of the tiny zipper on my back, and I question if I should just go with a different dress entirely. That would be easier than asking him for help.

A knock on my bedroom door makes me jump, and the zipper falls from my fingers yet again.

His eyes drop down to my dress when I open the door.

"I hate to rush, but my mom will—"

"Yeah, I know."

Her and her high standards. I'm not sure she knows that we're going together, in the same car. I'm not ready to face her wrath for it either, but at least I know I won't be alone in it.

The intensity in Miles' gaze makes my heart leap to my throat.

"What's that look for?" I rasp. Maybe he can see right through me, maybe he knows how dangerous that look really is, because he bows his head, breaking eye contact.

He shakes his head slightly.

"My self control is being tested here." His tone of voice sends a shiver down my spine.

As if we're not testing a lot of that every day.

"How?" I ask.

I watch his mouth pull up in the smirk that I go between wanting to wipe off or kiss off. It's ruining me at this moment, as if everything he's showing me is contagious. I don't know if I have *any* self control left when it comes to him.

Squinting my eyes closed for a couple seconds, I try to take a deep breath. We have somewhere to be, and we won't get there if I throw myself into his arms.

He's much closer to me when I open my eyes, and I feel light headed when he leans forward.

We won't get there if I faint, either.

His breath is hot above my ear, and if I was capable of sound right now, I'd probably moan. What he does to me without having to do much at all is dangerous.

"That dress," he whispers. "Makes me want to rip it right off of you, and forget every reason I have not to." A ghost of a kiss touches my cheek before he stands straight, and takes a step back.

He chose the worst time to decide that dirty talk was on the table.

"You definitely aren't allowed to say that."

The smallest lift of his shoulders is his answer. I move to stand before him again, closer than I should. I'm asking for trouble when I can't help but tip my head up and gaze into those beautiful brown eyes. I give him the softest smile I can, and return the kiss he gave me. Same spot.

It speaks volumes that I didn't have to stand on my toes to reach.

I take a step back before I ruin my makeup. It's the only reason I can find to do so.

"Can you zip me up?"

The breath that whooshes from him almost destroys me, but he motions for me to turn around, and I do.

Once it's done, and our tension is at the highest it's ever been, I still somehow manage to step past him towards the front door.

"You look pretty hot yourself," I say.

The sounds of his footsteps instantly follow behind me.

It's going to be a long night.

There are even more people here than I anticipated. It's overly warm in the small space, and I'm shocked that Amelia didn't host this elsewhere. It's not as if people can flow outside where it's cold and windy, the kind that makes your nose run and then freezes the snot.

Miles' comforting touch is keeping me grounded, with one guiding hand on the back of my arm. It couldn't be a better place, because it'll look fairly innocent when Amelia's eyes inevitably fall on us.

"Wow," he says beside me.

I nod in agreement, feeling nervous.

"There were not this many people here last year."

His phone goes off in his pocket, and he rolls his eyes when he grabs it and reads the name on the screen. I can see who it is in the reflection of his glasses.

"We just got here," he says as a greeting.

I can't hear Amelia on the other end due to all of the chatter going on around us.

"Autumn." Pause. "What for?" Pause. Another eye roll.

Why is that so adorable?

Again, someone should tell this man.

"Fine, I'll be right there."

"Everything okay?"

He sighs. "Yep. She needs me in the back room... alone. Are you okay here for a minute?"

I shrug, because I don't think the answer is yes, but it doesn't look like I have a choice.

I assume it comes off casually enough because his palm slides down my arm and he gives my hand the smallest squeeze.

"I'll be right back, I promise."

I thought I'd have more than sixty seconds to prepare before we were separated, and as soon as he's gone it's obvious that I was *not* prepared.

I have no idea where my desk ended up, because there aren't any in the room right now. If it was, that would be exactly where I'd run to hide. I don't see another option. I don't even see Kaitlyn or hear her bubbly voice anywhere.

I just stand here and hope I don't look as uncomfortable as I am. I've never done well in big crowds, but I feel even worse being around Amelia's clients. I've already overheard a conversation about dragging her on a plane to visit someone's second home. I am so out of place. I obviously have no reason to join any of these conversations, and no one is trying to include me. The few that I recognize haven't even made eye contact.

My hands are already starting to shake and it makes me think I would like my odds better outside, despite the cold. Another couple minutes of this, and an anxiety attack will be crashing this party.

I cross my arms in an attempt to shield myself in some way. It only makes me more self-conscious to think I might look like I'm the awkward, grumpy teenager I try so hard not to be anymore. Moments like right now make me wonder if I'll always be that girl, if there's no escaping it.

I'm aiming for the door before I even realize I'm moving. I have to get out of here before these walls close in on me. Fresh air, freezing or not, will be better than that.

I attempt to step around a tight ring of people, when the sound of the back door alerts me. I've heard it so many times, it sticks out even behind all the noise. I stop and look up, noticing Miles and Amelia making their way back out. There are others back there too from what I can see. Amelia must not have had a choice but to use all the space this place has got.

One other person follows closely after Miles, watching him in a way that irritates me. She's pretty, probably around my age. Her short blonde hair is sleek and straight, looking like it belongs in a hair care commercial. Amelia turns back to the girl, touching her arm in a way that encourages her to move forward with them.

Right. By. Miles'. Side.

As if she already knew exactly where I was standing, Amelia lifts her gaze and it immediately locks onto me. The smile on her face feels malicious, and I have a feeling I know why she changed her mind about inviting me.

The girl is visibly happy about her place next to him. He glances down at her, saying something that makes her smile, but then my view is blocked by an older couple that stops them to chat.

Nothing like setting your son up in front of the girl you want him to stay away from to get what you want. I'm torn up even more about that night with Ben, because if Miles was as jealous then as I am right now...

Ouch.

The room is getting warmer by the second, and I think the walls are in the lead as far as who's moving the fastest. My feet thankfully do their job, and get me moving in the direction of the door. I try to stick to the outskirts of the room, but there are so many people standing against the walls.

I say, "excuse me," an obnoxious amount of times, not making any eye contact when I do.

Right as getting to the door seems within reach, there's another set of feet directly in my way. I move to step around them, but a hand is gently placed on my shoulder to stop me.

"Where are you going?" His voice is like a magic wand, easing some of the panic and allowing me to take a much needed deep breath. When I look up to meet his eyes, it's like I'm put back together for a split second.

As much as I wish he was a complete magical cure, it's *only* a split second.

"Are you okay?"

"I was going to get some fresh air for a minute, but—"

My words sound as frantic as I feel and he puts the back of his hand against my forehead like I'm a child with a fever. I must look like the sweaty, frantic mess I am.

"You're burning up, Autumn." If he didn't look so concerned I'd feel like he was accusing me of doing something horrible. He holds out his hand for me to take. "We can get out of here if you need to."

"Oh, there you are!" Amelia's voice interrupts right before she's nudging Miles to the side and standing before him. "You sure move quickly."

The blonde smiles up at him, with unhidden interest. Who could blame her?

"Doesn't she look lovely, Miles?" She gives him a pointed look that's only hidden from the blonde woman. She's telling him without words what she expects him to say. "If you don't ask her to dinner, I'll do it!"

The blonde laughs, clearly enjoying Amelia's pressure. She goes to lean in towards his ear, and she must be *much* taller than me, because the space isn't a challenging one for her to reach. I can't help the satisfaction I feel when she doesn't get the chance to say what she wants, because Miles takes a step away. He doesn't even try to play it off for anything other than what it was.

Amelia doesn't look happy. I start inching towards the door again, scared for her attention to turn to me. I don't have the ability to keep anything off of my face, and I'd rather not dig myself a deeper hole.

"Autumn is one of my assistants. Autumn, this is Chloe. Her parents are clients of ours, you'd probably recognize the inside of her house." She laughs as if she had made a joke, and Chloe does too.

"Only for a month more," she says, pointedly. "I can't wait to give you free rein in my new place." She doesn't acknowledge the introduction to me at all, but I'm not surprised.

I'm polite as can be when I speak up, although my voice betrays my current state. "Nice to meet you, Chloe."

She slowly drags her eyes over me for the first time, and gives me a slight smile. "Did Amelia say you're an assistant? I haven't seen you before."

"I only work—"

"Oh, that reminds me!" she exclaims, turning back to Amelia with more ass-kissing.

Neither of them show any hint of discomfort at the obvious interruption. Normally I would probably just shut up, let it slide, but I'm not feeling that way right now. I'm feeling a million things, and I have to channel it all somewhere.

"What's the point in asking a question if you don't listen to the answer?"

Chloe's mouth drops open as she turns to look at me again. You'd think I'd just insulted her. I'm sure Amelia's expression is comparable, but I decide not to look at her. I'm still feeling too vulnerable to handle that much.

"Excuse me?"

"You asked me a question and didn't let me answer it." I shrug. "I was just wondering why." She could have simply smiled and nodded, but she *wanted* me to feel belittled. The same way too many people have, to remind me that I'm not good enough for their time or energy.

She closes and opens her mouth a couple times, clearly not used to being confronted and unsure of how to respond. Most days that's my part to play, but there's something about the last few weeks that has flipped a switch in my brain. The *least* I deserve is to be acknowledged.

"Autumn," Amelia gasps. "Have you had too much of the wine?"

I blurt out a laugh in response, which probably makes it look like I did exactly that. Like I found time to get drunk within the first fifteen minutes of this little get together.

"I haven't had a drop to drink tonight, actually." My tone is polite, but there's no way it's fooling anyone other than the guests that might glance over from across the room.

Amelia gives Chloe an apologetic look, one I've seen on her too many times.

"You can't speak to our clients that way. Please apologize for being rude."

Before I can tell her that I have no interest in doing that, Miles speaks up.

"Come on, mom. Do you want to be the boss that doesn't let your employees stand up for themselves?" He briefly grabs my hand that's shaking even more than it was before. "Do you still want that fresh air?"

I nod my head eagerly, stepping past the two women.

"Good idea. You should probably leave for the night. You could call a—"

"I'll be right there," Miles tells me, interrupting his mom. His stern expression, not directed at me, stops me in my tracks for a second. There's something so awe striking about the fact that he's defending me. Looking out for me, even when it involves his own mother.

It's not like I *want* him to take my side over hers. Nothing good ever comes of the girl that gets in the way of a mother and her son. It's just a lot. It hurts me that he has to deal with two sides to begin with.

The shocking cold of the breeze outside hits me, and forces me to give in to self pity for a moment. I wish I wasn't here where my only options are freezing my ass off in this dress, or having to deal with the people inside.

Is it even worth this job, really? Every day it feels like working with Amelia is hurting me more.

I walk around to the side of the building, where the wind can't hit me so harshly. This space between two buildings is actually quite peaceful, lit with street lanterns along with a trail of sidewalk that eventually leads to a small dog park. I discovered it on one of my lunch breaks, and found myself wondering if Miles had ever taken Freddy there. I could picture the two of them running around each other, surrounded by nothing but trees and grass. It was a warm and cozy image, although most everything about Miles usually is.

I get lost in my thoughts, zoning out in the direction of that trail. If only it wasn't so dark, and the weather was on my side. I would walk in that direction until this weight on my chest went away.

If that were even possible.

26

AUTUMN

I know Miles is walking up behind me before I even hear his footsteps. My shoulders sag with relief when I turn to see him walking in my direction. I didn't doubt him, but I couldn't be sure that Amelia wasn't finding some way to trap him in there with Chloe.

"Everything okay?" I ask.

As gloomy as his expression was, a smile cracks through at my words.

"I think I should be asking you that."

I shrug. It's better now that he's out here with me. Now that I know I don't have to go back in there.

"I just really want to leave."

He sighs loudly, and I watch his breath cloud in front of him.

"Yeah, me too. I don't want to be found out here after the scene I just caused."

"Oh?" I ask, and he nods. "What happened?"

"Well... Chloe knows I'm far from interested, and my mother is more embarrassed than I've ever seen her. I'll never hear the end of it."

He rubs the back of his neck.

"I'm sorry, Miles." Before I can say more, he blurts out a laugh. One of his arms reaches out around me and he's pulling me into him. I don't overthink it, I just let my cheek rest against his chest. I never want to move.

"You have no reason to be sorry," he says into my hair. "It's not your fault that my mom wanted to set me up in front of all of her clients. I've told her so many times that I'm not interested in dating anyone, and she doesn't listen. This was bound to happen eventually."

It makes me sad to hear. Not just that she's been pressuring him, but the reminder that he's alone. Not dating, not trying.

"Chloe's pretty," I say without thinking. It makes me glad I can't see his face and vice versa.

Miles scoffs, and I can't deny how satisfied I am by that reaction.

"I couldn't care less."

"Why?"

Then his hands are on my shoulders, and he gently puts space between us in order to look down at me. I try not to let my feet give out beneath me when those hands move up to hold my face.

Any chill this night has given me vanishes. It's possible I might actually be on fire, but I can't look down to check because my eyes are locked onto his.

I think he might be about to do something crazy, but he changes the subject instead.

"I liked seeing you stand up for yourself. She was rude."

I respond with a nod, still transfixed.

"And my standards are higher than pretty," he says, answering my previous question.

I don't think I'm imagining that his body crowds mine more than it was a second ago. He moves one hand just enough to tuck a strand of my hair behind my ear.

I have definitely gone up in flames.

It should be uncomfortable, holding my head back to look up at him, but it's not. I love our height difference. I love the way he looks down at me.

A small part of my brain is still somehow able to focus on the fact that we look awfully suspicious to anyone who might walk by. We're right outside the office, it wouldn't take much for someone else who needs some fresh air to wander this way. His mom, with her little set up, could come looking for him any second.

His face is barely inches from mine at this point.

"What are they then?" I breathe.

He shakes his head in a way that tells me he can't believe I have to ask.

"I want someone kind and funny," he says as if I'm supposed to know. "Someone my dog gets along with. But we both know he would hate her."

I smile. I could see that, little Freddy being a good judge of character. It feels like the world's biggest compliment that he's given me so much attention.

Miles returns the smile, probably remembering that same night. I don't dare let myself hope that it's his way of giving in. Of choosing me despite everything.

I can smell mint on his breath and all I want to do is kiss him again.

He has to be thinking the same thing. I don't miss the way his eyes drop to my mouth before he leans in, so slowly. His hand slides behind my ear, cradling my head. Holding me like I'm something special.

And then he does it. He finally fucking *kisses me.*

Every nerve in my body is alive and screaming, like it has *needed* this. It's not like the last time when we were both drunk and eager to have some fun. Everything that's happened between now and then, every word spoken between us has this kiss filled with emotion I've never experienced before. It's slow and smooth, like he's savoring the moment because he knows it will end.

There's something far more violent than butterflies in my stomach as his mouth gently caresses mine, as his stubble scratches my face in the best way.

He doesn't speed up, doesn't pry any further. I think he's as lost in this as I am, in the fact that we shouldn't be doing this, but it's been painful not to. It's like all of that pain has never existed. Not now, for these few seconds.

I don't hear a door open, but his mother's familiar voice echoes from the front of the building. "Miles?"

The fire inside of me is immediately put out. I'm grateful we'd been around the corner, out of sight, at least for now.

Of course she followed after him so quickly.

He leans away from me with a sigh.

"Stay right here," he whispers.

I nod, but on the inside I want to beg him not to walk away. I want to pull him back and pretend nothing in the world can stop us, not even her.

But I know better, and I watch him go.

27

MILES

"Hey," I say to my mother, trying to sound as casual as possible with my heart racing the way it is.

"What are you doing, Miles?" She sounds horrified, but I pretend not to notice.

"There was a lot going on, I just needed some fresh air."

A sharp glare bores into me, and I know she's beyond pissed. I might as well have said *There were a lot of witnesses so I came out here to make out with my brother's ex-girlfriend.*

She'd be just as angry either way, I think.

"I'm not an idiot, son. Neither are you, so let's cut the crap," she demands.

"I don't know what you mean," I lie.

Faster than I can react she rubs her thumb over my nose. I wince.

"Her makeup rubbed off on you." *Shit.* "Wipe it off before anyone sees you, and then get back inside."

It would be such a travesty if everyone that watched me reject Chloe knew it was for someone else, especially Autumn. A part of me wants to run in there and scream it, and see how my mother would deal with the scandal.

I wouldn't. I have a heart, and prefer when she's not as upset with me as she has been.

She starts to walk in the direction I came from, but I step in front of her.

"What are you doing?"

"Letting Miss Autumn know she's out of a job, and that she needs to stay away from my son." She steps around me but I can't help myself, I put a hand on her shoulder to stop her again.

"No, you're not." She scoffs a laugh, like she can't believe I have the nerve to go against her. "I really don't understand what your problem is. Autumn is one of the best people I know, and you act like I'm handing her permission to ruin our lives or something. You are always reminding us that we're grown men, but you only do that when it benefits you. You forget I'm thirty years old when it comes to making decisions that you don't approve of, and it's ridiculous. Justin isn't going to crumble if he finds out she's in my life. I'm not naive enough to assume he's going to love it, but that's *our* business. Between him and I." I run a hand through my hair as I try to collect the rest of my thoughts.

"I'm not some rebellious kid going against your wishes for fun. I tried to do it your way. I really fucking tried, but I can't stay away from her. I know you think that's her fault somehow, but that's so far from the truth."

She looks at me for a moment, as if I hadn't meant everything I just said. As if she needs to read my mind to decide what her next move is.

Whatever she finds isn't good enough.

"There are obviously some things you don't know, and I won't let you find out the hard way." Her voice is eerily calm.

"I think there's far more that *you* don't know."

She shakes her head. "You're going to get over this, sooner or later. When that time comes, she won't be working in my office. I might not be able to stop you from seeing her, but I can do my part to limit what's already too much."

"What are you going to do without the extra help at the office?"

"She's replaceable. You'll see that too, eventually."

The words break my heart, and then break it again a second time when I remember she's listening from a few feet away. Instead of stopping my mother this time, I turn and head for Autumn first.

But when I turn the corner, the alley is empty. She's gone.

I wonder which of the words sent her into flight mode, and a headache starts to pound at my temples.

"She was always good at running away," my mothers voice comes from behind me.

I turn to face her so fast. "You don't know a thing about what went on with her and Justin. You should talk to him about the *truth* before you keep throwing your judgment her way."

I don't even know the extent of it, but I paid attention. Justin didn't care about her, he just cared about the attention she gave him. Autumn has been through enough when it comes to my family, and I'm done letting it happen. I've failed for tonight. I've been failing for weeks, but I'll do better next time.

I start to head in the direction of the sidewalk, sure that's the way she went. She didn't pass us, and she's only on foot.

"Get back inside, Miles," my mother demands, ignoring my words.

"She shouldn't be walking alone this late."

"She chose to run off."

My fists clench, but I keep walking forward. I have to find her *now,* and make sure she's safe. I'm sure she's not okay, and I'll try to fix that too, but knowing she's safe is a good start.

My mother pleads behind me a couple more times before giving up. Probably because if she stays out here too long, a guest will come looking for her and find out that she isn't as perfect as she wants them to think.

Autumn

I didn't make it far before texting my girls and asking if anyone could pick me up. Vic came through like the angel she is, meeting me at that stupid park I'd wasted time daydreaming about. She had an extra coat in hand, and she didn't pry when I got into the car and exploded into tears.

I suppose I could text Amelia and let her know I'm quitting before she gets a chance to hurt me any worse than she has.

The pain is persistent, as if there's a physical wound where her words hit me. I knew she wasn't ever going to approve of Miles and I... but that wasn't the worst of what I'd heard from her. One would think I'd done something horribly wrong to her in the past, instead of just being the girl who had her heart broken by her youngest son. I don't know how she could excuse saying all those things about me. I can't imagine having a child and still siding with them if they hurt someone the way I was hurt by him. I'd buy the poor girl some flowers, apologize on his behalf.

Being around Miles has made it so easy for me to forget why we set our rules in the first place. I've been blinded by the way he makes me feel, his actions, his words, *him*. I've never loved being around anyone more, or craved anyone the way I crave him.

Is it enough to subject myself to Amelia's wrath? Or Justin's? It's funny how this has felt like it's so much about him, and yet he's so far out of the loop. I don't think it *is* about him anymore.

I wish I knew what it really was.

I pull my phone out, hardly able to see through the tears that are falling, and pull up Amelia's contact. My lack of vision makes the decision for me, and I simply hit the block button.

Enough is enough.

In my emotional state, I don't have the ability to think better of it when I pull up Miles' name and do the same. I should have tried harder to put space between us before. Before things got this hard. Deep down I knew there was never any hope for this to go another way, not since that conversation with Amelia at my desk. I've been so naive. I gave in. I fell for him.

Vic asks if she can stay and keep me company. I don't blame her for being worried, but I tell her I just want to be alone. I mean it.

Elaine and I curl up in my bed together, and she's the perfect companion while I crash, and break, and let the walls finally close in.

28

MILES

"I love you more than anything, Miles. You and your brother. I know it seems like I've been harsh, but please know I want you to be happy. I want all the best things in life for you. It would destroy me to see you give yourself to another—" I end the voicemail, I can't do it. If she's not going to spell out her reasons, I don't want to hear what she has to say.

"What's going on with you?" Justin asks. He watched me aggressively put my phone down, and I know I'm being less talkative than usual. There's no way I'm hiding my mood from him.

I shrug.

"You're acting weird, man. If I didn't know any better, I'd think Kara was giving you hell again."

It irritates me that everyone's first assumption is that Kara is still my problem. This feels so much worse than anything she put me through.

"No, we haven't talked in months," I tell him as I throw myself down next to him on the couch.

Part of the problem is that I haven't felt like I could just talk to Justin about it, or ask him any questions. Maybe, considering she won't answer my calls, I don't care what the consequences might be. It won't be worse than this.

"What was the deal with Autumn?"

He slowly turns to face me and blinks a couple times. "That's fucking random. What do you want to know about that for?"

I feign disinterest by gluing my gaze to the television.

"Just curious. Mom seems to really not like her, but she went and hired her at the office."

His posture becomes rigid.

"Are you serious? Why would she do that?"

"She needed help, I don't know. Probably figured you'd never stop by and find out."

"Yeah, well. The smell of flowers in there gives me a headache." He rubs his chin, clearly thinking something through. "Of all the people, why'd she hire her?"

I don't tell him that it's because of me, that I'm the one that told her about the job in the first place. I pretend not to know.

"That's annoying."

"Yeah, but why? I know things didn't end great, but you never really told me what happened. You just started dating Isabelle and never mentioned her again."

One glance at whatever is brewing in his eyes and I know he isn't going to tell me. I don't like that he feels the need to keep secrets about it even now. He must have done something pretty bad to not be able to own up to it after six years.

"I just moved on. Not much to talk about." I hate that I know he's lying, but he changes the subject before I can decide if I want to keep trying. "Speaking of moving on, you figured out how to do that yet?"

"Kind of," I admit. *Definitely* is a more fitting answer, but it's also one that would lead to questions.

Justin smiles widely at that. "You serious?" He nudges my arm. "That's great, man! It's about damn time."

"You think so?"

He nods. "Yeah, I do. I think Kara sucked the life out of you, and you've been taking your sweet time getting it back."

I smile at that.

"It does feel like I'm getting it back." It felt like I was *starting* to.

"So, there's someone responsible. How long have you been seeing her?" he asks.

I'm not the liar between us, at least not most of the time. I'm just keeping a portion of things to myself. I can offer him pieces.

"Only a couple of months," I admit. "But she's..." I shake my head. I can't even find the right words, and I'm just reminded of how much I miss her when I try.

It's been difficult to act like everything is normal, between going to work and now seeing him.

"Oh, you're down bad. Didn't anyone ever tell you not to fall for the rebound?" He turns away before he can notice the way his words make my jaw clench. I hate it. She's so much more than that.

"I already had a rebound."

"That one night with that one girl? You seriously believe that counts?"

It really has just been one night with one girl, but I don't bother arguing that it was enough for me. I didn't want to sleep around after my divorce. I didn't need the distraction. I was just so happy to be me again. It felt like that was all I needed, me and Freddy.

Until Autumn.

Now I don't know if anything will be enough without her.

"I think we should take a shot," is all I say to him. I abruptly stand to collect the bottle of whiskey that's been hiding in a top cabinet for months. I knew there was a time I'd need it, and now is a more than appropriate time.

One leads to two, two leads to four, and so on. We talk, laugh, and catch up. It's been too damn long since the two of us have just hung out. My brother is a busy guy, working full time, raising two kids. Dealing with his failing marriage and not knowing how to talk about it. We see each other at the occasional family dinners, but it's not often the two of us hang out on our own.

I only wish it wasn't tainted by the ache of missing Autumn, and the guilt I feel about hiding that from him. I'd be lying if I said that wasn't what motivated me to see him today.

"So, how'd you meet her? What's her name?" he asks the question once I'm too drunk to control my responses. I should've known he wouldn't drop it that easily, the jackass.

"I can't tell you. It's a secret."

The remote he'd just grabbed falls from his hand. "What? Why the hell is it a secret?"

"I can't tell you," I repeat.

I watch as the shock of keeping something from him surely turns into a look of suspicion. I am so fucked.

"It must be bad, huh? What if I guess? Is she related to Kara?"

I shake my head and laugh at him.

"Are you worried about what I'll think? Or is this girl trying to keep you a secret?"

Yes, I'm fucking terrified of what you'll think.

"We both have our reasons for not wanting anyone to know."

God, I miss her so much. I want to hear her voice.

I stand to grab myself a glass of water. I know I should try to sober up before I end up leaving her another, messier voicemail. They're already stacking up. It's been a miserable few days.

"She's not talking to me right now. I kind of messed up," I confess. "So if I never hear from her again, I'll tell you everything."

He frowns. "Fuck that, you have to fix it. You clearly have feelings for her."

I choke on the water I just tried to drink and it spews everywhere. Justin is slapping my back before I even notice he got up from his seat.

He probably thinks I'm shocked by the idea of having feelings for her, when in reality I'm shocked by the fact that he's the first person to say it out loud.

29

AUTUMN

Miles stops by my apartment multiple times in the weeks after I block him, once being on Thanksgiving. I hate that I'm responsible for interrupting time with his family.

I only know it's him because of his pleading voice on the other side of the door. It breaks my heart to ignore it, makes me feel shattered to my core. I've had to escape to my bedroom, and cover my ears with a pillow to shut him out. It's always soaked in tears when I finally pull it away.

In a perfect world, I'd open the door and grab him and never let him go. But it's not, and we're never going to get past the reality of our situation. There's another mother to add to the list of them that think of me as something they need to be rid of. I thought things with Amelia were bad back then, but I truly had no idea.

The pain of giving in to my feelings for Miles would probably equal the broken way I feel right now, if not be worse. It was nice to think I'd made all the progress I need, and become a stronger girl than the one my parents tossed aside, but I haven't. I've just avoided anyone I could disappoint for a long time.

The one good thing to come from all of this new free time and moping around is the writing I've gotten done. It's nice to escape into another world, be another person with every tap of my fingers against the keys. I'm grateful for my ability to immerse myself in my writing, even if it's short lived.

Sometimes it's not that simple. Sometimes my chest aches worse than I can convey in a fictional conflict. It feels as though I'm being harsh, wanting bad things to happen to the people I made up in my imagination. I know a lot of authors get a kick out of that, but my reasoning is much less complicated. It's a small way of feeling less alone in this hurt.

Kaitlyn has texted a few times to check in, or to ask if I've seen any of her posts. She made accounts for me on platforms I didn't have the courage to try, and I'm amazed at how much fun she has with it. We all have our hobbies, and hers happens to be really helpful.

The honest answer is that I haven't seen any of it, but not intentionally. Every time I open an app, I am *overwhelmed* by notifications. Likes, and comments, and tags. Hundreds of them, maybe even thousands. I'll read a couple of reviews that make me cry relieved tears and then I close the app before I can go any further. I don't need to see her posts, the result is glaringly obvious.

Kaitlyn is the best thing that came from working in Amelia's office.

It's after midnight, hours after Miles last showed up and begged me to talk to him. I haven't calmed down, even after two mugs of sleepy tea. I'm desperate to shut my mind off. If sleep isn't the way, then I at least need to find a distraction from the reason I'm not sleeping.

I end up on the couch, and throw on the first show that looks interesting. Some rich couple looking to find their dream house with all the bells and whistles. All it does is remind me of the times Miles has sat here next to me doing just this. Watching something that was mindless and easy to talk over. Whatever it was, it was so nice to have him here. His presence brought out a peacefulness in me that I never had before. It's hard not to doubt that I'll ever find it again.

My current train of thought is only going to do further damage, a fact proven by the tears already welling up in my eyes. I turn the television up to a volume that sufficiently blocks out the voice in my head.

When I lay down and rest my head against the furthest cushion, it still smells like him. I feel trapped by my inability to get away from him, but I don't think I really want to. There's comfort as much as there's pain in all of the pieces of him that linger.

"Don't make me break a window! You're going to let us in *right now,* Autumn!" Reya pounds on my door with the force of a hurricane, and I have no choice but to open it for my friends. They know I'd be too embarrassed to let them go on so loudly and disturb my neighbors.

I'm stunned to see two tiny faces right alongside them, Amira and Dahlia.

"What are you doing?"

"We're having a girls night," Vic replies with a bright smile and pushes past me.

It's nice of them to force me to take a shower and feel somewhat normal again. It's been too long since I did anything other than curl up in bed with Elaine, or venture as far as the front door for the food I ordered.

I haven't talked about everything that happened, but whatever Vic is guessing has her pretty angry. Every time we make eye contact her initial emotion seems to be rage before she gets herself in check and smiles at me. The pitying kind of smile that is a large factor is what has been keeping me away from my friends.

I love her for caring, I really do.

Reya does my dishes while I shower, and Vic seems to have pulled every blanket she could find to the living room. We all work together, chaotically, to make a cozy looking bed on the floor.

They even go as far as to move a couple of chairs in an attempt at a fort. It's not great, but the kids get a kick out of it which makes me smile for the first time in days. Their laughter is medicine, reminding me that the world doesn't begin and end with one particular person.

There's popcorn, and gummy worms, and ice cream. We all snuggle, and laugh, and watch Disney movies until we can't keep our eyes open. The young ones are the first to fall asleep, and I look over Dahlia's sleeping face to see my friends already looking over at me.

"I love you, guys."

Vic reaches her hand out to rest on my arm. "We love you, too. Stop trying to suffer without us."

"I feel a lot better." I glance down at a sleeping, precious face. "They helped."

"I figured they would."

30

MILES

"Okay, get the fuck up." I hear the words echo in my half-asleep state. What an annoying dream. "Seriously, how are you still passed out right now?"

Why is being unconscious not enough for my brother to stop stressing me out? I have to deal with it in my dreams too? That doesn't seem fair.

I groan at the unmistakable sound of my curtains being thrown open, followed by a flood of light that hurts my unopened eyes.

Okay, definitely not dreaming.

What the fuck?

"No grown man should be asleep at one in the afternoon unless they're dying. Are you dying, Miles?"

"How the hell did you get into my house?" I grumble as I pull the sheets over my face.

"Mom has a spare key. I took it."

"You can't just let yourself into my house. This is why *you* don't have a spare key."

"Stop being so dramatic. We've been worried about you, dumbass. You can't even bother to text mom back?" he asks in a pissy tone.

"It's only been..." I trail off, not knowing how long it's been. It feels like a couple of days have gone by since I last saw him, but I've worked a lot more shifts than that. "Why isn't mom the one here yelling at me?"

"I haven't started yelling yet, Miles. I'm not that cruel. I'll give you a few minutes to prepare yourself. Putting on some pants would be a good start." I squint my eyes open to peer down at myself and of course, I'm only wearing briefs and my blanket is pushed to the bottom of my bed.

"Get out."

"Timer's going. Four minutes." He grants my wish and walks out the bedroom door, but doesn't close it.

Not that cruel, my ass.

It takes me at least five minutes to get dressed, brush my teeth, and run my hands through my hair until I look somewhat presentable. The extra time is the least I deserve for being rudely awoken.

He's sprawled on my couch with a bag of my favorite chips in his hand. I reel in my annoyance in hopes that it'll help this go quickly.

"Alright then. What do you got, little brother?"

He brushes his hands to wipe off some crumbs without lifting his head. The asshole does it right over my couch, too. My fists clench.

"Why are you being all pathetic and mopey? You're freaking everyone out, and it's somehow become my problem."

"Well, you just said it yourself. That's your problem."

He turns so fast I'm surprised he doesn't get whiplash.

"Who *are* you right now? Seriously, Miles, you're the one that's supposed to keep your shit together."

"Maybe I'm sick of it when it means that my mother still tries to control everything I do like I'm still a teenager who can't make my own decisions," I snap with complete and total honesty. The most I've given him in a long time.

He huffs out a laugh. "There you go, fucking finally. You think you're the only one? You think I don't get it just as bad?"

I only shrug because how would I know? It's not like we're in the habit of telling each other how we're feeling. I throw myself down on the other end of the couch.

"You know..." he starts. "I don't want to try with Isabelle anymore."

My eyes widen, this is definitely the first time I've heard him say anything like that. It's always been so crucial to him that they keep trying to make things work.

"I love my kids, more than anything. I let myself think that what was best for them was sticking things out. Making our marriage work despite everything. One guess as to who pushed that onto me so hard?" I don't have to say it. "Insisting she shows up to all the family dinners, mentioning more grandchildren. The reality is that we can't help but hurt each other. The kids know it, young as they might be, they still pick up on things. I don't see how that's better than giving them two separate homes to live in."

"I had no idea."

"Neither did I until recently." The sigh that comes out of him is the most stressed I've ever heard him. "But I'm going to do it. I'm going to sign the divorce papers and get this show on the road. I've already started looking into a new apartment. My point in saying all of this, is that I feel so much better now that I've made this decision. Maybe I can inspire you to make your own decision so you can knock off this zombie act."

There are too many things I need to address about what he just told me, but I start with the easiest one. "Have you told mom yet?"

He shakes his head. "Not going to until I have to."

"Fair enough."

"So?" he asks. "Are you going to tell me what's going on with that girl, and what the hell mom has to do with it?"

I contemplate it for a long time. Seconds tick by, and he doesn't rush me. We just sit there in silence.

"I'm not ready to do that," I finally say.

"Do I have to pry it out of mom? You two and your secrets are freaking me out."

I shake my head. "There's no way she'll tell you."

He throws his arms up, looking a lot like a defeated kid.

"Can you figure your shit out and let me know when you're ready? This is crap, Miles."

"It is," I agree.

My brother stares at me for a minute, taking in the bags under my eyes, the unshaved beard. He processes just how bad I look with an unreadable expression.

Then he surprises me by pulling me out of my seat and into a hug. That wasn't on my bingo card for the year.

Honestly, the only thing I knew was going to happen was my divorce. Everyone saw it coming. Just as much as we all saw it coming for Justin, even when he was determined to keep it from happening.

I never could've guessed the way I feel about Autumn Owens, and how much it hurts.

"What are the odds of two brothers getting divorced in the same year? I feel like that's pretty unlikely."

He pretends to shudder. "I have way more in common with you than I ever thought I would." I smack the side of his head *almost* hard enough to hurt. "Now go take a shower, you smell like shit."

He's not wrong, I don't even have to sniff myself to check. I realize how pathetic it is, letting myself go like this. If she was anyone else, this might have lasted half the time it has, but she's not.

"Yeah, thanks."

"And talk to her, dumbass. Fix it."

"She's not responding to any of my texts," I admit defeatedly.

"So go see her."

"I think it's frowned upon to show up at her front door unannounced as many times as I have."

He rolls his eyes dramatically. "You're down *so* bad. Start with a shower, figure the rest out from there. It's probably hard to think through all the stench."

"I'm going, get out of my house," I mutter as I head to my bathroom. "And put that key back, there's a reason you don't have one."

"Don't worry. I'll put it back as soon as I make a copy."

I ignore him, assuming he's kidding. I really don't want to think about having to change my locks. I have more important things to deal with.

31

AUTUMN

My fleece lined tights and little black skirt, paired with my favorite turtle neck make me feel human for the first time in a long time. Human enough that I leave the house before nine, craving some breakfast. I haven't been cooking at all, and I'm excited about the prospect. I could really go for some bacon and eggs, maybe even pancakes.

There's only so much fast food a person can live off of, and I'm reaching the limit.

I end up piling all the breakfast ingredients I can find into my shopping cart. I've *missed* hash browns, and sausage, and I make some amazing French toast. My mouth is watering in the bread aisle.

I'm deciding between cinnamon raisin and blueberry bagels when my heart flies out of my chest.

Miles stands to my left, looking like he's seen a ghost. We're both stiff, unmoving, unblinking. I take in all of the details I can without being too obvious. His hands in his pockets, his wrinkled sweater.

I can't believe he's in front of me. It takes so much effort not to completely lose it. I have the urge to do something drastic, and I'm stuck between collapsing to the ground sobbing or grabbing him and showing him how happy I am to see his face. There's no denying it, as much as I should.

"You can tell me to walk away if that's what you want, Autumn. But I'll tell you right now, it's the last fucking thing I want to do."

I shake my head in response and pretend his words don't force the air out of my lungs. Not even the smallest, most rational parts of me want to see him go.

He takes a step toward me, overwhelming my senses. My body is so aware of his, and every breath I take is filled with the calming, fresh scent of him.

"Why?" I manage to gasp the words. As if I don't know that he hasn't stopped thinking about the night of the office party anymore than I have. I still feel like breaking down every time Amelia's words ring through my head.

You'll see that, too.

He gives me the smallest of hopeful smiles, before leaning against the shelving next to me. All of my focus goes to the muscled arms he crosses. The crewneck he's wearing is tight enough to leave little to the imagination. Memories flash in my mind. What they looked like in his moonlit living room. How they felt wrapped around me.

"Your phone full of unanswered messages can answer that question for you."

"Fair enough." I don't tell him that I haven't gotten any of the texts or why that is. I regret my choice already.

I realize I'm still clutching the bagels in my hands, and throw them back down on their shelf. His eyes follow my movements, before scanning me from head to toe. I might as well be naked with how vulnerable it makes me feel.

"Are you okay?"

It's not a question I know how to answer right now. He looks nervous enough that he must already know that much. He must be as scared as I am that there's no easy way for this to happen.

When I don't respond, he nods.

"Yeah, me neither."

"I'm sorry," I whisper.

Before I can register the gentle touch of his hand on my jaw, I'm looking into those deep brown eyes only a few inches in front of me. They're heated in a way that tells me an apology isn't what he wants from me.

"Tell me what you could possibly think you have to be sorry for."

Thanks to the weeks I've spent alone and overthinking, I have plenty of words to get out.

"For everything. For all the times I didn't answer the door, and all the times I *did*. For letting things get as bad as they were, not being able to stay away from you. For not listening to your mom *months* ago."

His jaw clenches. "What did my mom say to you?"

"Nothing that hasn't been implied every time she sees us together. I'm something she wants to protect you from."

He shakes his head a couple times, but it's not an answer to me. He takes his time processing my words, thinking them through.

"She thinks she knows something."

I look up at him, and he sees the question before I ask it.

"She told me there's something I don't know."

"Which is?"

He shakes his head again. "I don't know, it was that night. We were arguing. I didn't ask."

I watch him continue to be stuck in his head. Of course I'm curious, I'd love to know why Amelia feels the way she does about me. Whatever the reason, it can't possibly be as bad as my brain is making it out to be.

But I'm not as curious as he is, losing the moment like he's a detective hoping for a breakthrough. I'm almost standing there long enough that it's awkward. I almost want to back away, but then suddenly he's present again. His eyes meet mine and he steps forward, putting his hands on my arms.

"You're not the only one who couldn't stay away. I'm the one that kissed you. Twice. Do you think I should be apologizing to you?"

"Well, no, but it's— We were just drinking that first time, and then—" I don't know what I was planning to say, the words aren't in my head.

We built a connection, it's obvious we did.

"It wasn't just because we were drinking. I didn't want to look away that first day at this fucking store." He gestures to the empty aisle beside him. "I didn't want to pretend I wasn't staring, but I did. I thought that was the right thing to do. If I could go back in time, I'd change things. I'd tell you that you were the most beautiful woman I'd ever seen. I'd ask you out on a date instead of to catch up. I'd hope my brother wouldn't be a factor in your response."

"He would've been," I say quickly. Before he gets a chance to keep making my heart swell. "I'd love to pretend he's not a factor, but that's our reality. It's too complicated."

"It doesn't have to be complicated."

"It does. We don't get to decide that."

"I *am* deciding it. I'm not going anywhere, Autumn. I'm choosing you." His grip tightens just enough to emphasize his words. "I want you. We can figure out the rest of it."

"I'm not worth it," I say shakily. "I'm not worth a single argument with your mom, or the million arguments you'd have with Justin when he finds out."

His eyes widen, and every cell in my body is begging not to stick around for his response. I am suddenly very aware of how often I end up in flight mode, and I don't want to anymore. I want to have this conversation, and hope it gives us what we need in order to move on.

"I want what you said to be true," I continue. "That I'll be wanted in any room you're in... but what if your family is in that room too? They will be. Often. As they should be, because they love you the way you deserve."

He's so lucky to have that.

He brushes a teardrop away as soon as it falls to my cheek. The simple touch makes me feel so alive, I'm tempted to forget the consequences and lean into his touch. But I don't, because my anxiety over the situation has settled deep in my bones. I feel it everywhere, it's everything. I don't expect him to understand, but I wish he did.

Miles looks around like he'd forgotten we were in public until now. The only people we can see are an elderly couple, but they're far enough away that they can't eavesdrop.

Still, he grabs my purse out of the cart with one hand, and my wrist with the other. He pulls me to a door that I think is surely for employees, but suddenly there's a bathroom door, and he's pushing it open.

He shuts it behind him, closing us into the cramped space that's only meant for one person at a time.

His fingers slide down until they're laced with mine, and he gives me a reassuring squeeze.

"I know things have been bad, but they're not unreasonable people. I can talk to my mom, I can help her see this for what it is."

"It's not going to be that easy," I whisper. Funny that I lower my voice now that we do have privacy.

"You're right, it won't be. We'll argue some more. Justin will lose his shit. Things will be tense at first, but nothing is going to happen that won't be worth it. If the only other option is losing you, I'll deal with all of it. They're not the unforgiving type, it won't always be like this."

I run a hand down my face, trying to reel in the explosion of emotion that's begging to be let out. I still think dropping to the ground and sobbing is a fair option.

"They'd forgive *you*. They'd get over the fact that you are with me, but I wouldn't get the same treatment. They'll always see me as his ex. Amelia knows how to hold a grudge, I heard what she said about me at the party." I watch him wince slightly at that. "She never saw me as a victim to her teenage son, she saw me as the problem."

"You don't know that."

"I can already see it. She'd only ask you to come over for dinner on nights I'm busy, and ignore me when I'm there for holidays. I don't think I have it in me to try to prove myself to someone that's been decided on her opinion of me since I was fifteen."

"It's not decided! Whatever idea my mom has stuck in her head can't be impossible to get out. She spoke so highly of you before she saw whatever this is between us."

He isn't entirely wrong. There's definitely a disconnect between us, but we've talked and joked around the office enough that it felt like old times. It felt like how things were those first couple of years after we met.

"Justin has enough shit on his plate already. He knows whatever he did to you was wrong, and he's getting his karma for it."

I wish that fact was satisfying.

Miles steps even closer to me, until all I'm inhaling is his spearmint breath. "I know you think it's easier to walk away, but I think it might be the hardest thing I'd ever have to do. I'm already in this."

I felt it, too. I felt his decision, felt everything that was holding him back fall away with our last kiss.

The man in front of me has the best heart. It's intoxicating, the way he's holding out for me. The way he doesn't want to let me walk away from it.

I have never and *will never* want to, but it's never been about what I want. If it was, I'd have let myself drown in this mess a long time ago.

His free hand slides back into my hair, and it feels so right. It makes me wonder why I'm holding onto this pit in my stomach like it's a lifeline. His touch feels much more like something that could save me.

I must be so transparent. Whatever he sees in my expression is enough for him to slowly lean in. Just the anticipation of it is the most relief I've felt in so long.

I watch, paralyzed, as he pushes right past my metaphorical walls, and his lips land on mine. The world falls off my shoulders in an instant, and I don't care about anything other than him.

"Please tell me I can do that again," he breathes after pulling away too quickly.

I close the distance, not thinking, just feeling all the need that hasn't stopped building in me. Need for him alone, that nothing and nobody has been able to sate.

He eagerly returns my kiss, and his hand grips the base of my neck, keeping my head tilted at the perfect angle. It's messy, and a little rough, and everything I could have hoped for when his body presses into mine.

Being stuck between the wall and his hard body doesn't feel like being stuck at all. It feels like being set free. Even more so when I push right back, and I feel the groan that vibrates out of him.

"I don't think I can keep my hands to myself," he tells me between breaths as his hands travel down, tracing my body until they land on my hips. He holds me in a tight grip to grind against me harder. The friction is enough to drive every single thought out of my head. Nothing matters but this heat building in me, and the promise of more.

"Then don't," I pant.

Neither of us care where we are, or if anyone can hear us on the other side of the door. The two of us are all that exists.

His solid grip shifts to my thighs and he lifts me up. My legs instinctively wrap around him, but it still doesn't feel like I could ever possibly get close enough. He moves us over to the small counter with ease, setting me down before him.

I don't protest when his hands slip under my dress, and pull on the waistband of my tights. They're cheap, and flimsy, and without intention he rips them right down the center. I see the flash of surprise, maybe even an apology, in his eyes before he takes advantage of it. Fingers tear further and brush against the inside of my thighs. He's making slow work of traveling to the place I need him the most. I let out a small whimper in anticipation, and he captures it with his mouth.

When his thumb presses through the fabric of my underwear and up my slit, I can't help the gasp that flies out of me.

I know he's feeling how soaked my underwear is.

"Was it like this when you imagined me in your book?"

My eyes widen, but he doesn't notice as his kisses trail down my neck and across my collar bone.

I had written a scene where Cam pulls Brenda into the bathroom at a college party, because he couldn't last a second longer without touching her. And I *had* daydreamed about Miles not wanting to go a second without touching *me* while I wrote it.

I'm surprised he read that far.

His fingertips dip under the edge of the fabric and pulls it to the side. The second he has access, he presses his thumb to me and begins to rub in perfectly pressured circles. I somehow manage to nod despite my head spinning.

I did picture this, his hands and mouth on me, our shared breaths as he tore me apart using nothing else. Except this is a million times better than I imagined, better than anything I could've written about a character I was pretending *wasn't* him.

I'm nothing more than a panting mess. Our kiss has gotten sloppier, my ability to successfully multitask being long gone. This is the first time it's actually happened, feeling so consumed by what someone is doing with their hands that I can't even kiss them properly. I was working from pure imagination when I wrote it.

He's going to destroy me before I even lay eyes on his dick.

I move my messy kisses down his jaw, to his neck, nipping at him and savoring the taste of his skin. I start to move against his hand, encouraging him enough that he slips a finger inside of me. It only makes me push my hips faster, begging for more.

The only sounds filling the small space are the heavy breaths and moans that fly out of me, and his fingers moving through my wetness. I'd be embarrassed if I wasn't so consumed by the way he feels.

When he slips another finger in, and curves them to hit a certain spot, I know I'm done for.

"You're so fucking beautiful," he whispers before nipping at my earlobe.

I want to say the words right back, because that's what he is. His curly hair has fallen forward, and his cheeks are just as flushed as I'm sure mine are. I wish I could take a picture, and forever remember the awe written on his face. The determination.

More curses fly past his lips when he feels my core tighten around him, seemingly just as lost in this as I am. His thumb pushes down even harder, moving back and forth on my bundle of nerves and setting me off.

He muffles the scream that flies out of me with his mouth, like it's something he wants to keep for himself. I'm more than okay with that, I want to give him every orgasm if this is how they'll go.

My body sags back against the mirror as I catch my breath. I can still feel how hard he is against my thigh.

He lazily kisses my face, my neck, my chest. The neckline of this sweater is so stretched out, and I don't care. I'd ruin a hundred sweaters for him.

"Please let me do that a hundred more times," he pleads. "I don't think I'll ever get sick of the sounds you make."

If my core wasn't still throbbing, it would have started up again at those words.

"I'll be so disappointed if you don't," I admit, still panting.

His relief is palpable as he presses a kiss to my forehead.

"We can do this, A. I promise. Whatever you need, I'll do it."

I believe him. And I decide I'm going to let him, although I'm not any less scared of what the future holds.

32

MILES

"Boy!" Patty yells, causing me to jump back from the windowsill. I was so lost in thought that I overwatered her plant, spilling water down the wall and onto the carpet.

"Shit, Pat. I'm sorry." I waste no time grabbing a towel from the kitchen to soak it up. The plant is doomed if I don't do something about that as well, so I bring it back to the sink with me. The old woman just watches me as I go, clearly amused by my flustered state. To be fair, she's had the plant a lot longer than I've been around. I can't be the reason it dies.

Two alarms go off at the same time, one on my phone and one on hers. It means it's pill time.

"Pill time!" she yells from her seat. She's always yelling. I'm used to it by now.

Patty sits herself up, using the remote to her chair.

"You seem like you're in a good mood today," she points out as I hand her the medications and the cup of water in my hand. "Too good, in fact. You almost killed Jolene with your daydreaming over there."

"Jolene?" I ask, intentionally avoiding the rest of what she said.

"You know damn well I have a name for every plant in here, don't try to distract me. You spent weeks looking down in the dumps, and now something's changed. Update a poor old woman that can't even leave her home."

"You can leave whenever you want. You want Ella to take you to the mall?"

She glares at me, not at all oblivious to my bullshit. "You're killing me."

Maybe it's my lucky day, because she actually lets it drop.

My mom calls me on my way home. I find myself wishing I'd never let her memorize my work schedule. Things have never been this tense between us. I know I need to talk to her about Autumn, but I want that conversation to be on my terms. I don't want it to be over the phone. She has to know how serious I am, there's no other choice here. If she wants to stay mad, I won't feel guilty about it.

I'm going to protect Autumn from her either way.

"Hi, mom."

"Hello, child of mine. How was work?"

"Always a blast, how was yours?" I'm only half sarcastic, I could have worse things to deal with than a nosy grandmother.

"It was a good day. Chloe came in with pictures of her house, it's just gorgeous. Suits her perfectly. I can't wait to get started."

"That's nice," I mumble.

"Which reminds me, I would love it if you'd come with me next week. The shopping is always fun isn't it? And we can have lunch with her beforehand to—"

"Why would I go with you for lunch?"

"You know how much I want you to be comfortable around the office."

She's always thought I'm too good for my job. It's been impossible to get her to see that I don't want to do anything else. I'm happy where I am.

"And wouldn't it be nice to chat with her some more? You barely got the chance."

And there it is. I don't miss how carefully she words it. How she wants to act like the reason wasn't that I told her point-blank that I was not interested.

"It's such a shame you didn't even get her number, but I could give it to you. She'd love to hear from you."

"I don't want her number."

"You haven't even tried to get to know her."

"I don't want to get to know her."

She groans like I'm a disobedient child she can't get under control. "Did your brother do nothing to get you out of this funk?"

"I'm not in a funk." Not anymore.

"I don't see the problem, then. You could at least try, give her a chance. She's successful, and smart, and—"

"You do know what the problem is, and I don't have the energy to pretend it doesn't exist for your sake. Love you, mom. I'll talk to you later."

I hang up before she gets a chance to argue.

Autumn and I are going to have to talk soon about where we're going from where we are. I know I love being around her, I can barely stand when I'm not. I know she's the best person I've ever met. I know she's everything and more I could want for myself.

She's clever, and funny, and kind, and... may or may not ever be able to face my mother again.

A text comes through as I pull into my driveway.

Mom: *You can do so much better.*

The words make me feel sick to my stomach. They couldn't be further from the truth.

She *is* better.

— *ele* —

The sound of fingers hitting the keys is extremely soothing.

One of the hardest things about the last few weeks was knowing Autumn wasn't a phone call away anymore. I missed hearing her voice before I fell asleep.

Part of me was worried that she would overthink the morning we shared, and not answer when I called. I did have to leave for work sooner than I had wanted to. It wasn't easy to go.

But she did answer, very cheerily. She's been writing all day, feeling inspired, which makes me feel good. I know the time she spent ignoring me wasn't any easier on her than it was on me.

She was still going strong when I called, but she let me stay on the line. I'd rather be there, watching the concentration on her face, and all of her cute reactions.

It's doubtful that I wouldn't ruin her productivity the second I would walk through the door. Not because she lacks self control, but because I might. When it comes to her, it's actually a guarantee.

I don't speak. I just listen.

She's clearly on a roll, only pausing occasionally to mumble something to herself. I even heard her let out a small squeal as she went, trying to cover it with a cough. It was adorable.

The typing slows after a long while and she sighs.

"Damn, I'm good."

"I know you are."

She laughs. "I almost forgot you were there. Having fun?"

"I'm having so much fun that I'm almost half asleep," I confess.

"Oh no, I didn't mean to bore you. I can text you in the morning?"

"No," I say quickly. "It's nice. Don't go."

I hear the smile in her voice when she says, "Okay."

It's quiet for a long moment, as my thoughts drift to the morning we had. The way she was so lost to everything but the feeling of my fingers inside her. I need more of that.

"Autumn."

"Miles."

"Should we talk about it?"

She lets out a little hum, like she's thinking. I don't breathe while I wait for her answer.

"You're amazing, you know?"

"A lot of people start breakups with that line, you know."

"We can't break up, we aren't together."

I know it's nothing but the truth, but I still feel it hit me like a blow.

"Yeah."

"I do want to try," she says quietly.

"So do I."

"I just want to make sure you know that's all I can do. I can't promise anything."

"I can make enough promises for the both of us until you're ready. I promise," I tell her with a smile.

She chuckles into the phone and it's a sound I'll never get tired of hearing.

Amongst others.

"Deal."

"What are you doing right now?"

"Wrapping up what I'm working on so I can get in the car and come see you." Emphasizing her words, I hear her laptop slam closed.

"I'd love that. A lot," I tell her.

"Should I plan on staying the night?"

"I'd love that a lot," I say again. I'm short on words because all I can think about is getting to sleep next to her again, and maybe even finishing what we started this morning.

My dick wastes no time rising with that image in my mind.

33

MILES

Before I know it, she's standing in front of me holding an overnight bag. She looks like a dream come true, even more so than usual. I know she puts a lot of effort into her appearance during the day. Her hair and makeup are always done, her outfits are always color coordinated, but *this...*

The sight of Autumn in an oversized sweatshirt, leggings, and a messy bun on top of her head? It's my favorite look of them all. It's evidence of how comfortable she is with me, and that she didn't want to waste a second coming over.

I'm frozen in place as I study her, suddenly nervous. I don't want to make the wrong move. I don't want to be too forward or not forward enough. I want to do whatever this woman wants.

She smirks at me, as if reading my mind.

"You look a little conflicted."

"A little?" I breathe out a laugh, and so does she. "If only you knew."

"I might know," she says, dropping her bag, and closing the distance between us. "If it's anything like what's going through my mind."

"Which is?" I ask, watching her eyelids flutter as she feels my breath on her face.

She shakes her head. "You first."

I play with the one piece of hair she doesn't have up, a small curl that brushes her cheek. Her hand raises to my arm and grips my bicep. As if I could read her mind, I know what a request it is.

"I'm not going to waste time on words when it should be pretty fucking obvious," I say right before leaning down and capturing her mouth with my own.

She tastes so sweet. Even sweeter is the small whimper she lets out when my hand moves to the back of her head possessively. I hold her to me, loving the way our height difference helps me take what I want. She gives just as fiercely, nipping at my bottom lip and deepening the kiss when my mouth opens for her.

My other hand has a mind of its own as I bring it down her back and over her hip, gripping her like my life depends on it. I use my hold to pull her into me, pressing our bodies together. She gasps when she feels how hard I am against her.

When Autumn pushes back into me, creating the smallest amount of friction, I lose it. Both hands fly to the space just below her ass, which feels incredible in these leggings, and I lift her up. She wastes no time wrapping her legs around me, and grinding those perfect hips into mine.

"Fuck." The word involuntarily slips past my lips.

"Please," she says, and then kisses me even harder.

She moves her mouth down my neck and chest, as I carry her into my bedroom and shut the door behind me with a kick.

There are some things pets just shouldn't see.

I lay her down on the edge of the bed, my body covering hers. My hands don't want to stay in one spot, they long to touch every inch of her. Her breasts, her waist, her thighs. I love the feel of all of it under my grasp.

I push my hips against hers with even more fervor now, wondering if this is enough to make me finish. It feels like it might be. The sounds that fly out of her are so fucking delicious, that I'm encouraged to up my pace. It didn't occur to me that she might be just as close until I watch her eyes squeeze shut.

There is nothing in this world like watching her fall apart, the way her grip on me tightens, and her mouth falls open on a soundless scream. That image will be stuck in my head for the rest of my life.

I pause, letting her catch her breath. I watch her, in awe of the way she's done that for me twice today.

"How do you do that?" she gasps.

"Do what?"

"Make that happen so easily."

"Maybe we're meant for each other."

There's a second where I regret letting those words slip out, not sure if it's okay to come on that strong. The only thing I know for certain is that she's willing to try, to see where this can go.

When her eyes meet mine, I breathe a sigh of relief. I don't see any hint that she disagrees.

Her fingers begin to fumble with the edge of my shirt, but she's still coming down and doesn't get very far.

"Off. Please." I do as she says, pulling it over my head faster than I ever have. She watches with a hungry expression, her eyes landing on my chest with appreciation. I smile down at her.

"Your turn."

Her eyes only widen for a second before she pulls her sweatshirt up with one hand. I try and fail not to laugh when it gets caught on her head, and she keeps tugging, clearly frustrated. It gets her nowhere.

I easily help her out of it, and when she lets out a frustrated breath as she's freed, I'm right there devouring her with a kiss again. I can't let her have a second to feel embarrassed, not when there's nothing she could do to ruin this.

I don't stop there. I slip the straps of her bra down her shoulders, and admire the curve of her breasts before reaching around to unhook the back. I'm momentarily hypnotized by the sight of the perfection splayed out beneath me.

My fingers slide underneath the waistband of her leggings and start to peel those off, too. I could come in my jeans at the sight of her pale thighs, and the contrast of the lacy red fabric against them. Even more so when I notice the wet spot I can see along her center, waiting and ready for me.

"Are these the same ones you were wearing earlier?" I ask, pulling on the band and letting the elastic snap back against her hip.

I'd been so caught up in her face, watching the way her eyes squeezed shut and how her mouth parted as I brought her closer and closer before she came around my fingers, that I didn't even see what color her underwear were.

She shakes her head.

"Why not?"

I watch her cheeks grow red, even more so than they already were. "Because I got a little more up close and personal with a public restroom than I'd normally have liked. I had to strip and sanitize."

Fair enough.

"Speaking of stripping," I tell her as I press a kiss to her hip bone, teasing her as my mouth trails along her stomach to the other.

"No," I hear her say, just before a hand grips and tugs at my hair.

I lift my face to look up at her, giving into her pull. "No?"

"I appreciate if your intention is to get me off again, but it's your turn." She tugs a little harder and I follow through this time, capturing her mouth again.

"We don't need to take turns, sweetheart. I was looking forward to burying my face in your—" I'm interrupted by her palming me through my jeans, and I let out a harsh breath. I feel like a virgin, the way I move against her hand, desperate for any touch she'll give me.

I take it as a sign that I'm not undressed enough, and fix that problem quickly. Her body shakes with a silent laugh, amused by my enthusiasm. It doesn't last long, not once I'm towering over her, completely naked. She doesn't hide her ogling.

"Fucking hell," she breathes underneath me.

The head of my cock brushes the center of those lacey underwear and Autumn lets out another delicious sound. I'm barely hanging on, and even though I'm nervous I'll last a total of five seconds inside her, it's where I need to be right now. I blindly reach for the nightstand, where I know I have a condom.

I'm stopped by a small hand and fingers lacing between mine, pulling it back to her. I grab her where she leads me, which happens to be a perfect handful of a breast.

There's not a single part of us that doesn't fit together.

"Birth control?" I ask her, kissing her neck in between the two words.

I feel her nod against me. "And I used protection when..." She starts and then pauses. I can feel her anxiety spread to me in a second.

I lift my head to meet her eyes. I know what she's not saying, and I'd prefer if she didn't. I don't want anyone else's name to come out of her mouth right now.

"Okay," I say, and grind myself into her again. I'm sick of the remaining barrier between us. "Same. I mean, I always have."

She responds by grabbing onto the back of my neck and pulling me down for another kiss.

"Sorry in advance," I whisper over her lips, before slipping two fingers under the fabric and pulling hard and fast. The thin material doesn't resist much before tearing right off of her.

This time when I come back down to her, I'm met with nothing but her wet heat, and I can't resist it anymore. I capture her bottom lip between my own at the same moment I grip her waist and I move.

I don't stand a chance of lasting very long.

I look down at her, in awe of the view I have. Her hair is a mess of waves spread out on the sheets around her, her cheeks are tinged the perfect pink.

She moans, taking me in, and I have to make myself pause. The sound alone has the power to end this right here and now.

The pace at which I have to pull out and slide back inside is painfully slow. I can't help but marvel while I do, at how we fit together like this was always supposed to be where we ended up.

Her legs wrap around me tightly then, using their hold to pull me into her faster, and I give in.

Over and over again.

"I'm going to fucking explode if you keep that up."

She responds with another delicious cry and I steal it away with my mouth on hers. I up my pace, giving into her wordless demand.

Her noises become quicker, but shorter, and I know she's already as close as I am. I lower my hand to press a thumb to her bundle of nerves and feel her tense around me. I watch intently as her eyes squeeze shut again, and that's all it takes for my own release to find me.

I feel like a man possessed, burying my face in her neck, and groaning into her skin.

By the time I'm too sensitive to move, I notice the heavy rise and fall of her chest that tells me she's just as spent as I am. I pull out of her, instantly missing the feeling, and fall to the bed beside her. Our legs are still hanging off the edge.

She's still panting, when she looks over at my face.

"You're too perfect."

"The amount of times I've thought that about you today is almost embarrassing."

"Almost?"

"It's only the truth."

I kiss her lazily, sloppily, as we come down from the high. I simply enjoy the taste of her and the fact that she's *here*.

I might not have any control over what happens outside of this bubble, but it's enough. She's enough.

We eventually find our way to the pillows at the head of the bed, but we don't sleep. In between talking, laughing, and cuddling,

I find myself buried inside of her more than once before we're completely spent and our bodies beg for rest.

"There goes any chance of my night routine," I hear her mumble sleepily.

"What?" I ask, glancing at her. Her eyes are closed, and her chest moves with every sated breath. She's awake enough to smile sweetly at me.

"Nothing. Good night, Miles."

"Good night, sweetheart."

34

MILES

I wake the beautiful woman in my bed by pressing kisses to her shoulder and along her neck. She hums at the realization, and it makes me want to rip off her clothes again. As if I'm not sleep deprived from my inability to stop touching her last night.

Not that it matters. I'd give up sleeping all together for her.

"Why?" she groans. "I'm tired."

I laugh softly, not enough to agitate her sleepy state. "Freddy wants to go on a walk." Emphasizing my words is the sound of his paws at my bedroom door. "Come with us?"

She peers at me through her squinted eyes. "But it's cold."

"Yeah it is."

"I didn't bring the right clothes."

"I have clothes you can wear."

Her eyes stay squinted as she scoots into a sitting position, giving me a better look at her messy hair against my tan pillowcase. It's the best sight I've seen this early in the day while still in my own bed. I wish I could see it every day.

"I'm gonna need coffee," she grumbles. I press a kiss to her forehead, loving this tired and grumpy version of the Autumn I love so much already.

Because yeah. I do.

"One hot coffee coming right up."

It takes me less than three minutes to have a travel mug in her hands, and be sifting through my closet for something she can bundle up in. It's not the hardest thing I've done, considering everything I own would be oversized on her. I get back to her with a sweatshirt, sweatpants, a puffy jacket, a scarf, and a pair of long socks. She looks terrified by the pile in my arms and it pulls a laugh out of me.

"No chance of you being cold with all of this on."

When she grabs everything from me, she studies the jacket like there's something fascinating about it. Before I can ask, she faces me.

"I have this same one, believe it or not."

Of course I believe it, I remember everything I gave her six years ago.

"It's my favorite," I explain.

Then I see the flash of realization on her face.

"Wait, you gave me your *favorite* jacket? Why would you do that?"

"It'll keep you warm, and I'll get it back from you when we're—"

"No, I mean *then*. The one you gave me then. You didn't have to give me *anything*, but you could've at least given me something you weren't attached to."

I was attached to everything I gave her, especially that blanket that currently sits on her couch.

I invade her space, and put a hand to her cheek.

"The only thing that mattered was knowing you'd have more than a thin sweatshirt to keep you warm at night." I tuck a strand of hair behind her ear. "I might have also thought we would have stayed friends, and it wasn't like I'd never see any of it again. And see? I was partially right."

"You can't have any of it back," she says, trying to hide her emotions.

"It's all yours, hence my replacement."

She decides to wear her leggings again, despite my protests that she'll freeze her legs off. The final result though? With my jacket reaching her knees, and my scarf wrapped around her neck? It's a look I have to capture and keep forever.

I make sure she knows it, too. The second we get outside I hand her Freddy's leash and back away, pulling out my phone.

"What are you doing?" she asks, frowning deeply at the camera.

"Making sure I'll never forget how cute you look right now."

Now that I've given myself permission to finally acknowledge it out loud.

"I look like a mess."

"You're the cutest mess the world has ever seen." I can see her try to hold back a smile, the corner of her mouth just barely quirking up. "Yeah, the fucking cutest," I confirm.

I snap another photo.

When I go to grab the leash back from her, she pulls it out of my reach, and walks backwards away from me.

"No, he's mine now." She looks down at him with a loving smile that honestly takes my breath away. "Isn't that right, Freddy? You're obviously sick of being stuck with this guy all the time."

I smile to myself, not about to argue as I follow after them. My heart feels so full, watching how comfortable they are together.

"Miles? Is that you?"

My steps falter. It's a man's voice that seems somewhat familiar, but I can't place it.

I look to my right to see a guy who looks around my age with long blonde hair, and I'm sure I don't know him. I rack my brain for anyone matching his appearance and come up blank.

He's carrying a box away from the giant moving truck that sits in the driveway. I hadn't even realized my old neighbors had moved out, not that it's a surprise. I haven't been paying attention to much these last few weeks, they could've bulldozed the neighborhood without me noticing.

A few slow steps closer, and I'm still not sure who I'm looking at or how they know my name. Autumn glances at me expectantly, waiting for me to answer. I give her a subtle shrug.

"Uh, hey?"

He sets the box down on the porch step as we approach, so he can throw his arms out in a question.

"Don't tell me you don't recognize me, man. It's just some hair."

I give him a look that I hope is apologetic because even when he's right in front of us— nothing. I don't know. There's a nagging feeling somewhere in the back of my mind that I should.

What are the places I'd know someone from? My job, my mom's office, the handful of friends I used to have before I shut them all out. He doesn't fall into any of those categories.

"I'm sorry, I don't..." I trail off, watching him smile in amusement.

"No hard feelings. It is *some* hair, huh?" That's for sure, it's quite the mane. "Wyatt."

Wyatt.

It clicks quickly, I've only ever known one person named Wyatt. He was a kid I went to high school with, really nice guy. Not popular, didn't have the easiest time, but I helped when I could.

I shake my head in disbelief. "What the fuck?"

He roars a laugh, and suddenly I'm being bear hugged. He pats my back a couple of times, harder than necessary, before pulling away.

It's not just the hair that's changed, it's about everything about him.

"It's been a decade!"

"I thought you were in—" I forget exactly where, it having been so long ago— "another country?"

He nods eagerly. "Yeah, man. I was all over the place, mostly in Australia. It was a hell of a time, but I missed my folks. My girlfriend was sick of flying out. It was time."

"Disappointed yet?" I ask jokingly. I don't hate my hometown by any means, but I do think about what it'd be like to leave. If I'd want to come back after seeing what more the world has to offer.

"Not the least bit. There are some pretty places in the world, but they're not home."

I glance down at Autumn. She's what comes to mind with the loving way he said that word. *Home.*

Fuck, we have so much to figure out.

"Wyatt and I went to school together." I look back at him. "This is Autumn."

"Great to meet you," he says and shakes her hand. "You two make a good looking couple."

I think her friends would like this guy.

She smiles instead of correcting him, and I like that way too much.

"Nice to meet you, Wyatt."

"You two will have to come over for dinner once we're settled in! Lacey's such a chef."

"Wow, you and Lacey are still going strong?"

They started dating when we were freshman, and broke up a million times before graduation. It was never safe to assume where they were at.

"Strongest yet. She would fly out and see me every couple months, whenever she could get a break from work. It was good, I think, the time away from each other made us appreciate the time we got together."

He waves over at the house behind him, a beautiful place. Very classic, freshly painted, white picket fence.

"I got here a day early to get some things done and surprise her. Can't wait to see the look on her face when she realizes she doesn't have to help me lift any furniture."

"Do you want some help?" Autumn offers beside me, echoing the same thought in my own head.

"We have to get this guy around the block and home, then we can come back?" I say.

Wyatt shakes his head like he can't believe what he's hearing. "You'd want to do that? I don't know man, there's a lot of crap in there."

"All the more reason you could use some help, right?" Autumn smiles wide.

Wyatt returns it. "You're good people. Where's your place?"

I point two houses down to the only house that actually looks like it belongs on the edge of the woods.

He whistles in appreciation. "What a beauty. Makes me want to run to a cabin in the mountains."

It does have that effect.

"We should get moving. Don't want him to shit on your nice, new lawn."

Instead of responding, Wyatt drops to his knees and gives Freddy attention that's well deserved. He's getting a treat for not jumping all over the man during our conversation.

"Freddy," I tell him before he can ask.

"Oh, Freddy. You're a cool guy," he coos, scratching him behind the ears.

"He's the coolest," I agree.

We promise to be back shortly, and continue on our walk. I'm grateful that my dog waits until we're in front of someone else's house to take care of business.

"That guy used to be so nerdy."

Autumn laughs. "In what way?"

"Not in a bad way, but so much different than what we just saw. He was really into Star Wars— Okay, *way too* into Star Wars. He got picked on for it, but I always thought he was cool." I lean in to whisper. "Even if I couldn't stand those movies."

She gasps dramatically. "I'm going to tell him."

"I'd rather you didn't," I say with a smirk.

"I think it's great luck that he's one of your new neighbors."

"I think so, too."

We both seem to fall into our heads, and I don't notice when we're almost done until we're crossing the street.

"You haven't talked a lot about your friends."

I let out a long breath, but most of the unease at talking to her about it has faded. Maybe at first I was nervous she would judge me, or think I was pathetic. Now I know she's not capable of anything but understanding.

"Yeah. I don't really have any left," I admit. "It's not completely Kara's fault, I could have tried harder... It was just so complicated, it was easier not to."

"Why?"

I shrug. "I don't even have a sure answer. She was unhappy when I brought them around, and she was unhappy when I went out without her. It felt like I couldn't win. I *needed* a win, I tried for so long, but I never got one. I eventually just gave up on everything."

She stops me when we're at my front door and pulls me to face her. Before I can assure that it's okay, her arms are around me. I squeeze her back, realization hitting me hard. Now that it's out there, it feels a little easier to move forward.

When she pulls away, she tries to be subtle about wiping under eyes. I grab her hand, and take its place with my mouth. I place a kiss under one eye, and then the other. She starts giggling, because I'm sure it tickles, but then I silence her with my mouth on hers.

"Now you have at least two," she says quietly.

"At least?"

She puts her hand up to count on her fingers. "Me and your new neighbor, that's two. Then there's Reya and Vic, who will probably never leave you alone from this point forward. Good luck with that."

I laugh against her mouth before kissing her again. Doesn't sound like a problem to me.

35

AUTUMN

Spending every other night with Miles might have been a mistake, because I am addicted after only a few days together. I could happily spend every second with him, and not just because the sex is mind-blowing. Everything from making breakfast together, to playing with Freddy, and all the laughs in between have me wishing we could do this forever.

Being the thoughtful guy he is, he felt guilty being the reason that my cat was home alone those nights. We stopped at the pet store to get her toys, even though I told him she would lose interest quickly. He didn't care and I'm glad. It was too precious to watch the two of them roll around on the floor, her chasing toys on strings that he happily threw around.

I find myself hoping she and Freddy will get along that well. I want to introduce the two of them.

Miles has encouraged me to feel comfortable staying at his place when he's at work, but I've been in the mood to write, and I can't pass that up these days. I've been trying to get used to the fact that there are suddenly people who care when another book happens, and it's unreal. I don't want to disappoint anyone by dragging my feet.

Sure I could bring my laptop with me sometime, but I weirdly feel like the energy in my apartment has really contributed to my flow.

Everything I had been writing was gloomy, and sad, and I guess that's a good thing when writing a third act breakup. I did happen to like the direction things were heading in, and it's nice to finally be in the mood to write a happily ever after.

Things are light enough, hopeful enough, that I've actually been *consumed* by writing this happily ever after.

I physically feel the relief hit my body when Miles' smiling face appears in his front doorway. His joy is contagious as he sweeps me up into a hug. You'd think we had spent much more than twenty-four hours apart.

"Good day?" I ask him.

"It's always a good day when I get to hang out with those two," he says, referring to his niece and nephew.

A phone call from Justin interrupted our own this morning, and he needed a babysitter. Miles agreed with no questions asked.

Everyone he loves is so lucky. I already see how much his family asks of him, and he happily helps whenever he can. No complaints.

There are toys on the floor in the living room. Baby dolls, stuffed animals, and what looks to be plastic food. It melts my heart to picture him sitting there, goofing around with them. Serving plastic fruit to two giggling toddlers.

"You love them a lot," I say with a hint of awe in my voice.

"I do, they're a blast." He smiles as he begins to pick things up. "You know, if I didn't enjoy my job so much, I think I'd probably want to be a teacher."

I could see him doing that, leading a room. With his knack for taking care of people, and how fun he is to be around. A classroom full of kids would absolutely adore him.

"Do you want kids of your own?" I'm not sure why I blurt out the question, but I regret it instantly. This isn't the most ideal time for this conversation, and the look that flashes on his face tells me he agrees. "Oh, you don't have to answer that."

He takes a deep breath, and looks down at his shoes.

"No, it's okay. It's just hard to think about sometimes. I definitely did. I mean, I still do. Kara didn't." He grimaces, as if saying her name is still hard in itself, let alone remembering that they wanted such different lives. "I told myself that was fine, and I'd just have extra love for my niece and nephew but... I'm running out of time now anyway, it doesn't matter. I'm going to spoil those two forever." He's careful with his words, not putting any pressure on the possibility that he could still be a dad someday.

I put a hand on his shoulder, an attempt to be comforting.

"For what it's worth, I know you think you're ancient or something—" he cracks a smile— "but it seems to me like you have plenty of time."

"I guess I'll find out, right?"

Our eye contact feels intense.

"Right."

"What about you?" he asks softly. "Do you want kids someday?"

I nod my head. "I do, but I don't know. It kind of felt like I was going to run out of time, too."

He gives me a skeptical look.

"What are you, twenty?" he jokes.

"Basically," I reply. Although it's always felt like the opposite. Like I'm years and years ahead of where I'm comfortable with. "Not that I'm getting old or anything, but even with all the time in the world it was hard to imagine I'd ever find the right person. It's easy to decide to do it, but since my parents are so..." I trail off, but he nods in understanding. "I wasn't going to take that decision lightly."

"It *was* hard to imagine? Easier now?" he asks with a smirk.

My cheeks heat when I realize what I did, speaking in past tense. "I didn't—"

"Relax," he says, pressing a kiss to my temple. "I'm just teasing."

I say nothing else, not wanting that conversation to get deeper. Not yet. I'm not even sure what tomorrow will bring when it comes to the two of us. I just want to enjoy what we have while we have it, without any pressure.

I join him in picking up the mess, keeping my eyes down.

It's his turn to be comforting and he stops my reach with a hand over mine. His thumb brushes against my skin.

"I think that's great. Plenty of people are parents that shouldn't be." He could say that again.

We're quiet until everything is back in its place, and we head for the kitchen. Miles grabs a bottle of wine, one of my favorites, and then two glasses from a cupboard. I never even told him, it's either a coincidence, or he noticed that little thing about me too.

"What really happened there? If you don't mind me asking. I never understood why you were so young and had nowhere to go."

I exhale sharply, and take a seat on one of his barstools in an attempt to get as comfortable as I can while telling a story that makes me feel the opposite.

"They never wanted to be parents. My mom didn't find out she was pregnant until it was too late. I guess her period was never regular so she had no reason to think anything was off. Didn't get sick, didn't get much of a bump until the end. She went to her doctor one day for something unrelated, and then she left feeling like that was the worst day of her life." I clear my throat, refusing to get emotional over a reality I've faced plenty of times. "I never understood why they didn't just put me up for adoption, but they never changed their minds on me. I was an inconvenience. I was left home alone all the time, way younger than I should've been. When I started staying with my friend most days, they were pushing pretty hard to make it permanent."

I don't look up to meet his gaze, which is surely horrified.

"How did they get away with that?"

"I let them." I shrug. "Linda, Jade's mom, let me. She wanted to help, and she knew getting them in trouble wouldn't help anything. I didn't want revenge. I was just happy to be somewhere I wasn't alone." I smile at that, hoping it covers up how deep that pain still goes. I'll always be insecure about my place in other's lives. There's nothing worse I could be than an inconvenience.

"You deserved so much better." He shakes his head. "I don't know how the hell you kept it together."

"You think *that* was keeping it together?" I try to make it sound like a joke, but he sees it for what it is. "It wasn't easy, that's for sure.

I was always so jealous of my friends with their tight-knit families. I was definitely jealous of yours."

"I wouldn't call my family tight-knit."

I raise my brows at him. "Even after you moved out, you got together for dinner once a week. That's more than I could've imagined from mine."

He pulls me by my hand, out of my seat so that our bodies are pressed together.

"Speaking of more than you could've imagined."

His arms wrap around me, pulling me even tighter into him as his lips travel down to meet mine.

The best kind of hug.

"You've got family now," he whispers. "You have people that would do anything for you."

"I know," I whisper.

And I mean it, too.

With the fork in my hand, I stab a syrup covered bite on my plate and shove it in my mouth.

"I really do hate waffles," I say around a mouthful.

He chuckles and shakes his head.

"You sure do look like you're enjoying these for some reason."

I take another bite, giving myself time to come up with a snarky response. He's so good at everything he does, I honestly doubted him when he said he made the world's best. Now I'm questioning what other foods I could end up liking if he's the one that makes them.

The doorbell rings before I come up with anything. It takes a minute for the realization of what that means to hit me, but then I freeze. We both do. I hear muffled voices on the other side, none that I think I recognize right away.

I wait for Miles to move, to go answer it, but he doesn't. He looks even more panicked than I'm feeling.

"Miles?" I whisper.

"Miles?" A voice echoes mine from outside.

"It's Justin." His wide eyes lock onto mine.

Oh, fuck.

I thought we'd have more time. I thought we had a *lot* more time before we had to face *him.*

"What do you want to do?" he asks in a loud whisper.

I could kiss him for making it my choice.

Except I don't *know* what I want to do. I just know that every possible alarm is going off in my head, and I think it's too much right now. There's got to be a better time for this, a time when I'm better prepared.

At least I hope.

"Miles," I hear Justin's voice yell from the other side of the door again. It's familiar, but I also notice how much it's changed over the years. "You're lucky I gave that key back. My girl has to pee!"

I jerk my head towards the bedroom and hope the look on my face says what it needs to. That I'm sorry I can't do this right now. He says nothing else when I walk away, and I can't read his expression.

I lean against his bedroom closet, sliding my back down until I hit the carpeted floor.

I'm not happy with myself. I feel so guilty. This step isn't negotiable, but I don't know when I'll have the courage to face this.

This time with him has been blissful, it's been easy to ignore what the future holds. What if I'm just setting myself up to be hurt even worse down the road? What if I realize that I don't have the courage to face his family, despite the feelings that have me clinging to him and needing more? Or maybe I'll find that courage one day, but they'll never get over it. I can't picture them ever being okay with me in his life. The way that would hurt *him* is something I don't think I can even entertain the thought of.

"Jaz, no!" a woman yells. I assume it must be Isabelle. The thought of her still dredges up memories I'd rather forget. "Let go." A pause. "No, put it down. You have to pee, remember? Let's put it down and go use the bathroom."

I close my eyes and try to tune out their chaos.

It doesn't work.

She's apologizing to Miles for bringing her children into the house. He's reassuring her that it's always good to see them. After what's definitely more than a couple minutes, Justin asks him about some things they left behind the other day when they were over.

"Yeah, I have them in my room," Miles pauses, seeming to catch himself. "I think. It's kind of a mess. Wait here."

When he pushes the door open the rest of the way, his eyes immediately find me.

"*I'm sorry,*" he mouths.

I should be the one apologizing.

He grabs what looks like a diaper bag that's sitting right by his door, and closes it behind him when he walks out. I appreciate how it muffles the voices.

Eventually they fade out. I've probably been sitting on the floor for twenty minutes when Miles barges into the room.

"I am so sorry. I didn't think they'd stick around that long, especially not with Isabelle and—"

"It's not your fault."

He takes a step towards me, lifting his arm out like he's going to help me up, but I abruptly stand on my own and step to the side.

I had a chance to take a weight off of his shoulders. I had a chance to keep him from having to hide this from his brother, and I didn't take it. It terrified me.

It's not fair.

"I think maybe I should go home."

His expression falls completely, and I immediately want to pick it up again.

"Please don't. Let's just finish breakfast and have the day we planned. I want to spend it with you."

"I want that too, but—" My voice cracks, and the second he hears it, he grabs my hand.

"I see you trying to shut down on me. Do you think you're the only one that's scared, Autumn? We're in this *together*. He just surprised us, it's okay that we weren't ready." His dark gaze latches onto mine. "We have time."

"What if I can't ever face them?" I whisper.

His head shakes. "I'm willing to bet that you will. I want to prove to you that you're capable of more than you, or anyone else gives you credit for. Even if it takes months, I want to be right here while we work on it. I'm not going anywhere."

I start to disagree but he stops me with a gentle hand to my cheek.

"You are worth it. You can't change my mind. Whatever this ends up looking like for us, it's worth it. As long as the day comes where I'll get to hold your hand and show you off, regardless of who's around or what they think, I'm okay with however long it takes."

When it hits me how hard I'm crying, and my body shakes with the force of it, his arms wrap around me. I feel grounded by the kisses he places on my head and the calming lines he strokes down my back.

I want that more than words can convey.

"I love you."

For once in my life, I don't doubt those words being said to me. They don't even surprise me. I can feel it.

I lift my head to stare into my favorite brown eyes.

"I think I've loved you since I was nineteen, I just wouldn't let myself admit it."

His mouth curves into a bright, beautifully amused smile.

"I read your book, you admitted it plenty."

I feel my face go red as the embarrassment creeps in, but then he's there kissing it away.

36

AUTUMN

"I want a burger," Reya whines.

"We literally just ate."

"But we didn't eat burgers."

Everyone at Miles' table is looking at her like she's crazy, and not just because she's laying on the floor while she pets Freddy.

I don't think I've ever eaten so much in one sitting, I can't think of anything else. Not even my favorite dark chocolate brownies, which she brought us as a *Congrats for finally banging!* gift.

She wrote that on them with pink icing.

Wyatt and his girlfriend joined us for dinner as well, and I think Miles might have felt a little embarrassed by said pink icing. Maybe by Reya in general, it's no secret that she really doesn't know when to stop talking sometimes.

Everyone else at the table, including the two of them, were laughing so hard we felt like kids. Our new friends fit right in.

"I assumed you two were already going strong," Wyatt had said after things calmed down. "You just seem so natural together."

That pleased me to hear. Even Vic and Reya smiled their cutest smiles at his words, because they've seen it, too.

"How are you not full?" Vic asks her.

She shrugs, and sits up to take a sip of her wine. She's using her chair as a table, and it's rather amusing to watch.

"I don't think I ate as much."

I blurt out a laugh. "Yeah right! You went in for thirds and still finished before the rest of us."

"Who knew fake cheese could taste so good," she mumbled.

I did. I knew that.

Standing from the table, Wyatt places his hand on Lacey's.

"I think that's our cue to leave. If I even look at any more food right now, I'll burst."

The rest of us agree.

We exchange hugs with him, and Lacey gives polite handshakes. The best Reya does from her position is slap both of their hands in an upside-down high five.

"Let's make a habit out of this. It's good to see you, man."

"Yeah, we will. You guys have a good night."

It's quiet in the few moments after the front door closes behind them.

"Well you're in no shape to drive, so good luck getting that burger," Vic tells Reya as she stands from the table. She places a loving pat on her head as she passes.

"Oh, come on! You guys aren't being any fun right now."

"I don't think any of us should be driving," I tell her, having just topped off my own glass for the second time.

She eagerly points at Miles. "He can!"

I look to him, apologizing without words. I'm not going to—

"Yeah, sure. I can drive right now."

What. The. Hell.

"Really?" I ask.

"Yeah, why not?"

I look between the two of them.

"More importantly, why?"

"For the sake of spontaneity," Reya says and finally gets up from the floor. "Let's go, buddy!"

I look to Vic, grateful to see she's just as confused as I am. I'm starting to think Miles might be *too* perfect if such a thing is possible.

"If you change your mind, she'll get over it in about ten minutes and be onto the next thing," Vic tells him.

He laughs. "It's not a big deal, there's a drive-through around the corner. Are you guys coming?"

I quickly gulp down some of the wine I just poured.

"Well, of course I'm coming." I narrow my eyes. "But you're way too nice, you know that?"

"Might have been told before."

The four of us pile into his car, and I still can't believe we're doing this. Everyone but Reya seems to still be recovering from our full stomachs.

Miles turns on the radio, and doesn't realize what a bad idea that was. Not until the three women in his car are screaming Taylor Swift lyrics at the top of their lungs as if they're going through the hardest time in their life. One glance at his amused smile has butterflies fluttering through me.

I want to get used to nights like this.

The drive-through is a nightmare, to the point where it blocks most of the entrance to the parking lot.

"I'm not sitting in that," I groan at the same time Vic says, "Please, no."

"Going inside it is," he says.

Reya grabs my hand and holds on for dear life once we're out of the car.

"Thanks for letting your boyfriend take me to get a burger."

I pat her shoulder. "He's not my b— Wait, are you?" I ask, turning to him. I might be drunk, but I do realize what a terrible way that is to ask someone.

Still, I don't take it back. He's so entertained by us, he's already got the biggest smile on his face.

"Do you want me to be your boyfriend?"

I nod my head multiple times. Reya is also nodding next to me, quite the supporter.

He slides his hand back to that perfect place at the back of my head, pulling me out of my friend's hold. It's the one he uses to tilt my face up to look at him.

"I think that sounds pretty great," he says.

Both of my friends squeal. I think Vic claps, but I'm obviously distracted.

I try to stand on my toes, asking him for a kiss without words, but he suddenly goes tense.

That smile I love drops so quickly, I go into panic mode. He lets go of his hold on me, but he doesn't break our eye contact. It feels like he's trying to tell me something without words, but I don't pick up on it. Falling back on my heels, there's a question on the tip of my tongue.

"Are you fucking serious?"

A chill runs down my spine at that voice. All the hairs on my arms stand up.

How is he *here*? Of all places?

"Shit," Reya hisses. "I just wanted a burger."

"What are you doing, Miles?"

He turns to face the owner of the words, and I stumble backwards, closer to my girls. Vic's hand wraps around my arm when I do. It's a shame none of us can drive, because I feel like I need a getaway car.

"You can't even answer me?"

"Calm down."

"I'm not going to. Next? Anything else you want to say to me?"

I can see him shaking his head in my periphery. I dare a glance and he's... horrified. He looks like this is the worst possible thing that could've happened to him today.

I can't stand it. I want to shrink, to disappear.

"This has nothing to do with you," Miles tells his brother calmly.

"Apparently, because if it did then surely my *brother* would have had the fucking balls to mention it."

"I was going to—"

"Sure you fucking were. After making out with my ex-girlfriend outside a fast food joint, your next stop was my place, right?"

"That's not what—"

"I can't believe you. Weeks of pining, of being down about some girl you couldn't tell me about, and *this* is why you couldn't tell me!"

"It's been years! What is your problem?" I surprise myself by yelling. I hate seeing him go off on Miles, interrupting him and making him feel like he's done something wrong.

Vic remains holding me, and I think it offers me some strength I wouldn't normally have.

"This isn't your conversation."

"Sure it is! You've been complicating things between us without even knowing it. Now that you finally do, *get over it!* You didn't even like me, you cheating asshole!"

Yeah, I am drunk. Sober Autumn will be appalled tomorrow.

A shocked laugh comes from him. He doesn't know how to respond to that, because I'm right. I might sound a little ridiculous, and look like a total mess, but I'm right.

So his attention goes back to Miles. "Maybe I'm mad because you could have told me weeks ago. It seems like of all people in your life you have to confide in, maybe I'd have been a good one." He decides he's done talking, and shoulder checks Miles on his way past.

"Will you three go inside? Or to the car?" Miles asks quietly.

"I'm not hungry anymore," Reya whispers.

I nod slowly, making my feet move to grab his keys. He follows after his brother when I do.

By the time he catches up, we're in the car watching through the windows. The red neon light coming from the building beside them makes the interaction look even more intense.

Mouths move, but we can't hear from here. There's head shaking, and chest poking, and at one point I think Justin might punch his brother.

I am not mentally prepared for that to happen.

"You think this is fucking funny?" Justin shouts loud enough that it reaches us.

Miles is laughing, and I don't get it. I don't see how there's anything to laugh about. When he stops, it appears to de-escalate for a minute, and the two just talk. We just keep watching, quietly and anxiously. There's not a single sound in the car.

Until Reya starts snoring. I can't help laughing when Vic and I share a look. Our girl is going to be disappointed when she wakes up tomorrow and finds out she missed this.

"She's refused to say a single negative word about you!"

The bubble is popped by Miles' voice. I can't help my curiosity, I roll the window down, just an inch.

"How fucking great that you get to take advantage of the new and improved version."

It's the last thing Justin says before walking away, and Miles lets him go this time. He doesn't look at me when he gets back in the car and my chest sinks.

"You two are more than welcome to the guest room," he tells Vic.

We drive home in silence.

I hate every second of this. The look on Justin's face was too familiar, pulling me back to a time where I was convinced I deserved it. I was convinced I deserved every ounce of anger and disrespect he threw my way.

It was easy to believe I've moved past that, but here we are. I feel like I deserve this feeling right now.

"Are you okay?" I ask my boyfriend once we're alone in his room.

I won't forget any part of the night we just had, but especially not that. No matter what happens.

Miles Mason Cress is my *boyfriend*.

"You're asking me?" He laughs. "You're something else," he says, pulling me into him. I reside happily nestled into him when we fall down against the pillows.

"Yes, I'm asking you. That was a lot."

He's smiling, not looking like he was just a part of that argument.

"Are *you* okay?"

I shrug. "I think so. I'm more worried about you."

"We must really love each other," he says.

"We must."

He sits up then, grabbing a water bottle from his nightstand. I fall even more in love when he hands it to me.

"You'll need this more than I do." Only once I've started guzzling it down does he say, "I'm relieved."

I nod slowly. "I was hoping you would be. I mean... when this came out eventually. That was scarier than how I pictured it."

"I didn't want him to find out like that, but what's done is done. He'll get over it."

I set the water down, and Miles pulls me into him again. My back ends up against his chest, and he begins to rub my shoulders with the most incredibly placed pressure. I moan, overwhelmed by his magic hands. I love that I'm in a position to feel him slowly rising against me.

"You are so hot, you know that?" he whispers the words against my ear. "Even hotter when you're telling someone off."

"You enjoyed that?"

"Very much."

I'm going to keep him.

37

MILES

I walk through my mother's front door, knowing how much I'm not going to love this conversation. But it's going to be worth it.

"What were you thinking?" she yells as soon as she sees me. She's not really asking.

Justin stands with his hands down against her counter, his shoulders stiff. I'm searching for the words I need to make them understand. How to make them understand I'm not doing this to them, I'm doing it *for* me.

I know if I ran into anyone else that day, or let my mom set me up, I wouldn't be this happy. I'd be settling without even knowing it, and the thought makes me feel sick. If being married to Kara for years has taught me anything, it's that I never want to feel like that again.

"I need you to tell me exactly what your problem is with Autumn." I say it to my mom, and ignore my brother's presence.

She blinks in surprise. "What?"

"Why do you hate her?"

"I don't *hate* her, Miles. I let the girl work for me. You think I'd do that if I hated her?"

Justin shakes his head in disbelief, still clearly upset he wasn't told about that.

"Yeah, I did think that," I go on. "I can't explain why else you'd be so hell-bent on wanting us to stay away from each other."

"Do I really need to explain?" The look I give her makes her continue. "All those things she lied about with your brother, the way she treated him? I will not believe it's a coincidence that she's lured you in."

I can't even speak for a few moments, while trying to wrap my head around every ounce of bullshit that just came out of her mouth. Even when she gives me her expectant brow raise, I just stare back at her.

Justin is silent.

"Is it finally snapping into place? I want what's best for you, Miles."

I shake my head, over and over.

"No, mom. *No* to everything you just said. She hasn't *lured* me in at all."

She frowns. "That's what you believe right now, honey. Didn't you once believe Kara was the love of your life? We're all blinded by our feelings every now and then. I don't want you to wake up in a few years and realize you've let this girl manipulate you." Her eyes are an intense stare to solidify her matter-of-fact tone.

"No. You can't compare the two of them. I *saw* the red flags with Kara, and I actively chose to ignore them. Autumn is... she's got the best heart. She's a good person, who would rather try to ignore her feelings for me than upset you. That's what was going on when you couldn't get a hold of me. I was missing her, because of *you*. You got to her that night." I realize my voice has gotten louder the more I've gone on so I pause to let out a shaky breath. "I personally don't get it, if I were her I wouldn't care how you felt. Not after the way you've spoken to her. She has no reason to respect you and yet she *does*."

"Or it's an act. Girls are good at that sort of thing."

I'm so close to losing my patience.

I turn to my brother. "I think you're the liar."

"What?"

"Don't play dumb. I overheard enough conversations to know you were in the wrong. What did you do?"

She called him a cheater. I know that much, and it makes my blood boil.

"I—" he stops, seeming unsure.

"Justin."

He glares at me like I'm about to ruin his life.

"What did you overhear?" he asks instead of answering. Except it is an answer.

I didn't hear enough, apparently.

"What did you do?"

He scoffs. "She's already told you, you just want to hear me say it."

"Justin Thomas, if you don't just say it already," my mother snaps.

He's wringing his hands and refusing to make eye contact with her. We're the epitome of patience while he fights his internal battle. It's been such a long time, there should be no reason for him to care anymore. I just want to move forward.

"I told you Autumn and I broke up," he starts. "That time you found Isabelle at our house."

"And?"

"We hadn't. I was doing it behind her back." His words come out rushed.

Mom shakes her head, her hand covering her mouth. I'm too frozen to react. Frozen, and shaking, and absolutely livid.

I could've guessed that's what it was, but hearing it from him? The way he took advantage of and betrayed her, sounding like such simple words coming out of his mouth?

"You piece of shit."

"I was a kid! I'd never do that now."

There's no way of knowing if it's the truth, considering he married the girl he cheated on her with. I'm not a violent person, but I have to clench my fists to keep from hitting him.

"I was so rude to that poor girl." She looks genuinely regretful. "Because of things *you* told me!"

He falls down into a seat at the table, looking exhausted.

"I know."

"Do you? Do you know how horrible I feel for trusting my son to tell me the truth?"

"I was a kid," he says again with less defensiveness.

We're stuck in our heads, processing what this conversation means for all of us. It's good that my mom feels bad, it means that she'll apologize. She'll make up for it. We can *move forward*.

I admit my next words on a nervous breath.

"I'm in love with her."

My mother takes the seat next to him at the table.

"So you've been seeing her this whole time?" She sounds tired.

"That's not exactly true." I go into detail, explaining what the last couple months have looked like. I can't emphasize enough how much it sucked when I was without her. How I've never missed anyone more, and how I never want to miss her again.

My mother's response is to grab me into the tightest hug we've ever shared.

"I'm sorry. I hate that I'm the reason you were unhappy. I just want you to be loved the way I know you deserve."

"I am."

She backs away at that, enough to look up at me.

"You know she loves you?"

"I do," I say confidently.

My mom straightens her posture and looks me right in the eye.

"And you're sure you love her? She's the one for you?"

I don't hesitate to nod. "She is."

You don't feel the way I do for something that isn't meant to work out.

She pulls me in for another hug. "I'm so sorry, honey."

"It's okay, mom. I just want to move forward."

"We can do that."

Autumn

The silence between us is heavy, but there's not a single word I can think of to say to Amelia. Not when I know how she feels about me. I could plead my case but I don't think she'd believe a word of it.

I realize she's taking me in like she's also questioning why she's standing at my front door. I let her. I just keep standing there, hoping whatever she comes up with isn't going to hurt me any worse than she already has.

"I don't know what to say," I admit.

She nods as if in agreement.

"I don't blame you. I'm sure this is a shock, me turning up like this." The smile she offers me seems almost apologetic. "I guess I'll just start. I know I haven't been fair in the way that I viewed you. I'm a mom before I'm anything else and being Justin's mom wasn't easy for a long time. I think you saw a lot of it."

I nod.

"He never talked to me, never looked at me. He was a stranger living in my house. I was so desperate for any crumbs he'd give me, and they were so rare. I missed the boy I read stories to at night, and made waffles for in the morning, but I settled for crumbs." She dabs at her eyes, removing unshed tears.

She's never seemed so vulnerable to me.

"Do you want to come in? It's a little messy..." I trail off, feeling self conscious about the interior design queen seeing my poorly put together place.

She smiles the warmest smile I've ever seen on her. I try not to look as surprised as I feel when she nods and says, "I'd like that."

We sit at my dining room table, and it's weird. Not because of her or our conversation necessarily, but because I never sit at this table. I thought it would be more appropriate in this scenario than plopping down on my couch. It's like I'm seeing my apartment from a whole new perspective.

"I don't think you know what happened that day," she continues. "I was sick. Coughing and sniffling so much that I had to leave work early. I could barely keep my eyes open by the time I walked through the front door, but then I saw them. It was shocking, I had never seen him with anyone but you. My first reaction was that it was wrong, because he would've told me if you'd broken up. And Isabelle looked way too happy with herself. I didn't like her much at first." The admission surprises me enough to laugh.

"Next thing I know, my son who hadn't talked to me in years was confiding in me. I was on top of the world, despite the circumstances. I'm not a perfect person, I was finally getting all I'd wanted in so long. He told me he tried to end things with you, and you were giving him a hard time. Showing up to the house, and refusing to leave him alone."

She reaches over and puts a hand on mine. "All I thought when I saw you from then on was that I had to protect my boy. I had to do what I could to get more of those moments out of him, and it seemed like a good place to start. I can't believe how wrong I was, how cruel I've been to you."

Her eyes are expectant, and I know it might be the part where I'm supposed to tell her she's forgiven, but none of it is sinking in yet.

She adds, "I know it's no excuse, but being a parent is so hard. It's only one of a million mistakes I've made, but I can't stand how much you've been hurt because of this one."

I stop her. "Why now? What changed?"

"Both of my children had an enlightening conversation with me earlier," she explains.

Earlier today? Miles hadn't said anything. And *both* of them? It's definitely odd to picture Justin admitting to what he did wrong.

"I've never seen him like this, you know. He really loves you."

That's a lot.

She knows he loves me, and she doesn't look angry. She looks the least angry I've ever seen her, I think. Hope ignites in my chest.

"Kaitlyn misses you. She mentions you all the time."

I can't help but smile.

"I miss her too. She's messaged me a couple of times to check in."

Amelia pauses for a moment, zoning out and staring at the table. "I would offer you your job back, but from what she tells me it doesn't seem like you need it anymore."

I shrug. "No. I guess I don't, thanks to her. I've been utilizing my extra free time, getting this next book ready to be published."

"Do you have a date yet?"

"Not an exact one. A few months away at most."

"You should keep me updated. I'll get you something to say congratulations."

"That's sweet of you," is all I think to say.

She looks back down at my table, making me feel self conscious, but she lands on a stack of Polaroids. I'd forgotten about them, actually.

"Can I?"

I nod.

The picture on top of the stack is of Miles and I. The one where we both looked at Reya after she snapped a photo of... a moment.

The moment is the next picture she looks at, and she smiles. "That's a good one."

I haven't seen it since that night when I gathered them all, and back then I was trying not to look. I didn't want proof that there was something between us.

I am so happy to see it now.

"It is."

"That's a rare find, someone that can bring that kind of joy out of you. I'm glad you two have that."

I don't stop staring at the photo. "So am I."

She stands from her seat. "I... I really am sorry for everything. I always liked having you around, and that hasn't changed. You've grown into a wonderful woman."

I nod. "I know how much you love them. I always knew you were doing what you thought was right by them, even if I didn't understand it." Even if it was torture.

She nods back to me, a sheen in her eyes that proves just how sorry she feels. I believe her. I believe her more in this moment than I ever have.

"If there's anything I can do for you, Autumn, please let me know. I understand if you need some time after how I've behaved, but I'll be here." She leaves with that, giving a simple nod as a goodbye.

It feels too good to be true, like I'm not allowed to accept it. I want to, though. If she's being honest, then nothing is left to stop me from having what I want anymore.

Even if she's not, there isn't a single part of me that thinks Miles is something I want rather than something I need.

38

MILES

Late December is the best time of the year. The days are always filled with family. We have dinner together more often, we bake cookies, we get to shop for gifts. Most importantly, I get to watch my niece and nephew make core memories that'll leave them with this same feeling as an adult.

Even when Kara was around, complaining and trying to avoid it all, it couldn't take away from it. Nothing could ever ruin the bubble of joy surrounding us.

Not even last year when I confessed that Kara wasn't living with me anymore. There were a few uncomfortable minutes, and I let them think whatever they needed to. My mom abruptly stood and walked into the kitchen, and she came back with a bottle of sparkling wine. We toasted to having an extra piece of pie to fight over after Christmas dinner.

This year is different. Isabelle took their kids to her parents house a couple hours away. They've been gone for two days, and Justin is losing it. He's used to having them here with us, and I suppose that's also why he couldn't argue about it. We've always had them for the holidays.

I see how much it's devastating him, and we feel it half as bad. The days leading up to it haven't been the same without them. The house is too quiet, even with Christmas music playing around the clock.

Easing the pain of it slightly, is Autumn. She's still working up the courage to be a part of the festivities with my family, but I know it'll happen. I'm happy to let her take her time. My mom bought her a present and stuck it under the tree, just in case tomorrow's the day.

I can tell my mother is working on her overstepping with Justin. She stayed quiet about it for a grand total of twenty minutes today before she couldn't take it anymore. It wasn't my conversation to be in, and I hurriedly finished my plate and left them to talk it out. I care about my brother, but there are some things a grown man doesn't feel comfortable doing in front of anyone but his mother.

Like crying. I knew with one glance that he was going to. Neither of them protested when I headed home earlier than normal for a Christmas Eve.

I'm sitting in my car, staring out at the shimmering white of my front yard. There hasn't been any snow for the last few days, but the way everything is currently frozen over gives the illusion of it. I think I even prefer it, despite the fact that I have to try extra hard to keep myself from slipping and falling onto my ass. The camera on my doorbell had caught a couple too many times of me doing exactly that.

A shadow in the corner of my eye snaps me out of my zoning out, and I look over to see the silhouette of a person sitting in the swing on my front porch. I have a motion sensor light, so they had been there since before I pulled up. I'm already sure I know who it is as I hurriedly shut my car off and jump out of it, not thinking for a second about anything but her.

My eagerness bites me in the ass, literally, as I immediately slip on the slick driveaway. The angle at which my ankle twists sends a shooting pain up my entire leg.

Autumn

"Miles!" I yell as I rush towards him.

It only took me two seconds to get myself in check and not laugh, especially when I saw the direction his foot went. I'm fairly positive feet aren't supposed to do that.

"Careful, it's slippery," he hisses through gritted teeth and I noticeably slow my steps.

"Are you okay?" I ask the second I get down to his level on the ground. I can see that he probably wants to say no, the way he's harshly breathing through the pain. He still looks excited to see me through it all, and I can't help the butterflies that erupt.

"What are you doing here?"

I laugh in a way that hopefully tells him he's unbelievable before reaching for his hand.

"We should probably talk inside, where it's less dangerous."

He grins at that, despite the pain I know he's in.

"I'm going to need a second, sweetheart."

My mind flashes back to concern.

"That was a hard fall. Do you think you broke something?"

He nods. "I'd be surprised if that's not what just happened. I guess we'll know when I try to walk."

But fuck, I really don't want him to. I wish I was capable of carrying him so I didn't have to see him in even more pain.

"Take your time. I'm not going anywhere," I tell him with a patient smile.

"A—" he starts to say, but I interrupt him.

"I wish I had gone with you tonight."

"It's okay. I'm not rushing you to do anything you're not comfortable with."

I just look at him, so grateful. Of course I'm not going to be comfortable, how does one face their ex in this situation, and his mother at the same time? It's a lot.

But it doesn't make me anxious enough that I'm not going push through for the man I love. I need to rip the bandage off, and start this new chapter.

I nod. "I know, but I sat at home regretting it."

"Does that mean I can bring you over there tomorrow?"

"You want me to crash your Christmas?" I ask with a smile.

"Yes," he says without hesitation. "What would you normally be doing?"

I shrug. "Reya's dad is a great cook. She brings me leftovers."

"So you usually spend it alone?" He sounds devastated at that.

"No, she always brings them to me that day. Sometimes we'll watch a movie and make hot chocolate. Vic shows up when she can, but she has a lot of family to visit."

Honestly, some years are worse than others, but my girls are the best. I couldn't ask for a better family.

"How many years have you done that?"

"The last three."

"I'm glad you have them."

I wrap my arms around his shoulders and squeeze. The way I pull him into me somehow manages to move his ankle where it rests and I hear him let out a hiss.

"Shit, I'm sorry. I'm so dumb," I say with my hands on my cheeks. "It's getting too cold out here, can I help you get up?"

He grabs my wrist before I can stand. "You're not dumb."

My response is a quick nod before I carefully stand and reach out to help him up.

We get him to his feet with a groan, and I feel ridiculously short next to him as I pray that neither of us slips like this. I don't have the strength to stop him from going down again and vice versa with his injury. I'm not sure how he's going to do this without putting any pressure on the left side, but I tuck myself under his shoulder and hope it's enough to get him to the front door.

"You don't think it's a problem if I go with you tomorrow? I don't want to get in the way of your family stuff." He turns his head towards me with a questioning look.

"Not at all. If anyone makes you feel like you're in the way, they're going to get their ass kicked."

We both know he means Justin.

"Big words for a guy that just fell on his ass while stepping out of his car." We reach the front door and he pauses, smiling at me. I love that smile.

I snatch his keys before he can fumble with them to get the front door unlocked.

"My hands aren't broken, sweetheart."

"It's too cold for you to take your sweet time right now," I tease.

He puts his hands up in surrender because I have a point.

"I'll have to get a copy made for you," he says, pointing.

The fact that he wants to makes me blush. "I'd like that."

I waste no time when we get inside, carefully helping Miles to the couch. I place one of his red throw pillows on the coffee table in front of where he sits, and very gently lift his leg and set his foot on top. I see him wince, and then try to play it off with a smile.

"I'll get you some ice."

"Ice is what caused this in the first place," he grumbles.

I just laugh.

I make my way to the kitchen, and can feel his eyes on me as I comfortably move around it. I fill a gallon bag with ice cubes, and watch the apprehension in his eyes when I approach again. He doesn't say a word as I gently place it on his swollen part of his ankle. Gentle or not, I watch his eyes squeeze shut for a second and frown.

"You should go to urgent care," I say, taking a seat beside him on the couch.

He leans into me, and buries his face in my hair.

"You smell so good," I hum into his shoulder. I've been wanting to tell him that for months.

"I was just thinking the same thing."

"That you smell good? What is it? I'll buy some for myself." I smile up at him, and it's simply because I amuse myself.

He brings his face to my neck and sniffs loudly enough to make a giggle fly past my lips. The look on his face tells me that's quite the success for him.

I win my fight to get him to the hospital, and I'm sure he feels ridiculous having to let me help him walk. It's not the dynamic our heights are meant for, but I'm taking my job seriously. We get through the parking lot and up to the front desk with almost no incidents. *Almost* because he didn't see the curb until his injured foot was bumping into it. He's not a crybaby or anything, but it still upsets me to know he's in pain.

When the sweet girl at the front desk says he'll have to fill out some paperwork because he's never been here before, I blink at him in surprise.

"What?"

"You've lived here your whole life and have never been here before?"

He shrugs. "None of the care I needed has been urgent."

We sit and I watch as he goes down the lines, filling in his information. I like his handwriting. It's messy, but less boyish than I would've imagined. He doesn't seem to care that I'm being nosy. In fact, when he looks up and notices me staring, he places a hand on my thigh. He's so warm despite this chilly room with ceilings that are too tall and walls that are too white. He makes any uncomfortable place a comfortable one.

When he flips to the back of the page to continue with his information, he doesn't start writing. Instead he covers the print with his hand, blocking the questions from my view. I scrunch my brows curiously. I might be feeling the slightest bit insulted by his sudden change.

I'm about to ask what the problem is when he turns to me.

"Autumn?"

"What's wrong?" That's all I assume, just that something's wrong. His expression gives nothing away.

"I'm just wondering," he tells me. He pauses to search my eyes, going back and forth between them. "If you wouldn't mind being my emergency contact?"

I freeze. I blink.

I feel tears gathering as I recall an afternoon we were sitting in his mom's kitchen, years ago. One where a deep, depressing realization that I had no one hit me like a ton of bricks. It genuinely felt like I was being buried in them, when he pulled me out. When a simple sentence fought through my panic and I was okay.

"You remember that?"

"Of course I remember that."

I shake my head once in disbelief. "You don't have to..." I clear my throat because the emotion in my words is too much. The way my voice cracks is embarrassing. "Wouldn't you rather put Amelia?"

"I think I'd rather put you." He says it with a small smile, like this is casual. Not life altering.

Okay, calm down.

All I manage to do is nod, not trusting my voice again. His hand travels to mine and our fingers lace together.

It's thankfully not a long wait before they're calling him back. I'm not sure at first if I should jump up to follow him or stay put, until I realize no one has given him crutches. I grab his arm, grateful for the excuse.

—ell—

I wake up to Miles' alarm. My first emotion is anger, my second is actually just more anger, and my third is concern. I doubt the man who is currently groaning next to me is up for walking around the block right now, even with the fancy boot on.

His ankle is, in fact, fractured. No surprise there.

"Well, shit," I mumble to myself.

"What?" The word is just a groan too. That kicks my brain into action, and I force myself to get up. I get as far as sitting up against the headboard, my body still needing time to wake up.

"I'm not a morning person, Miles."

"I am aware."

"I have to walk Freddy." The fake sob that comes out of me sounds very real in my exhausted state.

"You don't have to walk him." His tone doesn't sound so sure about that.

I want to roll my eyes at him, but only manage to squint thanks to the early morning sunlight.

"You're not doing it. He'd be dragging you down the street after a few seconds of impatience. How sad would that be?"

I climb out of the bed, although my entire body aches with the need to lay back down and wrap my arms around Miles until we fall asleep again. It wouldn't take me long.

"Alright then. I'll be back."

"Really?" he asks like he didn't believe I was going to. Understandably. "You're amazing."

I lean over the side of the bed and kiss him on the cheek.

"I'll walk fast, and be back before you know it."

When I'm bundled up in his warm clothes and feeling only slightly prepared, I look back at him. A feeling of familiarity washes over me— reminds me of that first perfect morning we spent together. It's obvious this isn't the time to jump on him and hug him until I can't breathe, but the urge to do so is intense.

"Don't forget the bags."

"Bags?"

"Poop bags."

This is why I have a cat.

"Right."

39

AUTUMN

It's colder than usual this morning, and I take a second to simply feel sorry for myself as I watch my breath cloud in front of my face. Freddy is the epitome of patience, gazing up at me with big brown eyes. If I had to be stuck with walking a dog, I'm glad it's this one.

At least that's what I'm thinking until two minutes later when I have to pick up warm shit off the cold sidewalk. It's literally steaming.

Litter boxes are so much easier to deal with.

"Good morning!"

I glance up to see Wyatt, looking significantly less miserable than I feel. He's sitting out on his porch, with a mug in his hand.

"Merry Christmas!" I call back, trying to sound like I'm not in pain.

"You guys doing anything fun today?"

I don't know if fun is the word, the reminder fills me with nervous energy. In a few hours I'll be sitting at a table with two people that genuinely terrify me. Amelia, slightly less so, now that she was able to explain her end of things. As for Justin, he's unpredictable. It still sucks to think of him, and the way he so carelessly hurt me.

As if I wasn't alone enough, he had to make sure his mom shut me out, too. He was such an asshole.

Miles said he calmed down since the night he saw us, but I'll have to see it for myself before *I* can calm down.

"Dinner with his family. What about you?"

"Two dinners with two families." He nods towards his front door. "Lacey and I have been meaning to get together with you two again. We were thinking about going for a walk around the neighborhood tonight, to check out all of the lights. You should come!"

If that's not the most adorable thing I've ever heard.

"Sounds lovely, but Miles isn't going to be doing much walking for a bit."

I tell him about the slip, and the boot, and he looks genuinely devastated to hear it.

"Is he doing alright?"

"I'd say so, considering he's the one still passed out in a warm bed." I lift the leash.

Wyatt laughs. "Maybe we can make it a drive then. He's got my number."

"Sounds like a good—" I'm interrupted by Freddy's second poop. Right on the edge of Wyatt's perfectly manicured lawn. "I'm so sorry."

There are few things in life more humiliating than knowing someone is watching you pick up shit. I try not to gag, to look like I do this all the time, but laughter fills my ears again. Full, hearty laughter that makes me wonder if he's ever had a dog before.

"Don't sweat it. It's good for the grass."

Once I've got the second bag tied, and my disgust under control, I wave at him.

"Well, I hope you two have a great day!"

"You too, Autumn. Hope to see you guys later!"

Miles is asleep when we get back, to no surprise. He looks so comfortable, so at peace, despite his injury. I waste no time crawling in next to him, and wrapping my arms around his torso. A pleased sound comes from him as he pulls me in tighter.

"Merry Christmas, sweetheart," he breathes the words into my ear.

There's not a doubt in my mind that we are exactly where we're supposed to be right now. There's no way this day could go that would change that.

I look up at the house I've seen so many times before, and it's never felt so daunting.

Scuffling comes from behind Miles and I while he patiently gives me the time I need.

"Hey," he says.

"Hey," Justin replies.

For some reason, with that, Miles walks inside without me. He gives a quick nod in his brother's direction, and I know I'm not meant to follow. We've always needed to talk. To have some conversation that helps us move from where we used to be to now.

It's weird, being alone with him. The air between us is filled with feelings from the past and the present, and they're all so complex.

"I'm sorry," Justin starts. "I don't have any excuses, I just wasn't a good guy."

I take the words in, I process them. I try to see through all of those complex feelings to just right now, this moment.

None of it matters anymore. Maybe it did take this small apology for me to finally realize it, but it's the truth. The only thing that really matters is where we are now, and how we're going to move forward. It's a beautiful conclusion to come to.

Still not the best with words, he ends it there. Justin gives me a small smile, and heads up to the front door. I think for a moment that he's just going to leave me to walk in there alone, but then he pauses with the door open.

I take advantage of the small act of kindness, and walk through it.

Everything is warm hugs, and greetings filled with love. You couldn't tell that this family had just seen each other the night prior, they are still just as happy to be together now.

Amelia gives me a kind smile as she leans in for a side hug. "I'm so glad you're here."

"Me too," I agree, and I squeeze her back. I'm still cautious, but I am glad. I'm relieved. I'm ready.

Miles hugs his mother, and they squeeze each other until I think one of them is going to get hurt. Thankfully, his ankle isn't bothering him much at all today.

He comes back to me, and kisses my cheek. I can't help the smile that spreads across my face. It's so good to be loved by him.

Justin looks back and forth between us with an odd expression. Miles takes a step forward like he's about to say something, but Justin interrupts him.

"I am fine with this," he says, pointing between us, "but that doesn't mean it's not gonna be weird for a minute."

I speak before Miles can.

"That's fair."

I think it would be weird if things *weren't* weird.

I can't help but notice just how *weird* it must feel for him to be here alone. Without Isabelle, without his kids. I find myself hoping his days of being a cheating scumbag are over so he can find the right person. As much as he wronged me, my romantic heart won't think any other way.

Amelia runs back to her kitchen, finishing up the extravagant dinner she's made for us. I'm distracted by that for a moment when Justin steps before me.

He surprises me by holding his arms out expectantly. I do it, I hug him, and it's not even remotely painful.

He leans in to whisper in my ear, still somehow keeping a distance given our position. "It makes sense that you end up with the better one of us."

The words take me aback. I always thought he disliked me, hated me even, for my response to everything back then. When someone's actions make you feel a certain way, you believe them, but... we *were* just kids. He was just a kid when he cheated on me.

When Miles moves forward to take my place, I step back with a smile up at him. He looks like an absolute dream as always in his green button up.

"Merry Christmas, little brother." Instead of the hug that's being offered, he places his hands on his brother's shoulders and quickly lifts a knee that smashes into Justin's crotch. Even I cringe upon impact.

Justin falls forward with a couple of coughs, holding the injured area with a grip that almost looks even more painful. Miles has a grin on his face, as he leans down to rustle Justin's blonde hair.

"I think you know what that's for."

He can't speak, still very clearly affected if his bright red face is any indication, but he nods. Miles tosses a wink over his shoulder, and I can't help the laugh that bursts out of me. I can't say I've ever had a man defend my honor before, but it feels fucking incredible.

I do wonder how much better it would have felt if I had dealt the blow.

Amelia sighs as she steps up to the scene, but doesn't look surprised or even upset.

"I'll get you an ice pack, dear. You two in the dining room, I'm about to set dinner out." She waves us over there as if anyone's in a hurry, but I know we're not.

I know that I've got all the time in the world to walk over to that table, to sit down next to the man I love, and to adjust to this new chapter with his family.

40

MILES

TEN YEARS AGO

I'm not surprised that Justin gave none of us a warning that his new girlfriend was going to be joining us for dinner. I'm not even the one cooking the food and I'm annoyed. I'm sure mom is feeling it even more. Why do teenagers have to be such little shits?

Of course I love my brother, but ever since he started high school he's gotten on my last nerve. He's moody and inconsiderate on a good day. Makes me really wonder what kind of girl could stand being around him long enough to date him.

She's quiet so far, doesn't seem super thrilled to be here. The two of them talk in hushed whispers. From what I gather just by looking at them, it's not a fun conversation. I know fifteen-year-olds are good at that, making a problem where there isn't one, but this would be a little soon for them to be arguing. He hasn't told us how long they've been dating, and we only found out she existed a couple weeks ago. I doubt it's been much longer than that.

"So you go to school together?" I ask, trying to make conversation. The second the words are out, her eyes widen like a deer caught in the headlights. The girl looks terrified. I didn't think I was that intimidating.

Justin speaks before she can.

"Obviously. How else would I have met her?"

I ignore his bad attitude for now, I can always give him shit later.

"Classes together?"

"Just English."

"I thought you hated that class."

"I do. The teacher is a bitch."

"When did you two start going out?"

"Last month."

"Who asked who?"

"I did."

"Are you gonna let her talk at all?"

"She's shy, okay? Stop freaking her out."

But the deer in the headlights speaks up.

"No, it's okay. I'm not freaked out."

I don't know how it's possible but saying the words has her appearing even more frazzled. I don't think shy is the right word for her.

"How did he ask you out?"

She plays with the sleeves on her noticeably frayed jacket, and I have so many more questions.

"Um," she gulps, clearly thinking hard about her answer. Shouldn't that be an easy one? "He asked me at lunch."

"That's boring," I say, giving him a disappointed look.

"Whatever. Is dinner almost done?"

"Does it look like I have eyes on the kitchen?"

He rolls his eyes, and I roll mine right back. Fucking teenagers. *Speaking of fucking...* "You guys aren't having sex yet, are you?"

Her face turns the brightest shade of red a person could be, it's enough to make me feel slightly bad for asking the question so bluntly. Until I look back at my brother to see him roll his eyes yet again.

"Why would I tell you that?"

"You tell me everything." Or at least he used to. Another thing that's changed recently and I'm hoping it's only a phase. I liked being the big brother he could ask for anything. "So?"

"No, jackass. Shut up."

"Let me know when you're ready for that conversation. I'll save you from listening to mom's version. It's not great." I wish I had another option at the time.

"I don't need that conversation from either of you."

I reach across the table and mess up his overly styled hair faster than he can duck away. "Not an option, buddy."

"You're such a dick."

"Watch that mouth, Justin Thomas. I hope you don't always speak like that in front of your girlfriend." Mom is carrying a big pot of pasta, using oven mitts to carefully set it on the kitchen table between us.

"I don't," he says defensively. "Do I, Autumn?"

Right. Autumn. That's her name.

Instead of agreeing with him, she shrugs her shoulders. Her face grows red all over again knowing our eyes are on her. I start digging into the food, serving myself with a big spoon and practically drooling over the creamy alfredo sauce that mom makes from scratch. I don't always love her cooking, but I'll definitely miss this one when I move out someday.

My mom swats at my arm. "Don't be rude, let our guest grab her food first."

Autumn shakes her head, and I swear she's suddenly about to burst into tears.

"I can't," she clears her throat. "I'm lactose intolerant." The words come out so quiet I hope my mom can hear her so she doesn't have to repeat herself. She sounds so sad. I don't think she should feel embarrassed, but I can feel it radiating off of her in a way that's almost contagious.

That fucking sucks.

"Oh, I forgot. I'm sorry babe." Justin doesn't look very sorry when he proceeds to serve himself, not even glancing in her direction.

It's my mother's turn to look horrified.

"Oh, no! That won't do, let me see what else I have. You have to have—"

Autumn shakes her head again. "No, it's totally fine. I'm not really hungry, I can get something later."

My mother isn't having that. "You came over here to eat, let me figure something out." She starts to stand, and Justin stops her.

"She said it's fine. Why are you getting up?"

I've never seen her glare such daggers into him, or anyone before. I'm genuinely scared for a moment, despite the fact that it's not directed at me. He deserves it, though.

That girlfriend of his should run away now.

Said girlfriend stands abruptly. The energy in the room is enough to make everyone uncomfortable, of course it manages to make her look *even* more distressed somehow.

We lock eyes for a total of one second, not long enough for her to see my attempt at an apologetic smile.

"I'm going to go, actually. Eat. I'm going to go eat. At home. Thanks." She says the last words with a tight smile in my mom's direction before heading for the door. I feel like I should say something, do something to let her know she doesn't have to leave. We've all been in awkward situations like this before, it's not a big deal to make something work out. Mom clearly thinks so. She tries to call her name and stop her, even takes a few steps in her direction, but it's not enough. The girl is fast.

"You should have just listened to her," Justin says.

"I'm so confused."

"You didn't need to make a big deal out of it."

"I wasn't just going to let her sit there while we stuffed our faces! It's rude! I can't believe you not only brought her here unannounced, but on alfredo night! How do you forget something like that, Justin?"

"We only hang out for like an hour every day at school. How am I supposed to remember this stuff?"

She looks torn between sitting down to eat and storming away. I don't blame her, I want to storm away from Justin too.

But this pasta is fucking delicious.

"It would've been fine. Next time just don't bother with all of your host shit."

I want to hit him so hard that the bite he just took flies out of his mouth. Who is this guy and what did he do with my brother?

"I hope there's not a next time, Justin. That girl should dump your ass if she knows what's good for her." *Hell yeah, mom.* "Go to your room, now. You're grounded for speaking to me like that."

He knows better than to say anything else, just scoops one more forkful of his dinner into his mouth and leaves the table.

I do the one thing I can think of and stand up to hug her.

She sighs when I do.

"I thought I raised you both better than that."

"You did, mom. He's just being..." I try to think of the nicest possible word to describe that little asshole. "Dumb."

She pats my back and lets me go. "Let's not let it ruin dinner. Eat up."

I go after Justin when we're finished eating and cleaning up. The kid has a good life, a family that loves him, and now a girlfriend that tolerates his idiocy. It's hard to imagine what's triggered this mood of his lately. I know teenagers will be teenagers, but I wasn't like that when I was his age. It doesn't make any sense.

He's playing video games when I walk in, and I grab the controller out of his hand instead of asking him to talk. I know how that would go, he'd tell me to fuck off. He says it anyway, and I shrug because I don't particularly care right now.

"You're done for a minute. We're talking."

"I don't want to talk. Go away."

"Not until you give me some answers, dude. Don't you know you're supposed to stick up for your girlfriend? Be the host that you wouldn't let mom be? What the fuck was that?"

He tries to snatch the controller back, but I'm much taller than him and it's pretty simple to raise my hand out of his reach. For extra measure, I go over to the tv and turn that off too. His game will still be there when it turns back on, but this way he won't be distracted

"Talk to me, you idiot."

"It's stupid, okay? I shouldn't have invited her over."

"So that we wouldn't know you're rude to your girlfriend? So we could live in blissful ignorance?" I ask, getting heated.

"Calm down. It's not like that, I'm not rude to her."

"Could have fooled me."

He rubs his eyes now, in a tired, sad way, but it doesn't deter me. He could start crying and I'd still need an explanation.

"Just don't fucking tell mom, okay?" he asks, way quieter than he was talking before.

"Sure, fine." I know there are things he's told me in the past he prefers she doesn't know. It's not because he doesn't trust her or love her. She can just be... judgmental. It even wears on me sometimes, but I know she means well.

"I just don't want mom to start acting like *her* mom or something. Autumn doesn't really have parents, and she struggles with approval and stuff. I just don't want her to look for it here. The only person I want to share mom with is you."

I shake my head in confusion. "What would it matter? It doesn't mean you'd have any less."

"I don't know, man. It's hard to explain. Maybe because dad... I don't know." I'm taken aback by his words for a second. We never mention our dad, but I immediately understand what he means. Why he wouldn't want me to tell mom.

Our dad left when we were both young. I couldn't have been older than six. All we knew about him for a while was that he had a new wife. When Justin was old enough to understand, I'd decided to try and find him on social media. I wanted my brother to at least know who he was, what he looked like. What I found was a man with a big, happy family. He had three kids with her in six years, and he really loved them from what I could see in photos. Two more boys, and a daughter. Completely replacing us and then some. I tried to keep the full truth from Justin, but he wouldn't give up until he found out every detail I did. It hit him worse than it did me, even though he never really knew our dad. I tried to imagine how I would feel if I'd never known him. If I never went to the park, or got ice cream, or had a movie night with my father. The memories weren't very solid, they were only small glimpses of what had been, but they were enough. Enough for me to know that my dad did love me, and there's no good enough reason for him to have left us.

"You know this isn't like that, right? Mom isn't going to replace you with some random girl you bring home."

"There's a part of me that knows that. Really. It's just... she was so nice to her right off the bat. She never talks to me like that."

"Because you're not a guest. You eat the food she makes every night without thanking her. You dirty up her house without cleaning up after yourself, or apologizing or anything. You barely talk to her."

"So I deserve to be replaced?" he asks quietly.

"No! Why would you even say that? Mom doesn't want to replace you, but that doesn't mean she doesn't need you to be a little more respectful around here."

He looks like he's thinking about my words for a minute before he finally responds.

"Okay." I know my brother well enough that the word isn't an agreement, more like a way to end the conversation, but I let it go. I got what I needed out of him, which is to understand why.

Epilogue

Eight Months Later

The wedding is chaotic, but I'm not sure what else I expected. When the bride is as much of a perfectionist as she is, there was no other way this could have gone. Everyone is running around the venue like headless chickens, hoping they don't bump into her before the ceremony.

I am one of those chickens.

She couldn't have picked a better place. A wide open, perfectly manicured field with an impressive display of rose bushes. Willow trees are in the perfect place to protect the couple from the sun as they say their vows. With the huge, poofy, princess dress that she's in? That shade is going to do her a favor on this hot summer day.

I'm wearing a silky, strapless little number and I'm still sweating my ass off. Thankfully, the makeup artist worked magic that's keeping my face from melting. Mascara running down my face would not make for very good photos.

I stand in my line, waiting for my cue to walk down the aisle ahead of the bride. Miles is across from me in his own line, but the two people ahead of us are blocking my view of him. I wonder if he's feeling the same way I am, hot and nervous.

I must be so zoned out, picturing him in his tux, that I don't notice as soon as the two people in front of us disappear, and I don't have to picture it anymore. My memory from minutes ago doesn't do him justice. He'll never look better than he does right in front of me.

His face lights up when our eyes lock, and I smile my widest smile.

"You ready?" he mouths to me. I nod, only because I'm ready for anything when it's with him.

We lock arms, and exit the doors that will take us to the stunning display outside. The white chairs, the small stage, and the arch that are all so perfectly matched it's a pleasure to look at. The pink and white flowers, the greenery, it all came together just right. I can only hope that my own, inevitable wedding is half as beautiful.

And only half as crowded, because *yikes*. There are too many people here.

He gives my arm a little squeeze with his own as we approach the point where we separate. I blow him a kiss, and giggle as he catches it.

It feels like the time goes by slower as I stand up there waiting for her to appear. It would be rude to yawn in front of all these people, but I have to really fight a few from happening.

When she finally does appear, it wakes me up from the bored haze I was sinking into.

Amelia looks stunning. The extravagant dress makes her dark hair stand out even more than usual. Her red lips and rosy cheeks pop. This is her moment, and I love it for her. I love that I'm here, and a part of this family. Tears well up in my eyes, and pour over when hers meet mine. She smiles at me, and it's filled with nothing but joy. It feels very representative of my life now, happier than I know what to do with.

Amelia met Sam at the beginning of the year, after he walked into her office as a prospective client. That didn't work out, obviously, because they hit it off immediately. After twenty minutes of talking, she closed the office early to go out on a date with him.

He proposed after a couple months, and none of us were surprised. Miles and Justin love the guy. We all see how happy he makes her, how well they fit. And he's a *hilarious* addition to family dinners.

The ceremony is gorgeous. The vows make me cry even harder, almost an embarrassing amount for how many people are in the crowd.

I'm not the only one. I peek over at my boyfriend, and even he's wiping tears away with the back of his hand.

Amelia and I have bonded a lot over the last few months. We've had tons of deep conversations, learned more about each other's life experiences. She became a single mom at such a young age, and she didn't know how to manage having her own life and raising her sons at the same time. It had seemed impossible to her, and it's obvious mistakes were made along the way.

But our mistakes get us where we need to be, none of us would accomplish much without them. I've accepted her apologies a hundred times by now, and I fully understand that her actions were rooted in her love for her son. There was no way for her to know how sincere I was. There was no way for her to truly know that I was genuinely in love with him.

There's no way for anyone to deny it now.

Another interesting new development is her relationship with my best friends. Reya, always insistent on being included in everything, and Vic, who's happy to go with the flow, have been to *plenty* of family dinners. Sometimes Vic's husband will join us, sometimes all of the children do too. Amelia basically has three new grandchildren that she endlessly spoils.

Justin and Isabelle split their weeks in half with their kids, so they're a part of the fun most of the time, thankfully. The last year has really turned us all into one big family. It's what my girls already were to me for so long, and I love that everyone is happy to have been brought together. There's never a dull day between us.

For the reception we eat delicious, fancy food that is entirely overboard, just like most of Amelia's taste. Miles holds my hand the whole time we're seated and we listen to everyone chat around us.

Until, of course, it's time for him to give a speech.

He's so happy to do it. So dedicated to everything he does and everyone he loves. I give him a quick kiss before he stands to take his place in front of the microphone. I watch his ass the whole way, not caring who notices.

"Hi, everyone." He turns his head away and clears his throat, his only sign of nervousness. "I'm Miles, the son of the bride. A very lucky son to have been raised by this incredible woman. She's taught me a lot with her words, and her stories, but even more with her actions." He goes on about her strength, and what a great job she did as a mother. I get choked up, agreeing with every word.

She did do a good job. Miles is proof of it.

He looks at her and smiles. "I'm so glad you found someone that you can complain to. Someone that takes care of you the way you take care of everyone else. Thank you, Sam. We're happy to have you."

Someone reaches a glass of champagne out to him and he laughs, realizing he forgot to grab his own on his way up there. I smile to myself.

"Cheers to finally finding the person you needed all along. I love you both very much."

I watch as everyone in the room sips their champagne, and realize a second too late that I should pretend to take a sip of mine too. There are way too many observant people in this room and I don't need anyone reporting *anything* to *anyone* until I'm ready.

Thankfully Vic and Reya are caught up in their own applause.

I place the glass against my lips and hope the fact that the liquid inside doesn't make contact with them isn't obvious to anyone around me.

I think I'm in the clear, because all the attention is on Amelia and her son as they embrace. I love seeing him so happy, and I can't wait to give him one more reason.

The night is calmer than I anticipated. The group of us hanging out in our hotel room consists of myself, Miles, my girls, and Justin.

Julian is happily on baby duty for the night. Last we saw, they were all half asleep in their huge bed, trying to keep their eyes on the princess movie that was playing.

The brothers have celebrated hard today. They're both a bit drunk, and talk over each other every time one of them unlocks a new memory they need to share.

"I think it might be time everyone switches to drinking water," I say as I stand. I've heard enough about the scar on Justin's butt.

Vic stands to follow me.

"I think that's a great idea."

It's a nice place, bigger than I ever thought I'd see myself in, thanks to Amelia's splurging. Instead of being one hotel room, it's more like three or four of them put together. We turn the corner to a full sized kitchen, and my attention goes towards the fridge. I am rather parched now that I think of it. I should have filled that champagne glass with water earlier.

"Today has been so great," she says from behind me. I look over my shoulder as I load four water bottles into my arms.

"It was everything she deserves."

"Agreed."

"How are you still wearing those heels?" I ask, impressed as always by her.

They're *really* high heels. I have not been so graceful in my much shorter version, and took them off as soon as we got back.

"They're my wedding shoes." She stomps in place a couple times, just to make them click against the tile. "I've been to a *lot* of weddings, babe."

I hand her one of the bottles in my arms and she thanks me as I take it. Then she proceeds to gulp it down like she's never had water before.

"Drink a little too much? Feeling dehydrated?"

"No, I haven't had anyth—" She cuts herself off, as if that was saying something she shouldn't.

"Haven't had anything to drink?"

She nods.

"Why are you..." I pause. "Not even the champagne?"

She shakes her head, and her eyes search my face.

I try not to gasp when she rests one hand over her stomach, and she uses the other to place a finger in front of her lips.

"Our little secret, okay? Don't freak out. We don't want everyone to know about her yet."

"Vic, shut *up*!" I whisper scream. "Her?"

"We found out a couple days ago."

She's so small that it's easy to miss, but there is a bump there. It's accentuated even more by the way she cradles it.

How did I not notice? Shouldn't I have some sort of pregnant radar given my current state?

I glance over in the hallway to make sure we don't have any surprise listeners.

"So Julian knows? Does Reya? Who else?" My questions come one after the one and she laughs at my curiosity.

"Just him. Just us. We wanted to wait until after the wedding."

"Well, this is going to be awkward," I joke as I point to my own stomach. I don't have a bump yet, I'm not even sure how far along I am. I took the test yesterday morning after my period was a few days late.

Actually, I took five tests. Just to be sure. We hadn't been actively trying, but we talked about the possibility. I got off my birth control months ago, and we felt like it would happen when it's meant to happen.

This feels like perfect timing. I just published my third book, and I can actually afford to pay Kaitlyn for running all of my social media. Miles and I have been living together since the Spring. And now I get to experience this with my best friend, who's practically a professional at being pregnant.

She slaps the counter. "Autumn Owens. Are you serious right now?"

"I am so serious."

She covers her mouth that's dropped open.

"That explains why you were pretending to drink the champagne!"

I should have known I wasn't that sneaky.

She walks up to me and wraps me in a hug.

"I'm already picturing the playdates. They're going to be best friends."

I laugh. "Without a doubt."

She rubs circles on my back as I start to cry on her shoulder, and I hear a sniffle or two from her as well. As if I wasn't emotional enough, this brand new development is already making me feel like a wreck.

"What did we walk in on?" Reya's loud voice echoes through the kitchen and we both giggle as we pull apart.

"Absolutely nothing," she says with a sweet smile.

"You okay, sweetheart?" Miles asks as he approaches me. His brows do that cute thing they always do when he's concerned.

I'm so full of love for him, and excitement for our future, that I just want to say it. I want to share this with him right now.

But Vic has been patient, and thoughtful, and there is no way I'm going to steal her moment. I look over at her, hoping to gauge her thoughts, and she's nodding at me. She jerks her head towards Miles, silently telling me to go for it with a huge smile on her face.

I don't know what I did to deserve her as a friend.

"Actually," I start.

Justin's gaze is suspicious as he looks between us. Vic tries to cover her mouth when a squeal slips out, but it's unsuccessful.

"What is it?" Miles asks, only sparing small glances at her.

I try to think of the right way to say the words and come up short. Mostly because I'm still crying and I know my voice is going to crack. I grab his hand, and pull him with me as I run to my suitcase in the bedroom. I hadn't planned on telling him until we got home, but I brought a test just in case. I wanted to be prepared for a moment like this one.

Reya protests, hating that she's not the first to hear what I have to say. Vic wraps her up in a hug, to distract Reya or to distract herself, I'm not sure.

I don't hesitate when we enter the room, I don't say a thing. I just pull out the stick I peed on and hand it to him.

His face goes through so many emotions in such a short amount of time.

Confusion, shock, wonder, disbelief, and back to shock.

"This is yours?" he asks in a voice that's barely a whisper.

I nod too many times.

"How? When?" I repeat everything I told Vic, and more. I give him a heads up that he'll have to be late to work on the day of our first appointment, because I'm not going without him.

He doesn't care, I can see in his eyes how little anything else means right now.

Suddenly I'm in his arms, and he lifts me off the ground with a spin.

"Wow. I fucking love you so much."

"I love you so much."

As soon as Miles is setting me back on my feet, Reya is running into the room.

"You're *pregnant*?!" She doesn't let me confirm before squeezing me tight enough to *almost* worry me.

Vic gives me an apologetic shrug, but I don't need it.

"The first one is the easiest," I hear Justin loudly whisper into Miles' ear.

They laugh, and he congratulates us. That leads to more champagne being poured and I didn't even know we had any here in the room. It's a long while before everyone says goodnight and heads back to their rooms.

"I don't know how I'm supposed to wait so long before finding out if we're having a boy or a girl."

He smiles. "That's what's on your mind?"

"Of course it is!"

"What do you want them to be?"

"I don't have a preference."

He lifts me into his arm suddenly and I let out a yelp. "Everyone has a preference at first."

"Then tell me what you're hoping for."

He grins, tauntingly. "A happy, healthy baby."

"Exactly."

The exhaustion hits me quickly, and it looks like he's on the same page.

We go through our night routine, one that we've gotten really good at *together*, before collapsing into the huge bed. He plants kisses all over my face, down my chest and on to my stomach, eliciting an uncontrollable fit of giggling from me.

"I think I want a girl," he whispers.

"Yeah? What makes you say that?"

"Because that laugh of yours needs to be passed on." I feel him smile against my stomach.

"Funny, I was actually hoping for a boy for that same reason." I run a hand through his silky brown curls, still amazed I can do it whenever I want. Even a year later, it blows my mind that he's all mine.

"May the best laugh win," he says as he presses one last kiss right above my belly button.

I fall asleep very easily, and it has everything to do with his body wrapped so lovingly around mine.

ACKNOWLEDGEMENTS

What an emotional, incredible journey it has been to write my first book. I have known from the age of five that this was a dream of mine, but I spent too many years assuming I didn't have what it takes. I tried and failed countless times. I had a first chapter here, a blurb there. Plenty of writing done over the years, but never anything I could finish. I know exactly what changed in order for me to have this determination, and it's because as a twenty-two year old, I felt safe and comfortable for the first time in my life.

I have so many people to thank for the various steps along the way, so let's get into it, shall we?

First of all, my dear, sweet, supportive husband, Dominik. Thank you for making me feel like I can do anything. Thank you for all of the coffee and kind words you've handed me throughout this process. This book wouldn't be what it is without you letting me read my favorite parts aloud while you faced the wall because I was too nervous to let you look at me. I love you.

Alex Kettell! Thank you for being one of the first people to read this book as a work-in-progress. You're always the first person at a lot of things, like sharing my posts and responding to all of my babbling messages. I appreciate you so much, and I'm so glad the clock app brought us together.

Erica Grimes! You're one of the smartest people I know, and you've been such a crucial part of this for me. I couldn't have done this without you. If only you knew how much every single Snapchat video has meant to me. Thank you, thank you, thank you.

To my editor, Becca, you're amazing. Every note you had was a lightbulb moment. Thank you for caring about this book, and helping make it the best it could be.

To my cover designer, Sam, your talent is unmatched! Thank you for bringing this entire thing to life with your art, and thank you for making things so easy for a brand new author that had no clue what she was doing!

I can't finish this without mentioning the love I've been showered in by Delaney Schwantes and Ashley Orton in particular. Thanks for being the best cheerleaders. Thank you for every single encouraging word. I freaking love you both, and I feel extremely lucky to get to share this time in my life with you.

˜nes UK
˙tent Group UK Ltd.
˓2049040124
˧UK00016B/447

9 798989 286102